Passion of Isis

Sun-warmed sand clothed her naked body. Adie lay on a blanket of silk in a square stone room whose ceiling was open to the sky. The flick of something soft caressed her thigh. It tickled. She tried to wriggle but her body didn't respond. It was as though she was pinned down, but she felt no weight above her, nor cuffs about her wrists.

'An extraordinary find,' an individual at her feet said, and she smiled inwardly, knowing he was referring to her, as her head was cushioned and her hair confined in an elegant headdress.

The sun shone red through her eyelids. She felt the whisper of the desert breeze across her skin, and tried to move her toes. There was still no response, but strangely, she felt no panic.

'Exquisite, and perfectly preserved,' said a voice she recognised. The soft caress continued, meticulously sweeping the golden sand away from the underside of her breast. Her nipples tightened in response.

'She looks so real,' said the first man. 'If she weren't made of gold, I would say she was only sleeping.'

Gold? What is he talking about? She peeped from beneath her eyelashes at the length of her body and saw that they spoke the truth, for her skin shone with metallic lustre in the sunlight. Gold! she wanted to say, but she couldn't speak.

She trembled with anticipation, and awaited his next touch.

By the same author:

A Gentleman's Wager

Passion of Isis
Madelynne Ellis

BLACK LACE

Black Lace books contain sexual fantasies.
In real life, always practise safe sex.

First published in 2005 by
Black Lace
Thames Wharf Studios
Rainville Road
London W6 9HA

Design by Smith & Gilmour, London
Printed and bound by Mackays of Chatham PLC

ISBN 0 352 33993 4

To Lisabet, Belinda, Maddy,
Amanda and Virginia, my critters.
And to everyone at ERWA:
too many to list.

1

'Damn it!'

Adie slammed her fist into the desk, causing the dodgy lamp to flicker. It was past nine and she was still no closer to deciphering the dog-eared hieroglyphic manuscript. 'Ask Joe,' she said, more calmly, and shuffled off the high stool onto her feet. Her supervisor would still be at his desk. He was rarely anywhere else.

She trudged along the main corridor in semi-darkness, camouflaged with stripes of shadow that the security lights cast through the blinds. At this rate, she'd never convince him that he'd trained a maverick genius when she had to ask for help with an inscription – even one this complicated. Adie glanced again at the paper. She hated admitting defeat, especially to the gruff, bushy old professor who'd taken her under his wing during her doctorate. Her hopes of a permanent position in the department were foundering; all her fellow students had moved on, mostly to clerical jobs. One or two had scraped in as archivists or curators, but Adie wanted more. She wanted a place on an excavation team.

The light in the office was on; the door wedged permanently half-open. Her supervisor sat hunched over his desk in his shapeless brown suit. Professor Josef Levine was nearly 70 and ripe for retirement, something he swore he'd never consent to. 'If they push me out, Adie –' he'd confided one afternoon, '– they'll see me dead in a year. Work's the only reason I get up in the morning. All my other passions are long withered and gone.'

To Adie, he was the eccentric uncle she'd never had.

She was still a few feet away from the door when Joe raised his head. 'So you're back at Saqqara,' he said to an unseen figure across the desk.

Adie halted mid-stride, surprised to find anyone with him at this late hour. She checked her watch then leaned against the photocopier, resigned to a wait.

'I had to face it someday. Besides, the prospects for the new site are good.'

'And it's two weeks into the season. So why have you come to me?' asked Joe.

'Staff shortages. I was hoping you could recommend someone.'

Adie stopped breathing. An opportunity to work at Saqqara's desert necropolis would be hotly contended, and if she kept quiet, she might get the chance to apply before anyone else even heard about it.

'Come now, you don't need my help. You could have anyone you wanted.'

'Perhaps,' admitted the stranger. He shifted position in his seat, so that the aged springs creaked. 'But then, you know the problems I have with publicity.'

'You mean you can't risk advertising because you'll get swarmed by tourists and amateurs.' There was a heavy disdain in Joe's voice.

The man gave a gentle cough, while the furrows in Joe's brow deepened. He took a long, slow sip from his stained coffee mug. 'You know I hate picking favourites. Besides, what makes you think I've got anybody you'd want?'

'Because you have high standards, Josef, just like me. Just like you taught me.'

The reflected praise brought a smile to Adie's lips. This was more promising than she'd hoped. But to her dismay Joe just hunched his shoulders and grimaced, either at the coffee or the flattery. Adie suspected the latter. She wondered who the other man was. Joe seemed to be treating him with a lot of respect, so he must be important, and there weren't many famous Egyptologists about any more; the days of Howard Carter were long past. She strained to see him around the edge of the door, but his chair was set too far back and all she got was a glimpse of freshly pressed trousers.

'I want someone competent that no one will miss.' His voice was unfamiliar, and rang with rich low tones. Adie suspected he spent a lot of time speaking Arabic, though he sounded English. 'A new post-doctorate with some field experience would do.'

Adie's head started pounding. This was perfect for her. She'd received her PhD two months ago, and had worked on a summer dig in Cyprus. Not the same as Egypt, admittedly, but it was still fieldwork, and she could start immediately. She held her breath waiting for Joe to say her name. Instead, he shook his head. 'There's nobody. I'm sorry, Killian, I really don't think I can help you.' He sat back in his chair and folded his arms across his chest.

Adie gave an incredulous snort, but they didn't hear her muted outrage. What did he mean, there wasn't anyone? He knew she was looking for work. The wilful part of her wanted to march straight through the door. The sensible part made her stay put as soon as she realised Joe had given his companion a name.

Killian – Dr Simon Killian Carmichael to be precise – was the leading authority on the Early Dynasties, and had headed high-profile expeditions to Giza, Abusir, Dahshur and, most recently, Lisht. Rumour in the department was that he'd once been one of Joe Levine's students, and now she'd heard it from his own lips. Adie had never given it much thought until now, when the chance of working with him was slipping away.

'Why do you need extra staff, anyway?' asked Joe.

'Not extra, a replacement. I've sent Bill Harris home with a broken leg. He slipped down some steps at the dig and won't be on his feet again for months.'

Joe's lips thinned to a tight line. 'Assuming you'd want him back.'

Killian made no audible response.

Adie tried to imagine his expression. She'd never seen him, but she'd heard of his work. What student of Egyptology hadn't? His books and papers littered their rooms. He'd been the most requested guest for end-of-term lectures for the last five years. Not that he'd ever given one.

Joe pushed a stray paperclip towards the small silver mountain by his work tray. 'All right, I'll think about it, but I'm not making any promises.'

'Thank you. You can contact me at the hotel.'

Joe nodded. 'I'll let you know.' He rose, their discussion apparently at its end. Adie scrunched the inscription into her pocket. There was no way she was going to walk in and ask for help now, not even for a glimpse of Dr Carmichael. She wanted this job, and with that thought in mind she pulled out her keys and headed for the exit, determined to confront Joe first thing tomorrow.

Joe was marking essay papers when Adie arrived. She placed a fresh mug of coffee at his elbow, before finding a seat opposite him – the same seat Dr Carmichael had occupied the previous night.

'What do you want?' Joe greeted her, gruffly but with a friendly smile, and without breaking the flow of ink from his pen.

'I wondered if you'd heard of any new projects I might apply to work on?' she asked, having decided to try a subtle approach.

Joe's red pen stopped mid-sentence.

So much for subtlety.

He peered inquisitively at her from beneath his bushy

eyebrows. 'No,' he said, too slowly. 'Not that I can think of.'

Adie twisted her hands in her lap. The scratch of the pen nib resumed. 'What about the Saqqara project you were discussing last night?'

Joe sat back in his chair, and began to tap the pen on his desk. When he finally spoke, it was in a brusque whisper. 'Who told you about that?'

'Nobody. I overheard you. Dr Carmichael's looking for someone to work on his project, isn't he? He was here last night.' It was impossible to keep the excitement out of her voice.

Joe laid his pen across the top essay in the pile. His normally cheerful blue eyes seemed glassy. 'And I suppose you think you're just what he's looking for. I won't put you forward, Adie; you're wasting your time.'

'But ... I ... you...' She fell silent. Last night she'd assumed he'd overlooked her; now it was clear that there had been no mistake. She frowned. Joe wasn't being fair; he knew how much she wanted it.

'Why not?' she managed, with a little more composure. 'I heard you. He wants a PhD and some fieldwork experience. I've got that, and nobody's going to miss me.'

'Adie, you've never even been to Egypt. Besides, I've already made my recommendations. I'm sending Murphy and Longford. They both worked on the Luxor project last spring.'

Adie raked her fingers through her long hair in exasperation, then slapped her hands down forcefully on his crowded desk. It hurt her palms, but at least an ornament and his pen jumped. 'This is bullshit! How experienced do I have to be? Chris Longford's not even qualified.'

Joe regarded her sternly.

'Please, Joe, at least give me a chance. I can't stay here forever fixing other people's broken pots. My brain's turning to mush.'

Joe pressed his fingers to his temples. 'Adie, you don't know what you're asking. I'll help you find something else, I promise, but Carmichael's team is not for you.'

'Why not? Aren't I good enough all of a sudden? Does it have to be a man?'

'No, it does not. I just don't think you'd work well under Carmichael. You're too intuitive, and it's not his way. He'd stifle you, and I'm afraid he'd ruin you.'

Adie didn't understand him at all. 'That's the best you can come up with? He's one of the biggest names in the field. I can't just let it go. Besides, isn't it my choice who I work for?'

Joe shrugged his shoulders and coughed meaningfully. 'It's my decision and I've already made it. Now please, I have lots of marking to do.'

Adie bit her lip and remembered Killian's need for discretion. 'I'll leak news of the find,' she blurted.

'Don't be stupid. You don't know what you're talking about.'

'I do.'

A heavy silence fell. Adie stared stubbornly at the essay papers. She couldn't bear to see the anger in his eyes, but she wanted a shot at this job. She had to hold out. Back down, please, she prayed, because if they fell out over this she'd be packing her bags in the morning.

Joe flicked a speck of lint from his corduroy jacket. 'I don't believe you'd go to the press. Some of my students, yes, but not you.'

'I might,' she said, in a voice less convincing than before. 'Even a couple of emails to some of the more sensational websites would do it, or one of those lunatic fringe writers. You know, *Cadillacs of the Gods*, that kind of thing? Are you willing to take that chance?'

For a moment, Joe actually looked worried, and she wondered if she'd touched on a sore subject.

'You'd ruin your career.'

'I don't have a career. I'm going nowhere. What's there to lose?'

The crow's feet around his eyes softened, then his lips twitched as he shook his head.

'Please, Joe,' she begged. 'All I want is an interview.' She hung her head. This had already gone too far, and if he didn't give in soon she'd have to do something dramatic like run crying from the room. The tears would be real enough.

Joe sighed wearily. 'I'm not happy about this, but if it means so much to you, I'll call him. Now get back to work. I'll talk to you later.'

'Thanks, Joe,' she said, relief dissolving her tension. She scampered around the desk and flung her arms around his shoulders. 'You won't be disappointed.'

'We'll see,' she heard him growl, as she skipped through the open door.

By the morning of the interview, Adie's excitement had turned into a bad case of nerves. She felt completely numb apart from her stomach, which churned every time she thought about anything to do with archaeology. The worst part was not knowing what to expect. She didn't know what he was looking for, what the project was about, or even what he looked like. Her friends had speculatively described Dr Carmichael as a daring, darkly attractive Indiana Jones type, but she'd guessed he was going to look like one of the guys off *Time Team*. Of course, she secretly hoped they were right; a bit of excitement and adventure would make a nice change.

She arrived at Joe's cottage twenty minutes early. The rickety wooden fence was thick with ivy and moss, and weeds besieged the small vegetable patch. The back parlour was equally untidy, and dusty as well, with faded brown furnishings that matched their owner's scruffy, comfortable style. Adie fidgeted with the fringe of one of the overstuffed chairs, while Joe's ancient tabby cat eyed her suspiciously from a battered cushion.

Joe made her a cup of tea, then retreated outside to take a brush to the dead leaves. Adie sensed that he was still unhappy, but didn't understand why. She wished he'd stop being so secretive. If there was something dodgy about the project or Dr Carmichael, she'd rather be forewarned.

It was another ten minutes before Dr Carmichael arrived. By then, Adie was so anxious that she could taste her own bile, but she forced a calm expression when she heard the doorknob turn.

His appearance shocked her.

Dr Carmichael was so unlike anything she'd expected that she forgot to rise and greet him, and instead just stared at him in amazement. Of the many faces she had imagined for him, none had come close to the truth. Killian Carmichael was an elegant businessman wearing a very expensive-looking black overcoat, and although he had startling white hair, if he was a day over 35 she'd give up chocolate forever.

'Killian, this is Adie Hamilton,' announced Joe as he entered the room behind his guest, and his bushy eyebrows danced like two fat hairy caterpillars, reminding her to rise from her seat. The light cotton shirt she'd put on was clinging to her back, and she realised that her palms were sticky just in time to surreptitiously wipe them on her skirt before offering her hand.

'Dr Carmichael, I'm pleased to meet you at last.' Her voice was unsteady, and she could feel herself blushing as she spoke. He was surprisingly attractive, even beautiful in a poised, masculine way.

Killian accepted her hand. His grip was firm but his touch was icy, and his accompanying smile didn't reach his eyes. He wore no jewellery on his slender fingers, but

Adie noticed the expensive wristwatch. Everything about him spoke of measured aesthetics.

'I'll leave you to it.' Joe retreated through the patio doors into the garden. Adie was dimly aware of him disappearing into a tumbledown potting shed. Get your brain in gear, she told herself as she returned to her chair; you really want this job, and you need to impress this man.

Killian settled into the chair opposite. He crossed his long legs and withdrew a smart leather notebook from his briefcase. It occurred to Adie that he was obviously wealthy. She felt shabby in comparison, in her one interview suit.

He tilted his head to one side and regarded her coldly. 'Professor Levine tells me you threatened to go to the press.'

Adie gave a sharp cough. Joe had really dropped her in it. She was amazed that Killian had chosen to interview her at all.

Killian awaited her answer patiently.

'I wouldn't really have done it, Joe knows that.'

Killian leaned forwards in his chair as she spoke, and her image filled his pupils. His irises were grey, the colour of dove feathers, and held a strange inner warmth. 'Good. I just wanted you to confirm it for me. Josef wouldn't recommend someone he didn't like. I suspect he likes you an awful lot.'

'I suppose,' Adie said. She'd thought so too, but then why was he trying to wreck her chances of getting this job? And why did Killian seem to think this made her special?

Killian turned his gaze back to his notebook. 'Why do you want to go to Egypt, Dr Hamilton?'

Still shaken by his first statement, she took a breath and tried to form her thoughts. 'Egyptian culture and society fascinate me. I want to see the foundations that the theories are built on.' She knew she could have done better.

'I dislike theories,' he said intensely. 'I work only with concrete facts. Adventure stories and daydreams don't interest me.'

'Oh!'

Could he read her thoughts? Had he guessed that she dreamed of finding lost tombs and spectacular treasures?

He made some notes, and then began to interrogate her on all aspects of Egyptology. She answered with a degree of clarity she'd never found in exams, but struggled when it came to naming four of Ramesses II's 30-odd sons. Their names just eluded her.

'I could look them up,' she said. A tiny half-smile flickered across his lips. It made her want to reach out and touch his mouth. She quickly swatted the thought away.

'Is that your thesis?'

Adie handed over the leather-bound copy. He closed his pad and began to flick through the heavy volume, pausing to ask the occasional question. He seemed genuinely interested, and with his focus shifted away from her, she was free to gaze at him.

Now she knew why the press made so much fuss over him. Success and good looks were a rare combination outside of show business, and this man had both in abundance. She felt drawn by his cool laconicism, and aroused by his aloof beauty. Adie pressed her thighs together, only to find that it rubbed her cotton knickers against her cleft, and she was wet. She flushed, realising that she'd grown aroused watching him, and tried to regain her composure by taking a gulp of her stone-cold tea.

Eventually, he handed her thesis back. 'I've one last

question for you,' he said while she did her best to look alert and clever. 'I'd like you to imagine you are in charge of a dig and that you need to recruit a team member. You'll interview dozens of recent graduates and at best, their experience has been polishing the exhibits and gluing the pots. What could possibly interest you about any of them?'

'Depth of knowledge,' suggested Adie.

Killian shook his head. 'They all have that. Try again.'

'Team spirit.'

'This isn't an IT company. One last try.'

Think, Adie, she told herself as she tried not to scowl. Then for a split second she was back in the dingy classroom of the first lesson of her A level History course. 'Never forget,' her lecturer had said, as he wrote an important word in big chalk letters on the blackboard. Adie had copied it on to her pad while he'd underlined it and put a full stop at the end with such vigour that the chalk had crumbled between his fingers.

'Objectivity,' she said, knowing that it was something she frequently lacked.

Killian observed her calmly for a second or two, then said, 'That concludes your interview, Ms Hamilton. I'll let you know.'

'Wait, don't I get to ask you any questions?'

His intriguing half-smile reappeared. It was a very disarming smile; the sort that knocked you off balance and left you feeling that whatever he said was right. Adie wondered what the effect would be if he ever broke into a real smile.

'No,' he replied. 'If I decide to employ you, I'll give you all the information you need then.'

He shook her hand and, before she knew it, Joe was escorting her along the gravel drive to her car. He didn't ask how the interview had gone, and Adie didn't offer an opinion. She was too busy wondering what to make of Dr Carmichael and whether she'd get to see him again.

Six hours later she was still wondering the same thing. The interview was a grey blur and she couldn't remember half of what she'd said. The phone rang. 'Hello,' she said, as she absently fiddled with a piece of the pottery jigsaw that littered her desk.

'Adie, it's Joe Levine. Congratulations, you got the job.'

'I did!' she managed to gasp, almost dropping the receiver in her surprise.

'Yes. Killian's prepared to offer you the position provided you can be in Cairo by the end of next week.'

'That soon!'

'Yes. If you're not certain, I'm sure he'll understand.'

'No. There's no problem. I'll be there.' She bit her lip and frowned at the receiver. Joe's voice sounded unusually throaty. 'Is there something wrong?' she asked.

'No, of course not. I'm happy for you. It'll be a wonderful experience. A step in the right direction, eh?' He was trying to sound jolly, and Joe was never jolly. She guessed that he resented being proved wrong. At least, she hoped that was it. 'Killian will email your instructions. Good luck,' he said, 'and call me if you need any help.'

'I will. Bye, Joe, and thanks. Thanks for everything.' She hung up.

'Yes!' Too quiet, so she said it again loudly and punched the air for emphasis. She forgot about Joe's odd tone, and instead stared at the telephone suspiciously, wondering if it had tricked her. 'Congratulations,' she mouthed to herself. 'You actually did it.'

Adie grinned wickedly, and imagined long shadows cast over the still desert sands, and unearthing lost treasures with Killian. He was rich, famous and bloody gorgeous. Life had just improved immeasurably.

She surreptitiously glanced around the empty workroom. It was Friday afternoon, and she was unlikely to be disturbed. She crossed to the door and flicked the main light switch off. Inky shadows instantly suffused the windowless room, leaving just the warm pool of light around her desk lamp. Adie stepped out of her knickers and stuffed them into her desk drawer. She straddled her stool and lifted her skirt at the front, so the she could slip a hand between her legs.

The cool air on her thighs made her nipples tingle. She was taking a risk by indulging her fantasies at work, but the thought of working with Dr Carmichael was too deliciously enticing. She deserved a little celebration, and she knew that her friends would insist on taking her out as a treat.

Adie closed her eyes while her middle finger found her clitoris. Her lips parted as she gave a low sigh. She summoned Killian's image and he gave her that intriguing half-smile, then she pictured him loosening the buttons of her blouse and lifting her breasts free of the lacy cups of her bra. He was dressed as before, but he'd discarded his overcoat, and pristine white cotton emphasised the breadth of his strong shoulders. 'Can't you concentrate, Ms Hamilton?' he asked her, mid-interview, while he plucked and teased her nipples. He was knelt between her thighs and her neat skirt was bunched up. Waves of golden sensation loosened her knots of tension; she arched her back and thrust her sensitive teats towards his mouth. His breath whispered over their surface. 'Do you remember yet?'

'Khaemwese ... Merenptah...' Adie gasped as she recalled the names of Ramesses II's sons. In response to each answer, he flicked his tongue over her steepled nipples. Adie dredged her memory for more names. Inside she was burning, soaring above the blue skies of the desert, with the sun warming her skin. 'Amunhotep ... Mery-Atum.' His touch switched to her clitoris. Her image swam in his inky pupils, drawing her closer. Pleasure coiled around her nub, became more intense, more focused. Liquid heat swirled through her body, and rose to her skin like tiny effervescent bubbles, bringing the chase nearer and nearer to its ultimate goal.

'One more, one more, Adie, and I'll give you what you want.'

'I don't know any more.'

'Just one more.' All that stood between her and the subtle brush of his fingertips that would yield her the ultimate reward.

'I don't know,' she gasped again, frantic and clawing at his shirt. 'Ramesses, after his father.'

'A good guess.' The pad of his thumb quickened the spark of bittersweet pleasure that prickled in her clit. Adie clasped the stool in a vice-like grip and rode her climax to its pinnacle, before she slumped and pressed her burning cheek against the cool surface of the desk. Her throat felt hoarse from her strangled gasps, and she coughed tentatively. All was quiet around her. She sighed, then smiled to herself. If only the interview had gone the same way.

Across town, as Joe Levine replaced the receiver in its cradle, Killian's gaze lingered on the row of dusty photographs above the parlour fireplace. He knew Josef didn't approve of him appointing Adie Hamilton to the team, and he had a fair idea why. His past was a constant threat to his future, and Josef Levine never forgot that. He was being overprotective.

Joe crossed the room in five strides. His craggy face was set and his eyes were blazing. 'Why her?' he demanded. 'You knew I was against it. She doesn't have the right attitude.'

'Hasn't she?' Killian thought Adie Hamilton was exactly what he normally looked for, young, bright and self-assured.

'No.' Joe's eyes shone with fury. 'She's impetuous and far too romantic. She wants to find secrets and treasures.'

'Don't we all?'

'You used to.' Killian flinched at the brittle tone. He watched Joe's arm reach out towards the mantelpiece, and immediately knew what was coming. The old man was getting predictable.

Joe thrust a photograph into his hands. 'Do you even remember what it was like to have such hopes and idealism?'

Killian glanced at the photograph; he knew every detail of it. He had a copy of his own somewhere. The picture was of two young men posed either side of their professor on graduation day.

'She's just how you were in those days. Do you remember you couldn't wait to get to Egypt, even if you had to dig with your bare hands? The young Dr Carmichael and his faithful sidekick.'

'People change,' Killian said dismissively. He carefully replaced the picture back in its impression in the dust.

'Have you seen him since?'

'You know I haven't.' He turned his back on the old man and walked to the window. He couldn't fear the future because of the past. 'She'll be a good worker, Joe. You've told me so yourself, and that's what I need right now. If she's as ambitious as you say, she'll be heading her own projects in a few years. You should be thankful I'm giving her a head start.'

'If that were all, I'd be grateful. You have the respect of your peers at the moment, but you know very well how fast you can rise and fall.'

'Josef, it's in the past. Let's leave it there. I wouldn't employ her if I thought it would harm her.' Killian drew a heavy breath. When he spoke again, it was with a softer voice. 'And I promise I'll try not to ruin her with my cynicism.'

Joe bowed his head sadly. 'It's out of my hands. What can I do?' He sat down in one of the over-stuffed armchairs, and the cat leaped on to his knee. 'Just look out for her, eh? She doesn't really have anybody.'

Just over 100 miles north of Joe's cottage, in a badly heated sports hall, the raucous applause ceased abruptly, to be replaced by the clatter of people leaving their seats. Dareth Sadler crushed the plastic cup in his hand and left his seat without even a nod at his fellow panellists. It was just a crappy little convention anyway, full of sci-fi geeks and ditsy women who passionately believed in elves and dragons, and whose only talent was to knock you dead at 40 paces with the stench of their perfume. He didn't need to be here, he could still fill auditoriums anywhere in the world. Fuck that idiot and his derivative cyber-fantasy drivel.

Dareth chucked the cup at a wastepaper bin. Plenty of his books were still being bought from high-street shelves; he wasn't consigned to the charity shops yet. In fact, he could produce another bestseller anytime. He'd been thinking it was time to go back to Egypt, and get in touch with his contacts out there.

'Mr Sadler . . . over here.'

Dareth reached the top of the podium steps. He peered down at the two pretty students holding out copies of his books, and paused to flick a speck of lint from his all-black outfit.

Not even nearly past it.

He reached the bottom and raised an eyebrow.

'We think you're great,' they gushed as they thrust pens and pristine hardbacks of one of his earlier works at him. 'That other bloke doesn't know what he's talking about. What did he mean, bargain bins?'

Dareth made a noncommittal grunt and scribbled his signature.

'I've been wondering,' said one girl, encroaching on his personal space. 'I've never really understood what you meant about positive and negative principles in Egyptian magic; could you explain it to me?' She played with her long dyed-black hair and gazed directly at him. As he watched, she brought her little finger to her mouth and sucked it suggestively.

Dareth finally managed a smile. He drew his fingers through his own blond hair and flicked his gaze down to where her perky breasts were emphasised by an ultra-tight-fitting T-shirt. 'It's rather complicated, much easier to demonstrate than explain, but if you've time, we could go back to my hotel room and I'll be happy to go through it with you.'

Her gaze flicked coquettishly away and then back to his face. 'That would be great.' She slid her arm posses-sively around his. 'We've been trying to go through some of the simpler rituals, haven't we, Kate?' She grasped her friend by the wrist and tugged her closer.

'Yes! But we haven't had any success,' Kate volunteered more cautiously. She bit her thumbnail then added, 'If you could show us that would be amazing.'

Dareth smiled benignly at the plumper redhead; she'd have been really pretty if it wasn't for the excess of piercings: six or seven earrings, a nose stud and a tongue bar. Too much metal, he thought, although he did admire the Sheela na Gig pendant around her neck.

The blatant image marked her as a witchy type, look-ing to reclaim her sexuality for the goddess. Except to the men she encountered, a shag was just a shag.

They were all looking for the same thing: a little bit of magic in their sad little lives. This meant they were prey for any goatee-bearded huckster in a black suit with a big silver medallion, and he wasn't the worst one out there. These days he avoided the psychic fairs. Too much com-petition, and besides the women only wanted to get stoned and talk all night. The girls at these fantasy conventions were more nubile, and easier to impress. All he had to do was insert himself into their fantasies. The predictability of their responses both depressed and delighted him.

They left the sports complex and the crowds of convention-goers in home-made cloaks, and crossed the road outside. 'What I don't understand,' said Kate, hesitantly, 'is why the establishment still aren't taking you seriously. I mean, your theories are really advanced.'

'They're just so narrow-minded and blinkered,' replied her friend, saving Dareth the trouble of an answer. He'd been through this countless times over his ten-year career. The simple fact was that people believed what they wanted to believe, and dry and dusty Egyptologists liked dry and dusty theories, while his readers preferred something a little more upbeat.

'This way, ladies.' He showed them into his room in the conference centre, a typically bland affair, with the usual wall-mounted trouser press, overpriced mini-bar and combined porn-pizza menu, which he hastily shoved into a drawer. Hell, he needed this distraction, needed to be able to think straight again, to get on the phone to his agent and speak rationally.

Dareth flicked on the bedside lamp and closed the curtains.

'Did you know there's a convergence of energy lines nearby?' He let the question hang for a moment. 'I insisted on this room because one of them passes beneath us. Come here.' He took the redhead by the hand and drew her to a spot near the centre of the room. 'Can you feel it?'

Immediately, and rather predictably, her eyes seemed to glaze as though the flow of energy was consuming her. 'Yes, yes. I can feel it.'

Dareth gazed at her pendant with its wanton promise,

nestled in her plump cleavage. If any of the 40-odd motels he'd stayed in was built on a ley line, then he was a druid. 'I knew you would,' he said. 'I thought when I saw you that you'd be sensitive to such things.'

She beamed at him. Dareth returned her smile, then stepped towards the other girl. 'Have we met before?' he asked, taking both her hands in his. He squinted contemplatively at her for a moment as she shook her head. 'No. At least, not in this life. You're the living image of Ankara, the third dynasty princess. Have you heard of her?'

'No.' Her eyes were bright and excited.

'You should try past-life regression. I'm sure you'll find you're connected.' He tapped his index finger to his lips, then turned away to close the topic. 'You asked about positive and negative aspects, we'll concentrate on that.'

Now drawing them both over towards the bed, where he'd left an assortment of masks next to the alarm clock, he picked them each out a visage.

'Kate.' He handed the shorter girl an ornate feline eye-mask. 'You'll take the role of the lion goddess Sekhmet in this cleansing ritual. And . . .'

'Judy,' the black-haired minx informed him.

'You'll be the goddess Nut. You both represent the negative principle. Later, I'll introduce the positive principle, but first it's necessary for you to cancel each other out.'

'How do we do that?' asked Kate. She scratched at her chipped black nail polish while avoiding his gaze.

Dareth unfastened his collar. 'To begin with you need to undress.'

Kate's mouth opened. 'You what!' She planted her hands on her hips. Meanwhile, Judy's grin broadened. Seeing complicity, Dareth targeted his reply to her.

'The sky goddess Nut doesn't wear a Marilyn Manson T-shirt.' He grasped the hem of the garment, and Judy helpfully raised her arms. She was wearing a half-cup violet satin bra. 'Set dressing is an important aspect of ritual magic, and possibly where you've been going wrong before. Trust me, you need to place yourself at the centre of events in order for the energy to flow.'

'Right,' Kate said, dubiously, but she still followed suit when Judy kicked off her jeans and underwear.

Dareth settled in the room's only chair, one elbow propped against the arm, and began to tap a slow rhythm on the upholstery. 'Before you, Nut, is the powerful daughter of Ra, the punisher of those guilty of irreverence.' He lowered his voice, modulated his speech, so that the syllables echoed the monotony of the beat. 'In order to nullify her strengths, it is necessary to seduce her with your body.'

He remained perfectly still in his seat and let his words sink in. Step by step, complicity would lead to surrender. He slowed the beat, now imitating the regular thump of a heartbeat during sleep. 'One ... two ... three ... Awaken, Nut, Sekhmet.' The two women shuffled forwards and clasped one another around the tops of their arms. Kate, perhaps emboldened by the mask, or empowered by her explicit pendant, drew her friend closer until their lips locked, just grazing to begin with. Then their hips met, and the kiss became more intimate.

Dareth considered reaching for a camera but rejected the idea as too risky. The flash would break the spell. 'Remember, Nut, it is you who must do the coaxing,' he said.

In response, the dark-haired girl tentatively touched her friend's heavy breasts, cupping their weight in her palms. Then, lowering her head, she closed her mouth around one steepled nipple.

Dareth unfastened the remaining buttons of his shirt, and rubbed a hand across the growing bulge at his loins. Sometimes things seemed just a fraction too easy. Of course, Judy had been willing from the start. Still, it was time to up the stakes. 'Lay Kate down and spread her legs,' he coaxed. 'Use your tongue to tame her.'

Obediently, they both rolled on to the crisp sheets of the bed.

'Sekhmet, you are a lioness, a wild animal, don't be lulled so easily.' Dareth shifted himself forwards in the chair and reclined so that he could unzip and push a hand inside his fly. It constantly amazed him how easily people were seduced by the old ritual-magic line and a little simple suggestion. Amazed, and gratified.

Judy slithered down the length of Kate's pleasingly rounded body, seeking out the sensitive areas with her lips and tongue as she moved, making her friend murmur in delight. She reached the base of the bed and knelt on the floor between Kate's splayed thighs. Dareth released his cock and shimmied out of his trousers and briefs. Precome had already beaded on the tip, and he rubbed it over the sensitive head as he watched Judy's dark head bob while she worked Kate's clit. It was almost time to take advantage of their arousal and introduce the positive principle.

Naked, he stalked across the carpet to the bed, his pale lean body faintly luminescent in the dim light. He reached the bed and traced a finger from Judy's shoulder to her neck. 'Enough,' he whispered against her skin. 'Work your way up again, so that she can return the favour.'

Dareth pressed in close against her bare rump as she stood, his cock seeking entrance between the apex of her thighs. Judy rubbed her bottom against him, urging him to impale her, but Dareth only teased her with his cock-tip as he slid an arm around her waist and sought her clitoris with the knuckle of his thumb.

Judy arched back against him and gave a sigh. On the bed, Kate lifted her hips towards them, her pale blue eyes behind the feline mask wide and pleading. Her breath sounded soft and deep, but there was also a looming urgency to it. Judy would have to wait.

Dareth urged Judy on to the bed astride her prone friend. He watched as she covered Kate's mouth with her neatly shaped muff, then availed himself of the warm wet heat of Kate's body. He briefly wondered if his fellow discussion panellists were having half as much fun, and decided that they weren't. Damn it, at 40 he was still hot, and he'd see that little prick eat his words before the year was out.

Kate was becoming breathless, her body sucking his cock deeper. As she reached climax, her whole body shook. She gave a single muffled cry then lifted Judy's leg and wriggled out from under her friend.

Dareth withdrew. Kate rose to her knees and pushed Judy on to all fours, holding her in a subservient position for him to enter. His cock butted eagerly against her, then slid in deep. His former anger melted away as the tingling sensation that started in his balls flooded into his shaft. He rode the high notes, letting instinct dictate his rhythm. Kate reached over and stroked his thigh; her fingers were fiery. Then, unexpectedly, she brushed a digit along the taut stretch of skin between his balls and his anus. The intimacy caught him off guard, making his spine flex and pushing his level of arousal to fever pitch. Fire streamed through his cock, and he let go with a roar of pure ecstasy.

Just the sort of cleansing he'd been looking for.

2

Adie slumped against a wall in a meagre strip of shade outside Cairo airport. She ignored the clamouring taxi drivers in dusty old Peugeot 404s and glanced around at the strange landscape. Just over a week had passed since her interview. Her arm and bottom ached from all the injections, and her nose was still a bit red from parting with her flatmate, but she had finally arrived in Egypt. Now she was looking forward to seeing her employer, the man who had brought her here. He'd been in her thoughts constantly since their first meeting. She'd studied all his papers just for the tiniest clue about him, but she'd found them curiously dry and impersonal.

To her left, a crowd of people milled around a dirty coach. Their milky tourist complexions, so much in contrast to the dark skin of the locals, had attracted a plague of guides and street vendors. A tall Nubian woman pushed a luggage cart through their midst, followed by a line of wide-eyed children whose lilting voices seemed to hang in the air. Adie clutched her overnight bag for comfort. She felt vulnerable and conspicuous, and home seemed very far away.

The stream of people gradually thinned to a trickle. Adie yawned, fatigued by the heat, and shifted her feet uncomfortably. Her clothes were damp with perspiration; a bead of sweat tickled her spine and rolled into the crease of her buttocks. She imagined the sharp cool taste of gin and tonic, sighed lethargically and closed her eyes.

Killian had contacted her only once, a single email that she'd read repeatedly. It had been brief and to the point, with no information about her role, her colleagues, or even where she'd be staying. She wondered if he thought of her as a woman, or just as another person able to dig dirt and sift rubble.

'Dr Adina Hamilton – Adie?' The soft voice of a woman broke her reverie.

'Yes,' she replied and opened her eyes. The woman before her was blonde, slender and delicate as a lily, but with sharp, appraising green eyes, and clearly defined triceps. She was also catching more than a few glances from the men nearby.

'I'm Siân Lawrence. Dr Carmichael sent me to collect you.'

'Oh!' Adie tried not to look disappointed as her heart sank. What chance had she with Killian when he employed such creatures? She immediately envied Siân her long, neatly plaited tail of hair and her sun-kissed, honey-gold skin. However, the woman gave her such a friendly smile that she couldn't hate her. Besides, she reminded herself, she was here to work, not to flirt.

Siân easily lifted her heavy suitcase. 'Sorry you had to wait. The traffic's appalling at this time of day.' She ushered Adie down the line of cars and donkey carts to a battered old Land Rover. 'Climb on board, it's open,' she instructed, while she hefted Adie's case into the back.

From the airport at Heliopolis they sped south towards central Cairo, past the exhibition centre and the outskirts of the Northern Cemetery, with the dry dusty wind whistling past the open window. Adie gazed out in awe at the city and the mixture of modern buildings and minarets. 'I never expected it to be like this,' she admitted.

'Nobody ever does. They think it'll all be stuck in the past. Cairo is the largest city in Africa and the Middle East. Believe me, it has everything any other city has, including the traffic.' To prove the point she leaned on the horn. Beep! She shot through a red light.

Adie jumped. Nobody on the street or in the other cars seemed even slightly surprised. A few of them even chased her through.

'Don't worry about it,' mumbled Siân. She hit the horn again as she slalomed between the two lines of traffic. Adie grabbed the edge of her seat; she'd expected a slow tour of the town, not Steve McQueen's reckless kid sister. Outside there was an answering cacophony of horns.

'Is this normal?' she gasped as they sailed past two huge bronze lions and out on to a bridge. The wide grey-blue stretch of water beneath them glittered in the early afternoon sun; along its banks date palms and flame trees flanked blue stone walkways which bustled with people. She was looking at the Nile, the lifeblood of Egypt since predynastic times.

Siân nodded as she leap-frogged the car down the lane of traffic.

'Where are we heading?'

'The apartment. It's on Gezira. One of the two islands Cairo spilled on to during the nineteenth century. It's mostly leafy residential, not very touristy. You'll get a chance to see some of downtown Cairo tonight when we have dinner.' They passed another pair of lions and reached dry land.

'Who's we?' asked Adie, while she struggled to absorb her surroundings. The buildings were less crowded here on the island and the landscape was now predominantly green.

'The team, of course. They're waiting to meet you.'

'Right. With Dr Carmichael?' She was sure Killian had said he'd meet her in person, but she could forgive him for staying out of the sweltering heat at the airport if he was going to be at the apartment.

'Afraid not. He's busy at the university.'

Adie tensed in her seat. This wasn't quite the welcome she'd expected. Siân seemed to notice her discomfort for she glanced at her curiously. 'Taken a fancy to him already, have you?'

'No.' Her answer was too sharp and a blush rose across her cheeks to contradict her.

'It isn't anything personal. He did plan to meet you, but something came up and it couldn't wait, since we're back on site tomorrow.' Siân's friendly smile became impish. 'You sure you're not interested in him? You must be the only woman who isn't.'

Adie shook her head.

'Honestly?'

'Yes.' She paused. 'I find him intellectually fascinating, that's all.' It sounded lame, and judging by the gleam in Siân's eyes, she wasn't fooling anyone. In fact, her companion was trying not to smirk.

'Right. Have it your way,' she said. 'Just don't hold your breath while you're waiting for him to make a move. It won't happen. And forget that romantic crap the media write, it's just not him. Discipline's more his style.'

'I see.' Adie had a brief vision of him cracking a bullwhip against her bare bottom. Was that what she was in for?

'He's also immune to seduction and keeps his cock in cold freeze, but I guess that's half his charm.'

'Are you warning me off?'

Siân shook her head vigorously. 'Hell no, just warning you. I wish you the best of luck, 'cause you'll need it.'

They waited to turn left at the end of a wide leafy avenue. 'What about the rest of the team, what are they like?' asked Adie.

Siân tapped the steering wheel thoughtfully. Outside someone was listening to a strange synthesis of eastern and western music on a tinny cassette player: wailing Arabic vocals layered over a Balearic beat.

'Full-time, besides Killian and myself there's Matthew and Lucas. Matthew's the dark, pretty one, and Lucas is the blond with the glasses. All you have to remember about them is that Matthew's good for a laugh, and Lucas isn't. He's an expert on ancient texts, but he's also a total square. There's also Jason and Samih; you probably won't see much of them. They're attached to Cairo University and do a lot of the cleaning and sorting. They hardly ever come out to Saqqara, which is probably just as well, because when they do turn up they always manage to upset Lucas.'

'How come?'

'Oh, you know, just by breathing mostly. They rarely take anything seriously and Lucas doesn't approve. You'll see.'

'So Lucas is fairly outnumbered, then? I mean by Matthew, Samih and Jason?'

Siân shook her head. 'You'd think so, but the three of them have never quite gelled. Not much in common, plus I think Matthew looks down on them a bit.' She shrugged, and turned the car through a gateway and on to a white gravel drive.

'What about Killian? How do people get on with him?'

Siân turned off the engine. 'As well as they need to. He's the boss. They do as they're told. Don't worry about him. Just remember to be professional and you won't go far wrong. But hey, you'll find out what he's like soon enough. Come on, let's see if they've saved us some ice-cream.'

Across the city in his office at the university, Killian studied the plans of the site one final time, then folded them and tucked the paper into his pocket. By now, Adie Hamilton would have arrived and the team would be sounding her out, sharing a few jokes and stories, building him up and playing him down. He swallowed some of the coffee that had gone cold an hour ago. The bitter taste reminded him of his angry parting with Joe. He hadn't meant to upset the man who had stuck by him even through the lowest point of his career, but he needed someone competent and keen, and he'd known even before the interview that Adie was something special just from the way Joe spoke of her. With some training, he was sure she'd make an excellent Egyptologist.

He frowned and rose from his chair. The evening sun was reflecting off the cars parked below his office window. He pushed it open and leaned out. The dry heat was pleasing against his skin after the grey, cold and wet English weather. Even after two days in Cairo, he still felt slightly chilled. He rejected the possibility that the chill was actually a cold prickle of fear dredged up by Joe's words.

Killian never pretended that his path to the top had been smooth. Far from it: his career had almost ended before it had properly begun, thanks to a nasty incident he preferred to forget. In those days, his colleagues had shunned him, but he'd struggled on tenaciously and now, when they lavished accolades on him, he felt like laughing in their faces. Of course, he was proud of what he'd achieved, but this season would be tough on him. Saqqara had become synonymous with his dreams; it was also the place he'd first seen them shattered. He knew that friends like Josef Levine feared for his reputation, even his sanity, if the past was brought up again. They already looked on Bill Harris's fall as a bad omen. But Killian refused to see it like that. Only by going back to Saqqara would he ever face his demon.

Below, a group of students crossed the car park. Two of them waved. Determined to be positive, he waved back, but the uncharacteristic response made them hurry away in confusion. Killian realised that Adie Hamilton was probably feeling just as confused. He knew he should have collected her in person, and while he could fool the team that he was too busy, he couldn't fool himself. He was avoiding her and he didn't know why.

She'd been on his mind a lot over the last week. Two nights ago, he'd woken in a cold sweat with her name on his tongue. Of course, Josef's admonishment was enough to fix a name in anybody's head. But it wasn't just that. He'd sensed it at the interview, a sort of excited energy about her that made him want to take her hand and show her all the wonders he'd seen. He wanted to see the light of discovery in her eyes.

Killian stopped himself before he got carried away. He also wanted her to work quietly and efficiently, his way, with no fuss.

He returned to his desk and flicked through his appointment diary: nothing until the next semester. He'd cancelled them all to give the project his undivided attention, but now he wished that he'd agreed to the lecture at the American University in Cairo. It would have taken his mind off tomorrow, but it was too late for regrets. He slumped forwards and pressed his forehead to the desk. Roll on tomorrow.

The smell of harsh tobacco and coffee mingled in the cool night air as Adie gazed with glassy eyes at the narrow, covered alleyway. They had eaten at a hotel overlooking the Nile and then moved on to Fishwari's – Cairo's oldest coffee house – where she'd drunk two cups of the thick sugary beverage that had left her feeling wired. She was still disappointed that Killian hadn't turned up, but the rest of the team were doing their best to make her feel welcome. Even 'straight and boring' Lucas was being warm and pleasant.

'Poor Bill,' Samih mused about their old work-mate, as Adie's attention came back to the rickety little table around which they were crowded. 'He was all set for his next race when he broke that leg. Now we won't see him again for ages. I had money on him!'

Bill, it turned out, had been the real black sheep of the team. An architecture graduate who'd ended up in the Middle East designing skyscrapers, he'd got involved with the Egyptian Antiquities Organisation on a few small projects and had somehow managed to wangle a permanent position on Killian's team.

'Adie's prettier,' Jason said. He turned his head and smiled at her. Samih's expression also brightened.

'That's true. Bill was a bit grizzly, especially first thing. I don't suppose you're any good at camel racing, are you?'

The two young Cairenes, she was rapidly learning, were something of a double act. 'I'm afraid not. I've never even been near one,' she replied.

'I'd keep it that way if I were you,' cautioned Lucas. His seat creaked as he shifted forwards. 'They're unscrupulous beasts, and their owners aren't much better. If you want to go exploring, hire a horse, or better still get someone to drive you.'

'Boring!' sighed Jason, while Samih nodded his head in agreement.

Adie looked to Siân, who shook her head. 'I'm with Lucas on this one. If you want to visit somewhere just let me know. I'll be happy to take you.'

'Thanks.'

Siân nodded. 'It's all right for these two, they're men and they grew up here. Cairo's pretty safe but I wouldn't advise going off on your own. Western women have an undeserved reputation among some of the men in these parts.'

'Too many Hollywood exports,' Lucas embellished. 'The image they're fed is that all western women are promiscuous and available. Some of the tourists don't help either, so be careful how you dress. Save your skinny fits and shorts for underground at the dig, where there are fewer wandering hands.'

'Which reminds me.' Siân dug into her pocket and pulled out a small box. 'Killian asked me to give you this.'

Adie took the tiny box; her fingers tingled with excitement at the unexpected present. The hinge opened with a snap to reveal a gold wedding band. She stared at it, gobsmacked. Siân chuckled and leaned in close. 'I've one too.' Sure enough, she had an identical plain gold ring on her left ring finger. 'It's a safety thing. You're less likely to be harassed by strange blokes if they think you're married. Present company excepted.'

Adie stared at the ring thoughtfully, then snapped the box shut and shoved it in her pocket. She couldn't bring herself to put it on just yet; maybe tomorrow. It presented a new spin on being married to the job.

'We ought to head back, we've work to do tomorrow,' Lucas said, to several groans.

'Don't be so boring, it's not even midnight yet.' Jason shuffled his chair closer to Adie's and placed an arm around her shoulder.

'You don't have to be up early tomorrow.'

'Yeah, but it's her first night. Come on, man!' he pleaded, but to no effect. Lucas merely folded his arms across his chest. Jason sighed, then turned his attention back to Adie. 'Don't listen to him,' he coaxed. 'You should make the most of it. Once you get to Saqqara that's it, no fun, no smiling, and definitely no alcohol. Killian's a real slave driver.'

'Too right,' added Samih. He leaned across the table conspiratorially. 'You've seen what Lucas is like; Killian's twice as bad. Why do you think we stay in town?'

Adie looked sceptically at them. They were both grinning mischievously. 'What about at the hotel?'

'There is no hotel,' said Matthew, who had been quiet

all evening. He smiled archly, and Adie noticed that his lips were stained from the wine they'd drunk earlier. Siân hadn't been lying when she'd described him as pretty on the car journey from the airport. Matthew was slender and fine-boned with a long straight nose and star-lashed china-blue eyes. He looked like an Art student or a refugee from a Hugo Boss ad, but certainly not an Egyptologist. Adie turned to Siân for an answer.

'It's true. Killian owns a *dahabiyya* – a houseboat. He has it moored close to the site. He says it's more convenient than living in a hotel or commuting from Cairo and I'm inclined to agree, although it does get a bit claustrophobic.'

'It's so he can keep a check on us,' Matthew added. Adie breathed a sigh of relief; for a moment she had thought they were camping. 'Just wait and see, it's all early nights and early mornings. The man doesn't have a single natural urge, and the only reason Siân's sticking up for him is because she fancies him. I hope you've more sense.'

'Ignore him. He's teasing you.' Siân wagged a finger at Matthew. Her voice became sharp. 'These two are bad enough without you starting as well. Lucas is right. We should be heading home.'

'Touchy!' Matthew retorted. 'What's the matter, Siân? Frightened of competition? I keep telling you, if you want to get his attention, paint yourself gold and get someone to bury you. He's only interested in older women. *Much* older women.'

Siân pushed the wooden table away from her chair, making their drinks rattle, and stood. 'Time to leave,' she said.

They stepped out of the cab at the gate to the apartment, while Lucas haggled with the driver. The neighbourhood was dark and silent, and pollution obscured the stars. The night was mild, warmed by the dusty southerly wind. Adie followed Matthew along the grass verge to the front door, avoiding the noisy crunch of the gravel. Siân unlocked the door and light spilled over the wooden slats of the veranda.

They all crowded into the kitchen while Adie considered Matthew's remark. Everyone's image of Killian was remote and dispassionate, but she was sure she'd detected real warmth beneath his cold professionalism. And was Siân that smitten? Adie somehow doubted it, but Matthew seemed to have upset her.

The kitchen was a mixture of Islamic design and western gadgets: more a magazine's interpretation of Oriental than the real thing. Siân opened the fridge and took out some orange juice, which she drank from the carton. She pulled herself up on to the workbench, while Lucas snorted disapprovingly. He poured himself a glass of water. Jason and Samih sat down at the table.

Matthew padded across the tiled floor to Siân. He stroked her thigh, and said something under his breath. Adie strained to catch the reply, intrigued by the interplay. The pair had been staring daggers at each other all the way home.

'I'm sure I don't know what you mean.' Siân grabbed his wrist, but Matthew easily twisted free and clasped her hand instead. He raised it to his mouth and kissed her knuckles.

Siân's catlike green eyes glittered. 'Show off,' she scoffed.

Matthew responded by hooking his free hand around Siân's back and pulling her forwards, so that she slipped across the polished worktop into his arms. Siân twined her legs around Matthew's hips. 'Is this what you had in mind?' she asked.

'Yep.'

They began to kiss. So they were an item, of sorts, she realised and turned away. That explained things.

'Grow up, you two. No one wants to see it,' snarled Lucas in irritation as their kiss became increasingly noisy.

'No, man, we're enjoying it. Live floorshow – you pay money for this in some places.' Samih grinned at Adie. 'Jason and I don't get out much,' he confided. His dark-olive skin had flushed a delicate shade of pink across his cheekbones, and his dark eyes were like saucers. Meanwhile, Jason was blithely stirring a third spoonful of sugar into his tea.

'OK, we'll leave,' said Siân. She slipped off the bench and tugged Matthew towards the door. 'You're just jealous, Mr Marsh. When was the last time you got laid?'

'About the same time as Killian,' quipped Matthew. Siân poked him in the ribs, but he continued regardless. 'Remind me to change careers if I ever get too good at my job.'

Lucas ignored the remarks. 'Hold it,' he said, bringing them both to a halt in the doorway. 'Aren't you forgetting something?'

Siân turned back with a scowl. 'I was hoping you'd forgotten.'

'Well I didn't. We still need to decide who's getting up early tomorrow for Killian.'

'Don't look at us,' chorused Jason and Samih. Samih gave a theatrical yawn. 'We don't start work 'til nine. Cut cards or something, it'll be quicker than the usual bickering.'

Lucas opened the dresser drawer and took out a handful of tapers. 'All right, we'll draw straws.' He held out the bundle. 'Choose.' They each selected one. 'You too, Adie. You're part of the team now, that means you get the same deal as the rest of us.'

Reluctantly, she drew a spill. It was the shortest.

'Bad luck,' said Siân. She patted Adie's shoulder sympathetically. 'Looks like you're greeting the boss. You'll enjoy it, he's always radiant first thing.'

'And you tell me off for teasing people,' muttered Matthew. He pressed a kiss to Adie's brow, which gave her a sudden whiff of his spicy cologne. 'Sleep well. And welcome to the team.'

'Yeah,' moaned Adie. She watched them leave and then stared at Lucas as he tidied the spills back into the drawer. 'How early?'

'Very early. He'll be here at five to load the trunks. You'll have to open the door, because it's bolted from the inside when anyone with any sense is staying here.' He glared at the two Cairenes. 'He'll probably need a hand moving things, as well.'

'You're really serious?' said Adie.

'Quite serious.'

'Jesus!' She yawned, and then pushed herself to her feet. If she had to be up before five she really did need to get to bed.

Lucas left the kitchen behind her. 'Remember to switch the lights off, you two,' he called.

'Sure. Goodnight.'

Adie closed the bedroom door of the room she was supposed to share with Siân, then stripped and snuggled under the cool sheets. She'd never been any good at mornings.

Sun-warmed sand clothed her naked body. Adie lay on a blanket of silk in a square stone room whose ceiling was open to the sky. The flick of something soft caressed her thigh. It tickled. She tried to wriggle but her body didn't respond. It was as though she was pinned down, but she felt no weight above her, nor cuffs about her wrists.

'An extraordinary find,' an individual at her feet said, and she smiled inwardly, knowing he was referring to her, as her head was cushioned and her hair confined in an elegant headdress.

The sun shone red through her eyelids. She felt the whisper of the desert breeze across her skin, and tried to move her toes. There was still no response, but strangely, she felt no panic.

'Exquisite, and perfectly preserved,' said a voice she recognised. 'She must have lain here over three thousand years, and not a scratch on her.' The soft caress continued, meticulously sweeping the golden sand away from the underside of her breast. Her nipples tightened in response. Apparently, she hadn't lost any sensation.

'She looks so real,' said the first man. 'If she weren't made of gold, I would say she was only sleeping.'

Gold? What is he talking about? She peeped from beneath her eyelashes at the length of her body and saw that they spoke the truth, for her skin shone with metallic lustre in the sunlight. Gold! she wanted to say, but she couldn't speak.

'She's so detailed,' said Killian, and he touched one puckered areola with the brush. A splinter of ice seemed to lodge in her skin at the intimacy; its cold arousal shocked the dormant seed of passion within her into life. She trembled with anticipation, and awaited his next touch.

'Astounding. I can't wait until you show her to the board. Speaking of which, one of us should tell them.'

'You go,' said Killian, whilst he stroked a finger over her hip. The longed-for contact made her vagina feel heavy and full. He began to circle her navel with the tip of his index finger, using slow nervous strokes that became bolder as the footfalls of the other man receded. One finger became two, and two rapidly became three, until he was running both palms over her warm torso.

Adie's skin tingled with languorous pleasure. The heat in her womb seeped like treacle through her limbs. She sighed noiselessly. He stared at her as though her beauty had enthralled him and expelled every other thought from his mind. Slowly, he dipped his head and pressed bow-shaped lips to her chin. The scent of him lingered in the air around them. He explored the shadows of her throat. His kiss moved to her parted lips and alighted like a butterfly, before the stab of his tongue drove deep inside her mouth. He tasted of coriander, slightly spicy, and subtly sweet. Adie silently purred; she strained to reach him, to return his caress, but her body wouldn't respond.

Killian drew back and gazed down upon her in wonderment. She saw the shadow of doubt in his liquid grey eyes, and wished she could reassure him. A telltale strain appeared across the zip of his trousers, and he glanced around nervously. Finally, he swept the last of the sand from the tops of her thighs, then drew a hand up between her legs. Her labia parted for his fingers and welcomed him with a sticky wet sound. He moaned to find her so wet, so ready for him. She felt his body tremble as he shifted position so that he crouched between her golden thighs. He wrenched open the restraining zip, and then ran a hand along his erection as if to prepare himself.

Adie sighed at the vision of his hard, red-tipped cock. A honeyed bead of arousal trickled from her vulva. She wanted to touch him, to beg him to give in to his desire, but all she could do was lie and wait.

'A statue?' he questioned himself as her flawless image swam in his dark pupils. 'Is this real? Ah!' He gasped as he pressed himself to her cleft.

Adie's senses leaped. He slid into her with the same liquid sensuality as ice-cream sliding down her throat on a burning August afternoon, deep into her until their loins nestled together. It felt so good, she wished she could save it, to experience it over and over again. He fucked her slowly at first, his penis moving like satin in her sheath. He stroked her cheek and kissed her golden lips. She felt every tiny jump of his cock, every hot breath against her throat, and yet she still couldn't move. There was no way of telling him that a few firm touches to her clitoris would make it complete.

He picked up the pace, and began to thrust with selfish pleasure, short strokes and fast. A sweat broke out across his brow. Then he pounded with deeper, harder strokes, but still fast, still building. He nudged into her G-spot and her stomach tightened. A crazy tingle began between her clitoris and her spine.

'Don't stop, don't stop, don't stop,' she repeated silently, urgently. The sensation built, pushing its way into her brain. She experienced a momentary sense of stillness, utter calm, and then her whole body shuddered as she came.

'Oh god!' he murmured in her ear, as her body contracted around him. His weight rested upon her, his heart hammering so vigorously she could feel it against her chest. He arched his back, and pushed his cock deep into her core. One final stroke. His eyes narrowed and then closed. His lips parted and his cock jerked as the intensity of his orgasm forced the air from his lungs.

3

The sound of his heartbeat didn't stop when she opened her eyes, but turned into the dull thump of the knocker against the front door. Adie blinked groggily at the darkened room, then found her watch – 5 a.m. Siân's bed was still empty, and the rest of the house was quiet. Somehow she managed to focus enough to snatch up her robe. The belt was missing, so she clasped the edges together in one hand as she staggered through unfamiliar rooms. 'All right, I'm coming. Take a chill pill.' The heavy bolt slid back with a metallic thud, and she turned the key in the lock.

'About time.' Killian swept past her, then turned back as she shut the door. He flicked the light switch on and wakened the room with a soft orange glow. For a moment his eyes relaxed, softening his expression. 'Do they have you answering the door already?'

'I drew the short straw,' Adie replied as she clutched her robe tightly around herself, aware that her nipples were still erect from her dream. Killian was leaner and more handsome than she remembered. The false memory of him gently brushing sand from her skin resurfaced, and she felt a distinct pulse of arousal.

'There's a surprise.' He cast a brisk glance over her near-naked body. Adie's cheeks burned as she realised that he could probably see straight through the thin cloth.

'Perhaps you'd like to put some clothes on,' he said.

'Yes!' She fled to her room, shut the door and pressed her forehead to the frame, afraid that he might follow, and disappointed when he didn't. She found the end of the bed and sat down. After a deep breath, she opened her case and dug out a pair of lightweight trousers and a vest top.

There was a firm rap on the door. 'I've made some coffee,' Killian called. 'You looked like you needed it.'

'Yeah, great.' Adie pulled on her boots and quickly laced them up. She was at the door before she remembered the wedding ring Siân had presented to her. She reclaimed it from the pocket of yesterday's clothing and slipped it on. The fit was good.

Killian was standing in the corridor when she opened the bedroom door. He handed her a mug and she took a hesitant sip of the strong liquid, then put it aside as her stomach protested.

'I hope they looked after you last night. Unfortunately, something came up.'

She nodded, and watched enthralled as his lips pressed against the rim of the mug. As before, she wanted to reach over and touch him, but she feared his reaction.

'Do you always start at dawn?' she asked instead.

'Mostly.' He turned away, killing the conversation. Adie watched him disappear through a doorway. He returned carrying a large case. 'Do you think you could hold the door open?' he asked.

Outside, the moon gazed down on the city like the left eye of Horus. Adie watched the moonlight play on his silky white hair as he slid the trunk into the back of a gleaming four-by-four. She tried another sip of coffee, and this time her stomach didn't argue.

'Can I help?' she asked when he dragged another trunk into the corridor. Her eyes locked on the open collar of his shirt. The fabric parted to reveal the shadowy line of his collarbone. His skin was several shades darker than the linen, and evenly tanned all the way down. She guessed he sometimes worked with his shirt off. That would be something to look forward to.

Killian looked her over again in his dispassionate way. She'd have to get used to that. 'If you want.'

Adie gripped one of the leather handles and helped him lift. It was heavier than she'd expected but she gritted her teeth, determined not to seem weak and useless. By the time they'd dragged it into the car, she was hot, sticky and breathing hard. 'Shall we get another?' she asked, hoping to look tough and capable.

Killian shook his head. 'I can manage. Why don't you collect your things instead?'

'All right,' she agreed. There was no fooling him, and she didn't really fancy lifting another case. 'What do I need?'

Killian's gaze dropped to where her damp vest clung to her breasts. 'With your skin and that outfit? Some factor fifty.' Adie flushed and turned away, feeling like a rank amateur. 'Bring enough clothes for a week, your toothbrush and a sun-hat,' he added.

It was quarter to six when they reached Saqqara. The early-morning sun washed over the desert landscape, turning it into a vast ocean of gold. Adie gazed at the necropolis in wonderment; it was very different from how it appeared on TV. Nothing had prepared her for quite how bright it all was. To her right, Djoser's pyramid rose to the heavens in six gilded steps, surrounded by the mounds of other crumbling pyramids and ancient mastabas, and over it all the *khamseen* wind raced in great hot gusts, blowing up dust clouds like swarms of incessant midges.

Killian stood silently beside her. At first glance, he appeared unaffected by the weight of history around them, but as they set out towards the excavation, she thought she detected a subtle gleam of emotion in his cool grey eyes.

They left the trunks in the car and walked past the

eroded pyramid of Unas – the last king of the fifth dynasty – and the pitlike entrance to Sekhemkhet's unfinished tomb, towards an uninteresting mound of rubble.

'Impressive, isn't it,' Killian commented dryly as they came to the pile of sand and stones. 'You can see why it's been ignored for the last hundred years.' He scraped away some of the ochre-coloured earth with his hands, and rolled away a couple of small boulders to reveal a solid iron door and a thick padlock. 'We had the door put in when we realised there was something interesting down here. It keeps the wildlife and the tourists out.'

'And presumably, the tomb raiders,' said Adie cheerily before lapsing into a cough, surprised by the dry taste of sand in her mouth.

Killian gave her a tight smile and fished a key from his back pocket. Adie stared at his taut buttocks as he unfastened the padlock. She thought about grabbing a handful, but apart from his cold rebuke there was a risk that he'd straighten up and knock himself out on the lintel, and she'd have a hard time explaining that to the team.

The door opened on to a small antechamber at the top of a broad stairway, and in a sudden rush of excitement, she pushed through the door after him. This was what she'd come here for. Years of work, weeks of pleading, threats of blackmail, all for this. Finally, she was standing inside an Egyptian house of the dead.

Killian pulled the door closed behind them, blocking out the morning sun and the roar of the southerly wind. No deathless mummies lurched out of the gloom, no giant boulders rolled into view, and no wonderful treasure glinted at her. In the black stillness, Adie's excitement ebbed. She hadn't really expected any of those things, but she still felt slightly disappointed by the plain stone antechamber. She shivered. The sharp odour of animal excrement filled her nostrils and made her gag. Killian's torch cast half-formed shadows over the walls, and seemed to declare them as trespassers. Which, she realised, was exactly what they were. The submerged tomb was the final resting-place of an ancient pharaoh and, whatever their motive, they were unwelcome.

'Careful of your footing,' Killian cautioned, his voice echoing dully. 'We've already had one accident and I don't want another.'

Adie nodded, and allowed herself to be guided further inside.

Stairs, the walls of which were powdery with white limestone, ran down to a stone doorway inscribed with hieroglyphs. Killian ushered her into a square room. One corner had partially fallen in, but the left-hand wall was virtually intact. Its surface was decorated with an extensive, intricately coloured relief of animal-headed beings engaged in some ritual. A section of the frieze appeared to have been hacked out, corresponding to the groin area of one of the figures.

'Wow!' She reached out a hand to the vividly coloured surface, but Killian jerked her back.

'Beautiful, isn't it?' he said into her ear, and she felt his breath buffet her cheek. Temporarily lost for words, she nodded dumbly. How had anyone missed this for so long? It was in almost perfect condition.

'The entrance was lost under a rock fall,' Killian explained, answering her silent question. 'We discovered it while engaged on a mapping project of the area. Tourists had been climbing on it and knocked some of the stones away to reveal a gap, but until we cleared the entrance we had to scramble through with just basic equipment.'

'And this is what you found,' she said, still transfixed by the mural.

'More of a rediscovery. We weren't the first to come down here, as you can see from the graffiti,' he said as he pointed out sections of the northern and western walls. 'And other archaeologists had reported evidence of a tomb here.'

'Yes, but . . .' Adie took a hesitant step forwards, wishing but not daring to run her fingertips over the ancient painting. 'What does it represent?'

Killian moved forwards a fraction. 'It's hard to say for sure because of the missing fragment, but the figure on the right seems to be the pharaoh as a manifestation of Horus, undergoing some form of ritual performed by the kneeling slave. The priestly figure in the background is Osiris, possibly imparting his worldly powers to his son.'

Adie nodded, recognising the distinctive features of the figures, Horus the sky god with his hawk's head and Osiris in his mummy wrappings, holding the symbols of kingship – the crook and the flail.

'Some believe it's a representation of fellatio,' continued Killian, and the ghost of a smile briefly softened his chiselled features. 'Others think it's a washing or embalming ritual, due to the presence of the jars. The team's divided. You're welcome to make up your own mind, but please refrain from broadcasting it outside these walls.'

Adie swallowed, imagining Killian as the pharaoh, herself as the slave, lips parted to receive his erection. He was standing very close to her and she could smell his scent, an exotic, slightly spicy blend underpinned by the faint smell of his own body.

'Are you all right?' Killian placed a firm hand on her shoulder. A quiver of excitement licked her insides at the contact. She fought the urge to lean into him, to force an embrace from his concerned gesture.

'Adie?'

'I'm fine. Just sleep deprivation, that's all,' she said breathlessly. 'What's your opinion of the mural?'

'I don't have one. There are other issues which are far more pressing.'

'Right.' Adie took an uncertain step back, surprised by the chill realism of his last remark. 'So what happened to the fragment?'

'A mid-nineteenth-century explorer called William Jacobs hacked it out. The story goes that after a successful season at Giza, he came to Saqqara in late December 1881, accompanied by his nineteen-year-old daughter and their native companion. He entered the chamber ahead of the pair and censored the image to protect her innocence.'

Killian shook his head sadly. 'The Victorians had some very strange values. They made some incredible discoveries, but they did a lot of damage too. No doubt you've heard of similar examples of mutilated statues, and severed genitalia.'

Adie nodded.

'Josef used to use one as a paperweight, until it was stolen.'

'So it does show fellatio,' concluded Adie.

'It shows a penis. That much is clear from Jacobs' diary. Which, incidentally, is in the Cairo Museum library if you wish to look.'

'What did he do with the bit he chipped out?'

'Who knows. It might turn up here, but frankly I doubt it. Possibly it was sold to a private collector. We're just lucky he didn't remove the whole scene and ship it back to England. That happened a lot back then.'

Killian turned and ran his torch over the walls. After the brilliance of the mural, the rest of the chamber seemed altogether drab. 'Through there, the corridor continues for a short distance before it becomes blocked by rubble, probably from a cave-in. Before that, it branches off into another corridor leading to a network of storage magazines. You'll see them later. To start with, you'll be working in here until you've shown me what you can do. See these plaster fragments scattered around? I'd like you to work on reassembling them, so I hope you've a talent for jigsaw puzzles.'

Adie stifled a sigh. More broken pots. Still, there was the prospect of some exploration and the chance of finding that fragment.

'Get some breakfast before you start. It's going to be a very long day.'

He hadn't been joking, thought Adie later that evening. The others had arrived shortly after six and they'd worked all day and into the evening fixing the lighting rig. It had been hot, thirsty work, while the tomb had warmed like a slow-cooker. Matthew and Siân had kept her going. Meanwhile, Killian seemed tireless, and inured to the heat.

The *dahabiyya* turned out to be a converted passenger boat. Built in the 20s to carry wealthy tourists down the Nile between Cairo and Luxor, it had been refitted with every convenience, including a modern workroom. Adie had tried to picture Hercule Poirot pacing the deck, but he would have tripped over the crates of equipment.

They ate communally. Lucas had made *fiteer*, a sort of stuffed pizza with a flaky pastry base. They'd all showered. Killian's white hair was slowly drying in the evening sun. He seemed more relaxed here, surrounded by verdant grassland and chattering wildlife, than in the heart of the necropolis. There was a distant look in his grey eyes, as if his mind dreamed while his body ate. Adie tried to catch his eye but failed. She suddenly felt awkward and new.

'Well done on getting through your first day without breaking anything,' said Lucas beside her. He gave her a gentle pat on the back. Adie recovered a little at his praise.

Siân leaned in and poured coffee. 'My first day was a

disaster. I was so excited I managed to put a pickaxe through my foot.'

'You're joking!' Adie said, horrified.

'Wish I was; I spent three months recovering and missed the rest of the season, but I've got a lovely scar to show for it. Remind me and I'll show you some time.'

'That's all right, I think I'll pass.'

Siân shrugged her slender shoulders, and moved along the table with the coffee.

'What are you dreaming about?' Adie asked Killian, opting for a direct approach. He seemed to come to himself, but his expression showed irritation.

'I don't dream. I plan, I investigate and I let the facts speak for themselves.' He regarded her coldly. 'Joe seems to think you're more intuitive than that. He also thinks I'll crush your eager spirit.'

Adie stared dumbly. Success with her was often down to instinct, and Joe had recognised and complimented her ability to see patterns where others could see none. She'd thought she had a valuable skill.

'I don't have time for ifs and maybes. Remember to keep any opinions to yourself until you can back them up with evidence.'

Adie nodded wordlessly, trying to digest this weighty morsel.

Killian remained at the table long after the others had left, as Siân knew he would. She'd got used to his habits, and if she couldn't read his thoughts, she certainly knew his moods. She could see that his mind was on the project and on Adie. After a few years working side by side in cramped conditions, you could tell when a man got horny. He wouldn't admit it, though, and thanks to his usual charm neither would Adie.

Once Siân would have been jealous, back when she'd

just joined the team and been infatuated with his good looks and outward confidence; since then she'd learned that he came with a lot of emotional baggage. She figured the sex would have been good, but she could get that from Matthew without negotiating for it. Besides, Killian's kinks weren't her own; she liked her partners to be equals, and with Killian there would always be that power differential.

She crept up behind his chair and pressed a hand to his shoulder. 'Siân,' he murmured. Nobody else on the team ever made such an affectionate gesture to him. He didn't stir or resist as she lifted the coffee mug from his hands and took a sip.

'Yuck! It's cold. How can you drink that stuff?' She put the cup down with a thump.

'I wasn't.'

'I'll make some more, shall I?'

Killian yawned. 'Not for me. I'm off to bed. I've been up since four.' He started to rise but Siân laid a hand on his arm to stop him.

'Hang on. Are you all right? You look like something's on your mind.'

Killian regarded her silently. Now that he was facing her, there was an obvious liquid sheen to his eyes. Siân didn't expect him to talk. He usually bottled up his temper and his passions, which still led to occasional messy flare-ups.

'I'm fine,' he replied, the even timbre of his voice well rehearsed.

'Adie should fit in well,' she persisted.

'Hopefully. As long as she doesn't get scared off.'

'Eh?'

'Matthew. He's been on the shark all day.'

'Oh, right.' So he'd noticed. Well, that virtually proved his interest in Adie. There was never a time when Matthew wasn't trying to get into someone's pants, but

Killian had never remarked upon it before. 'What are you going to do?' she asked.

Killian pushed his chair back from the table, and rose. 'Fall into bed. I want to start early tomorrow to make up for the time we've lost.' He scooped up his coffee mug and threw the contents overboard.

Siân watched him leave, then padded along the deck towards the prow.

Adie was resting with her chin in her hands when the sound of footsteps reached her through the dusty roar of the wind. 'I thought everyone had turned in,' she said to Siân, who came to a halt beside her. The blonde woman put her back to the railing as water sucked at the *dahabiyya*.

'Not quite. We've been talking about you.'

Adie's shoulders came up defensively. 'Anything I should know about?'

'Nothing bad. We were just trying to suss you out. And Matthew's taken a fancy to you.'

Adie shifted forwards a fraction on the box she was sitting on. 'I thought you two were an item.'

'Hell, no.' Siân pushed her long braid over her shoulder and faked outrage. 'We're fuck buddies. He's good for a laugh, but he wouldn't know serious if it slapped him in the face. And I wouldn't want to get serious with him. He takes too long in the bathroom, if you get me.'

'I think so. It was last night,' said Adie. 'I just assumed.'

Siân laughed. 'We were just making the most of it. There's no privacy here; everyone can hear everything.'

'I'll bear that in mind.' She mentally tore up her plans for seducing Killian. Besides, she was still smarting from his words at dinner.

'I'm turning in now,' said Siân. 'Killian wants to start at dawn, so you'd best do the same.'

'Will do.'

Adie watched her leave then turned her gaze towards the brilliant heavens. Killian's outburst had helped her to understand Joe's reluctance to send her here, but intuition told her there was something more. Presumably, time would tell. Meanwhile, she'd just have to grin and bear it until Killian gave her a permanent contract.

4

Adie stared dreamily at the rolling dunes beyond the tomb's narrow entrance. Her first six days in Egypt had passed in a blur of sand, sweat and suggestiveness; the latter from Matthew, who was taking advantage of his close proximity. As the two junior members of the team, they had the tedious job of sorting the fractured pieces of plaster from the antechamber floor. This meant long hours on her hands and knees, and she found herself easily distracted by the desolate beauty of the world outside.

'Are you skiving again?' asked Siân, coming upon her from behind. 'What's it like out there?'

'Windy.'

'Should have guessed, another choppy night on the river, and another dinner that tastes of sand. I hate this season. Still, it should be over soon.'

'I thought the *khamseen* was supposed to last fifty days,' Adie said. She'd been picking her way through the *Lonely Planet* guide.

'Is it? Storms usually blow themselves out after a couple of hours. You must be trouble or something. This has hardly eased off since you arrived.'

'Don't blame me.'

Siân shrugged and peeped over her penny shades. She squeezed into the doorway next to Adie to watch as a few brave tourists battled against the wind. In the distance, the three peaks of Egypt's most famous landmarks waited impassively while the storm softened their outlines by infinitesimal degrees.

'Killian's looking for you.' Siân ducked back inside the entrance chamber and took a long draught from her water bottle. Some of the contents spilled over her chin, soaking into her navy T-shirt to leave darker patches. 'He wants to know if you're making any progress. I'd get down there and impress him while you've got the chance.'

'Thanks for the tip.'

Killian had his back to her as she entered the mural room. His white hair was damp from the heat, and his moist T-shirt clung to his broad shoulders. She could understand how he seduced the media. It was all stage-managed. If they wanted Indiana Jones, he appeared dust-streaked and grimy from the tunnels. And if they wanted the immaculate scholar, he turned up cool and professional in a suit. Adie couldn't decide which image she liked best. She just wished he wasn't so distant. Instead of being full of stories of adventures on previous digs, she'd discovered that he didn't make small talk.

'Here she is,' Matthew said. He was crouched over a quadrangle he'd just cleared. Killian turned 90 degrees in response.

'Adie, I was just telling Matthew, I want you both to concentrate on the north-west corner. Try to reconstruct that section of the wall-relief. There may be a cartouche among the fragments that'll tell us who the tomb belongs to.'

Adie glanced at the area he meant.

'I said we'd get right on it,' Matthew elucidated.

'But what about the other areas? We might find the missing fragment of mural where we are.'

'Slim chance.'

Adie sucked her bottom lip. Killian's soft yet crushing tone made her feel like she'd just had her hand slapped. 'Is a cartouche more important, then?'

'Funding is important,' he responded dryly. 'And our sponsors will be happier once they have a name to drop.'

Matthew brushed the dust from the knees of his trousers, then checked his watch. 'There's not much time to start on this now. I guess it'll wait until tomorrow. Unless...' He licked his lips, whilst his gaze flickered across to Adie and then Killian. 'Unless we put in a couple more hours tonight. I'm game if Adie is.'

Killian raised a sceptical eyebrow. 'You do realise you don't get paid overtime?'

'I know.'

'Good. And Adie?' He turned his steely gaze upon her.

Adie fixed a grin. 'No problem.' She nodded her head enthusiastically, only to scowl at Matthew the moment Killian turned his back. As much as she wanted to impress, she liked a little time in the evening to recuperate.

'I'll arrange for someone to pick you up at nine,' Killian said. 'That should give you plenty of time to make an impression.'

'I could kill you,' Adie said to Matthew twenty minutes later, after the rest of the team had quit for the night. 'I ache all over, and I was first for the shower tonight. What's with volunteering me?' She rammed her trowel into the earth floor and jerked it out again, sending dirt flying.

'Hey, gently! Nobody's making you stay. You could have said no.'

'Right, like that was an option. I'm still on probation, remember.'

'Chill out, Adie, it's obvious he's going to keep you on.'

'How do you work that one out, genius?'

''Cause he fancies you, and who can blame him.' He gave her a cheeky grin as his gaze slid down to her breasts, which were straining the rounded neck of her vest and threatening to spill out.

Adie pursed her lips and prodded him with her trowel. All week, he'd been trying to convince her that Killian had a thing for her. It had become the boringly predictable end to every conversation. 'Next time, ask before you volunteer me,' she said. 'And stop staring at my tits.'

'Didn't bother you earlier.'

'It's off-putting.'

Matthew continued to stare, and Adie flushed. 'I told you. I'm not interested,' she said, trying hard not to smile at his playful grin. Despite her words, the first telltale signs of arousal were already clawing at her insides. Even a few minutes of being around Killian seemed to fire her senses. She wondered if she was getting a bit obsessive. Anyway, Matthew was playing on her desire. He insolently drew a finger over one flaming cheek, then along her jawbone and down to her neck.

'I remember, you're saving yourself for the boss. 'Cept you'll have forgotten what to do with him by the time he comes around.'

Adie stiffened at the thrill of his touch, and her nipples became visible through her vest. Play it cool, she told herself. She'd been rebuffing his offer of casual sex, saying it wasn't her thing. But maybe it would help her get some perspective.

'Getting a little hot and bothered?' Matthew asked, stroking her neck with his thumb.

'No.'

'You sure about that?' Matthew drew his finger down to her breast and circled one nipple. 'Hey,' she said, but didn't pull away.

'How about I promise you a massage to soothe away all the extra aches and pains?'

'You'd like that.'

'So would you.' He clapped his hands together, then blew on them to warm them. 'Think I should start right now, with these.' He touched her breasts, parting his fingers to trap the nipples. Adie moaned as the action caused a flux of dew to dampen her panties. Matthew leaned closer, until the tips of their noses almost met. 'Say no if you want me to stop.'

His tongue-tip explored her lips with a gossamer touch, parted them, and pressed gently inside. The sensation rippled down her throat like a heavily spiced wine, and coiled around her sensitive nipples. She reached out to him and tried to run her hand up his thigh, but he shuffled back out of her reach. 'Ah ah,' he teased. 'I haven't finished your massage yet. There are still several bits I want to get to grips with.'

Adie sat on her haunches. 'I think I deserve a turn.'

'You want to fondle my nipples?' he asked and lifted his polo shirt. Adie caught the glint of gold. To her surprise his left nipple was pierced.

'Not exactly.'

'Not even a little squeeze?' There was a distinct hint of disappointment in his voice, and she guessed they were one of his sweet spots. She wondered if he liked the feel of the metal rotating through the hole. Just the idea of it turned her on. Oh, what the hell, there was no one about. She crawled to him and, with timid curiosity, touched the precious metal with her tongue. He growled softly in response, and ran his hands down her back from her shoulder to her bum. 'Hmm, thong, is it?' he murmured, not finding any seam across her buttocks. 'I always liked them.'

Adie tilted her head to look up at him. 'I'm sure you look amazing in them. Are you wearing one?' She kissed his abdomen just above the navel, then loosened his buckle and the top button of his trousers. The rosy head of his penis strained against the waistband of his shorts. Matthew pulled his shirt over his head while Adie pushed down his trousers and shorts so that he swung free in a high upward arc.

'Suck me,' he said thickly.

Adie laughed, but then obeyed. She licked under the ridge, then planted kisses down the shaft to the root and back, before she took him into her mouth. 'Ah!' he gasped as she lavished attention on the top three inches of his cock. She cupped his balls with one hand and followed the motion of her mouth with the other. Fellatio was something she enjoyed. She loved the power of having a man completely at her mercy.

'Adie,' he hissed shakily. Sweat had broken out across the top of his lip. He bit down on the bottom one until the colour drained from it. 'Stop, unless you want me to come right now.'

'Really?' She cocked an eyebrow. 'A man who doesn't want to come in my mouth, that's a novelty.'

'Adie! Course I do, just not now.'

She released him, after giving him a sly lick across the tip. Matthew pulled her up into his embrace. He locked his mouth over hers for the duration of a deep wet kiss, then returned his attention to her breasts. He licked at her nipples until the fabric was wet through then pulled the vest over her head and released the clasp of her bra. 'Where'd you learn to suck like that?'

'Wouldn't you like to know?' Her technique had been perfected early in her college days to keep her boyfriends out of her pants. She hadn't actually gone the whole way with a guy until she was nearly twenty.

Matthew slid his hand inside her trousers. His palm was hot against the skin of her crotch. Adie opened her thighs, and he wriggled a finger between her sex lips. 'Have you got something to wear?' she asked.

'What do you take me for?' He reached down and dug into the right pocket of his trousers. 'Finest *kababit*, courtesy of the friendly Zamalek Pharmacy,' he said in a mock Cairene accent. He tore the foil with his teeth, then removed his hand from inside her clothing to do the rest.

Adie watched in fascination as he rolled the sheath over his erection. She loved the fact that he wasn't embarrassed or self-conscious about her looking at him, but mostly she wished he was Killian. Although she doubted her boss would be this relaxed.

'You've still got far too many clothes on,' Matthew said pointedly, as he held himself over her. His penis caught between the tops of her thighs as she kicked her trousers free of her ankles, and she experienced the sudden lick of pleasure even as it dilated his pupils.

'Closer,' she hissed.

'Like this?' His cock-tip pressed into her vulva.

'Mmm, closer.' An inch slipped inside. She gasped at the intense heat, and the sensation of being stretched. It was too much, and yet not enough. She wriggled to get him deeper, and felt the piquant thrill like an itch in her brain.

Matthew pushed her legs together with his knees, intensifying the feeling of restriction. A gush of cream lubricated her tight sheath, as he pressed in as deep as her straight-legged position would allow.

'Oh, that's good,' he panted, his breath hot against her ear. He edged further over her and planted a line of kisses over her face and hair.

The climb came swiftly, thundering through her loins like a runaway train.

'Can you come like this?' he asked. Adie nodded, as she soared on a high note. She knew from his jerky motion he was soaring with her.

'A bit faster,' she whispered.

He blew out his next breath. 'I'll try.'

Matthew dug his fingers into her bottom. He kneaded her cheeks, while he kept a tight reign on his self-control that seemed likely to fail any moment. Adie arched her spine. Her nipples tightened, puckered so that they rasped across his chest with each thrust. A buzz started deep within her and spread through her cunt like a grassfire. 'A little more,' she begged, in response to the mushrooming swell of the flames. She cried out at the delicious bittersweet pleasure-pain that licked at her skin, and gasped as her orgasm came, dimly aware of Matthew jerking in time with his own release.

Matthew still covered her, considerately balanced on his elbows. Adie gave a luxurious sigh, and stroked his shoulder-blade. His skin was damp with sweat and streaked with dirt, as was her own.

'Short but intense,' he muttered, then turned his head and planted a kiss on her nose. 'Whoa, I'm afterglowing.' Adie rubbed herself against his cheek, enjoying his warmth and closeness, until he started to lose his erection and hauled himself to his feet. 'Call of nature,' he mumbled, and whipped off the condom. She watched him pull on his trousers and zip them up. 'Won't be a sec.'

Matthew sprinted up the stairs into the night air. He rubbed his bare arms self-consciously, hyper-aware of every tiny sound that greeted him as he surveyed the horizon. The necropolis seemed unnaturally quiet, as if it were hiding something – holding its breath until he'd gone.

He found a secluded spot and relieved himself quickly, fearful of being caught. The growing sense of tension ratcheted up a few notches when he caught the sound of a motor humming on the breeze. Matthew zipped up sharply, then sprinted over the sandy ground towards the parking area. Sure enough, there was Killian's four-by-four, his profile just visible through the window in the driver's door. He must have dropped off the day's finds and driven back to Saqqara almost immediately.

Matthew swallowed the hard lump that suddenly formed in his throat. He hoped Adie had put her clothes back on or they were both in serious trouble. He had to warn her. He spun on his heels and made for the sub-merged pyramid.

The shadowy chamber was lonely without Matthew. Adie rolled on to her stomach and idly traced the carving down the wall. It appeared to continue below the level of the floor. Adie picked another part of the carving; it was the same. She sought her torch and turned the beam on to the space where the floor and wall met. Butterflies started in her chest. There was something here. She scraped the earth-covered floor with her trowel. Below the top few centimetres, where the dirt had been compacted by their feet, the earth was loose. She dug a little deeper and still the carvings continued.

'Matthew!' she called, although she knew he was out of earshot. Her voice echoed back at her in the empty sepulchre, but she was too excited to worry about it. She traced the pattern again, then scrambled to her feet, and raced up the stairs in search of him.

Just inside the door, she paused and shimmied into her fatigues and boots. The desert wind was slowly shifting the sand dunes northwards. The twilit sky was full of dust that stung as it hit her bare skin. 'Matthew!' She covered her breasts with one arm as she daringly ran to the nearest dune, where she expected to find him taking a leak. But there was no sign of him.

'Where the hell are you?'

She kicked a rock with the toe of her unlaced boot, and something moved beside it. 'Shit!' she exclaimed, as she frantically scrambled backwards. The scorpion she'd disturbed was encased in thick armour, with its tail held high. It scuttled forwards as she hurriedly stepped back, still trying to keep her breasts covered. The sand gave way beneath her feet and she abruptly found herself on her bum looking skywards.

The heavens were a deep iridescent blue. Adie's mouth

fell open as her brain digested the image of horse and rider staring at her from the crest of the nearest dune. He was swathed from head to toe in light-extinguishing cloth. In the seductive monochrome of moonlight, it was as if Rudolph Valentino had ridden straight out of *The Sheikh*. She blinked, and he was gone.

The shuffling motion of the scorpion tugged her vision downwards again. It was almost level with her toes; they instinctively curled in her boots. Horrified, Adie leaped to her feet and fled back to the excavation.

Matthew was standing by the door, fully dressed. 'What are you doing?' he hissed, gawping at her bare chest. 'Are you trying to get us both fired?'

'I was trying to find you,' she retorted, as he shoved her through the entranceway. 'I think I've made a discovery.'

'What, a topless beach?'

'A doorway, actually. I was looking at the carvings on the right-hand side and I had this feeling.' She stumbled over her loose bootlaces, and almost took the same tumble as Bill, but Matthew managed to catch her in time.

'That's really fascinating,' he snapped, and Adie finally saw the panic in his china-blue eyes.

'What is it?'

Matthew pulled her down the steps into the mural chamber, where he scooped up her discarded clothes and shoved them into her arms. 'Killian's just pulled up, and he's on his way over. For god's sake, get dressed before he gets here.' He rubbed at the thin line of perspiration that had formed above his lip.

Adie hastily fastened her bra, then pulled on her top. Above them, the screech of hinges was followed by the dull thump of boots on the stairs. Adie hurriedly raked her hands through her tousled hair, and a moment later Killian emerged from the corridor into the room. He paused just over the threshold and peered at them suspiciously, his chiselled features as stony as granite.

'All finished?' he enquired.

'Adie's made a discovery,' Matthew blurted. He kicked something into the shadow cast by one of the work bags. Adie glanced surreptitiously at it and was horrified to find it was her thong. She pressed her two front teeth hard into her bottom lip, but realised that Killian was watching her, and so forced a smile instead.

Matthew stumbled forwards. 'We stopped work as soon as we found it. We thought we'd better let you know about it.' His tone seemed a little forced and desperate.

Adie rubbed her nose. Killian was staring at her. 'The carvings continue below the level of the floor. I think it might be the steps leading to the burial chamber.'

'All from a glitch in the plaster. It's more likely the result of structural damage.' Killian took a step towards her and lifted a black beetle from her hair. 'Normally the burial chamber is at the end of a descending passage that opens from the south wall.' He turned and looked pointedly at the obvious downward-sloping corridor.

Adie ground her teeth, but managed to relax her jaw before he turned to face her again. His patronising logic really irked her. Sure, he was probably right, but did he have to say it like that?

'Show me.'

Adie guided him over to the wall. He knelt in the space where she'd recently lain bare and made a cursory examination of the carving, tracing his clever fingers over the ridges.

'You're right. There's something here. We'll take a closer look tomorrow, see if it's important. Collect your things together now and we'll head out to the boat.'

'What about the fragments?' asked Adie.

Killian glanced down at the thickly littered area by his feet. 'Just bring what you've got so far and we'll make a start on piecing it together.' He turned his back, allowing

Adie to scoop up her pants before following him to the exit.

At least he seemed to have accepted their explanation.

Just yards away, from the cover of his hire car, Dareth Sadler peered through his binoculars at the rubble mound that marked the excavation site. It wasn't much to look at, but first impressions weren't everything and he'd had it on good authority that Carmichael had a team working down there. Although he wondered what kind of work they could be doing, considering he'd just witnessed two of the team chasing around half-naked.

'So explain to me what's so exciting about this particular mound,' he said to his Egyptian companion. 'And why I should devote my next book to it.'

The man gave him a crooked smile that drew attention the hook-shaped scar etched into his right cheek. 'An early-dynasty pornographic mural.'

Dareth lowered his binoculars, and turned his head towards the driver's seat to find Jamāl grinning.

'I thought that might grab your interest,' Jamāl said. 'I hope you bought plenty of *guinays*.'

'And how did you find out about that?' Dareth demanded. He captured the tiny figurine hanging from the rear-view mirror and turned it between his finger and thumb, expecting to find a well-endowed woman, only to find his own stylishly attired image staring back at him. He raised an eyebrow. 'Nice toy. Not your normal thing. Bootleg?'

Jamāl nodded. 'A stall in the Khan. Associates of mine, they heard you were coming. And I thought you might like the touch.'

'I suppose I'm flattered. At least they've dressed me nicely.' He released the doll, and let it spin on its chain. 'The site,' he prompted.

Jamāl slid his hands around the steering wheel. 'I had

the good fortune to meet one of the team in a bar, drunk on Garden's Gin. I heard he broke his leg the next day, probably a result of the hangover. He described the mural as showing the pharaoh as Horus being sucked off by a kneeling slave, except the interesting bit is missing.'

'Go on.' Dareth raised his binoculars again for a second look at the mound. The mural sounded intriguing, but his previous books had all focused on more visually impressive monuments, like the six golden steps of Djoser's pyramid to his right, which were easily photographed. If he took on this project, he'd need interior shots, and that required far more ingenuity. Luckily, Jamāl could work magic when it came to circumventing Egypt's ever-changing regulations and hordes of paper-pushers.

'Apparently there's a journal in the Egyptian Museum, some Victorian who was kind enough to record his adventures. It might be worth a read.'

Dareth gave a dubious grunt. 'I'll reserve judgement on that. It probably just records how many sticks of dynamite he used to trash the place.' He returned his binoculars to their case. He wasn't about to entirely dismiss the journal; with luck it would contain a few floor plans and maybe some sketches. That was if Carmichael didn't already have it out on permanent loan. He sank back into the passenger seat. Maybe he could use what he'd seen of the other team members to gain some leverage. 'OK, I've seen enough,' he said. 'Take me back to Cairo.'

5

Killian woke to the first rays of dawn pouring between the slats of his cabin blinds. The warm sheets rubbed seductively against his skin, tempting him to remain in bed. He clasped his hands behind his head, content to laze. It was still only twenty past five.

Today was going to be busy. Alongside everything else, Adie's find would have to be investigated. The revelation that she'd found something still surprised him, since there hadn't been any signs of work in progress when he'd arrived. In fact, the physical evidence of her crooked clothing and unlaced boots, plus Matthew's look of panic, suggested they'd been up to something else entirely.

He sat up abruptly. The sudden vision of them writhing, half-naked among the scattered artifacts, brought an acrid taste to his mouth. He gulped spring water from a bottle at his side, but the taste remained.

Of course, it hadn't really been a surprise. He'd come back early because he didn't trust Matthew's motives. He'd been flirting outrageously since Adie arrived. Still, he wished he'd found things otherwise, that Adie was more selective, or maybe just less promiscuous than others on the team. He knew all about Siân and Matthew's sexual opportunism, and Bill's middle name had been girl trouble. Or maybe that had just been trouble.

A knock on the door derailed his train of thought. 'Come in.'

Lucas stuck his head around the jamb. 'I'm off to join Mark Leyham this morning. You haven't forgotten?' he said.

Killian pressed his steepled fingers to his brow, regretting his decision to lend Lucas to the team at Unas's pyramid. 'Actually, I had. How long does he want you for?'

Lucas stepped inside the door, but didn't close it. 'I'm not sure.' He pushed his glasses up his long nose. 'He wants me to look at some inscriptions they've uncovered in the valley temple.'

'Well, try not to be gone all day. We've got a lot on.'

'I'll try.' He backed out of the door.

'Wait!' said Killian, bringing the other man to a halt. 'Take Matthew with you. It'll be good experience for him.'

Lucas frowned over the rim of his oval glasses. 'I thought you said we had a lot on.'

'We have, but we'll manage.' It was time he put Adie Hamilton's skills to the test, and he suspected that she'd be more productive working alone.

'As you say.' Lucas glanced at his watch. 'I'd better go. I don't want to keep Mark waiting.'

'Send Adie along once she's finished her breakfast, will you?'

The door closed and Killian sank back into the pillows to sort out the day's activities in his head. With Matthew and Lucas gone, that left himself and Siân to stabilise the intact portions of the antechamber wall, while Adie cleared the rest of the floor. More than enough to keep them all busy – and to keep his recent dark thoughts out of his conscious mind. Joe's misgivings had woken an old demon.

Killian ran one palm down his torso. Saqqara – it was his first love, but it was also a vivid reminder of failure and disgrace. That thought, coupled with the honeyed sensation he felt as the sheet brushed the head of his cock, made him feel tetchy. He threw off the cover and padded across the wooden floor towards his makeshift dressing table, aware that he was half-hard. A faded square of red cloth lay crumpled on the surface. Killian stared at the ancient memento uncertainly for a moment, then scooped it up. Even after all these years, the old cotton texture and scent of it still worked its magic and made him smile. It seemed a lifetime since the dig in England, where he'd unearthed the fake banner planted by his undergraduate mates in the hope that he'd make a fool of himself. Except that he'd spotted it for a twentieth-century wall-hanging just from the reek of incense. The faint trace of sandalwood still lingered now.

He stepped under the shower spray with the cotton still in his hand, remembering the black-haired girl whose room it had once adorned and the nights he'd spent there, back when he'd had a social life and a sex life. She'd smelled of sandalwood too.

Adie Hamilton smelled of jasmine talc.

Caught up in the memory, Killian circled the cloth against his stomach. He closed his eyes and played his fingers over the sensitive head of his cock. Instead of his former lover, it was Adie – hair tousled and still drowsy, the outline of her body just visible through the silk of her dressing gown – that he pictured. He shook his head, attempting to dislodge the thought. She was off limits, against his principles, and wasting herself on Matthew. Besides, he'd promised Joe that he'd keep his distance. But the image taunted him.

He recalled her perched on the edge of her seat, trying to take everything in as they drove out to Saqqara on her first morning. The dawn sun had gilded her brown hair with auburn highlights, while her dark eyelashes had dusted her cheeks each time she tried to stifle a yawn. Killian had felt hot around the collar that morning for the first time since he'd left for England to seek a replacement for Bill.

The water tickled as it ran down his body. Killian lifted the cloth again. A thin thread of pre-ejaculate clung to it, stretched like spider silk hung with raindrops. He wondered what Adie would look like dressed in panties of the same shade of red, a thin thong-like strap peeping from between her neatly rounded cheeks. He closed his eyes again, saw himself plucking at the string, then gliding his cock down the warm cleft of her buttocks.

Blondes had never been his preference. Maybe that was why he'd never succumbed to Siân's persuasive charms. He wondered if he'd manage to find a similar excuse to keep his distance from Adie.

The images of her came faster as he no longer tried to banish them. Sensation coiled in his loins. He pressed himself against the cold tiles, imagining rubbing his penis into the shadowy valley between her cheeks. 'Yes,' he murmured, nuzzling against her neck, while he guided his cock towards his goal. 'Relax, Adie, trust me . . .'

The image of penetration was a potent one. His cock twitched, trapped between his body and the hardness of the tiles. His orgasm started in his testicles; it caught him like the bite of a whip, sending streaks of pleasure through his tensed muscles, and causing his seed to splatter over the tiles.

He slumped, and dropped the cloth. Exorcism over, he rubbed the water from his eyes and reached for the soap. It was just the novelty of a new person, and a relatively new site. It wasn't anything to do with Adie. She was just one of the team, nothing more, and he'd damn well prove it.

Adie paused before Killian's cabin and stared thoughtfully at the door for a moment. She bit her lip and wondered why he wanted to see her alone, so early in the day. Although it was tempting to imagine that he was inviting her to some erotic liaison, there were only two likely possibilities. Either he'd decided to reward her with a bit more responsibility after her discovery, or else he'd somehow found out about last night and Matthew, and this was a reprimand.

Adie hoped that she hadn't risked everything for a moment of fun. Certainly, she didn't consider it any more than that. She took a deep breath and knocked.

'Come in,' he called. His voice sounded typically even and neutral.

Adie opened the door and peered hesitantly around the edge. The only light in the cabin came through the slats of the blinds. The air smelled of water vapour. Killian was standing by the chest of drawers, towel-drying his white hair. He looked more delicious than ever, dressed in a simple Egyptian cotton bathrobe that clung to his damp skin.

Adie guessed from his state of dress that he wasn't about to give her a lecture. Somehow, she knew he'd be more formal about that. Relieved, she released a long breath of admiration and relief.

Killian turned his head towards her. 'Find a seat, I won't be long.' He slung his towel over a low stool.

Take your time, she thought as she sat down among the rumpled bed linen, I'll just enjoy the show. Killian opened a drawer and began to rake through the contents. She watched him pull on some underwear beneath his robe, noticing when he inadvertently flashed her that the skin of his naked cheeks was two shades lighter than that of his upper body. A sudden white-hot flare of desire intensified her hopes of skipping a turn at digging for the day, in favour of some horizontal shift work.

Killian pulled on his trousers then turned about.

Adie lowered her gaze, blushing furiously, sure that he was staring at her with that fixed frosty expression he adopted when someone was doing something he'd rather they didn't. When he didn't make any comment, she slowly let her gaze wander back up his body in time to watch his robe slither down his arms to settle around his feet. His body had been moulded by long hours of physical labour and was tanned to a delicious tawny brown.

'Would you mind?' he asked in a businesslike tone, drawing her attention back to his face. He handed her a tube of sun-cream and turned his back. Hardly able to comprehend this new turn of events, Adie hesitantly squeezed some of the cream on to her fingertips. It was cold, as if he'd been keeping it in the fridge, but his body was warm and firm as she tentatively applied the cream.

'You can rub harder; I won't break,' he muttered, and rolled his shoulders.

'Sorry, right.' Her voice sounded rather shrill. Adie licked her lips and made contact with her whole palm, still half expecting to find herself in her own bed, having overslept again.

She could feel his every breath, his heartbeat. Her own pulse began to quicken. The movement of her hands began to slow into languorous circles that she longed to follow with her lips. Killian shifted his bare feet on the boards. Despite his seemingly relaxed, blasé manner, there were definite knots of tension across his shoulders, and they appeared to be growing tighter in response to her touch. Adie frowned. Apparently, she made him tense. That wasn't a good sign.

'Tell me about the find,' he said.

Adie stared at the nape of his neck, her heart beating in her throat. Was he suspicious?

'Tell me how you came across it, and be exact.'

Adie took a step back from him, at the same time as he turned around. 'I was working nearby, and I noticed the carvings,' she said hesitantly, while frantically trying to place the reality of the find into a suitable context, instead of the aftermath of a sex scene. 'They seemed to continue below the level of the floor, so I scraped away some of the earth. I didn't go any further because Matthew said we should inform you first.'

Killian stroked his bottom lip with his curled fore-finger. 'I see.' He took the sun-cream from her and dabbed a spot on her nose where she'd caught the sun, before screwing on the cap. 'And what makes you think it leads to the burial chamber?'

Adie thought for a moment, then realised that he was testing her. 'Over-enthusiasm,' she admitted.

'I'm pleased you realise that. It's the sort of ill-considered remark that the press gets hold of and blows out of pro-portion. In future, think before you offer an opinion.'

'OK.' That would be simple enough. Only the shock of him walking in on them had made her say it in the first place.

Killian crossed to the window and tweaked the blind. 'I need you to focus on clearing those fragments today. The quicker it gets done, the sooner we can investigate your "steps".'

By lunchtime, Adie had cleared almost two thirds of the fragments from the earth floor, but her enthusiasm had waned completely. Killian was taking measurements at the far end of the southern corridor, where the ceiling had collapsed. She scuffed her knee for the third time in twenty minutes, swore and left her pitch. Her shadow leaped across the chamber wall like a demented moth as she came up behind Siân, working on the delicate mural.

'Are you finished?' Siân asked without taking her eyes off her work. She steadied her hand against the delicate plaster and inserted a long syringe full of epoxy resin into the wall.

Adie responded with a groan. 'No, but I'm giving my joints a rest.' She rubbed at the scuffed patches on her trousers for emphasis. 'My knees are killing me.'

Siân glanced up and smiled sympathetically. 'You'll get used to it. Hasn't Killian noticed? I'm sure he'd give you something else to do for a bit.'

'Nope, and I'm not about to beg. I want to know what I've found. Besides, whingeing is hardly likely to impress him.'

'And you think flogging yourself will?'

Adie frowned uncertainly.

'I've told you,' Siân said, 'I've been trying to catch his attention for four years, and all I've got to show for it is a Christmas card and a felt-tip pen he lent me. And I've spent more days on my knees than I can easily count. So, unless you're prepared to jump him and tie him down, you've more chance of finding this missing bit of wall.' She nodded towards the central figure of the pharaoh, and the gap in the plaster. 'But hey, it'd still be a cock.'

'Siân!'

Siân lowered her tools, and shuffled along the floor to the next spot. 'Old pharaoh must have at least twelve inches. You can't turn your nose up at that.'

Adie stared at the fractured mural. 'Wanna bet? There is such a thing as too big, you know.'

'If you say so.'

'I do. You're worse than my old flatmate, and I don't think she's ever slept with the same bloke twice.'

Siân nodded her head sagely. 'Wise. You can't be too careful about them getting the wrong idea and treating you like a doormat.'

Adie crossed her arms defensively. 'Yeah, assuming you can get them interested in the first place.' Still, the mural had given her one thought. If she somehow managed to locate the missing fragment, that would guarantee Killian's attention. She could start by scouring Jacob's journal for clues, and meanwhile it was just about possible that she'd find the missing piece amongst the rubble. Enthusiasm renewed, she bounded back across the dingy chamber to her work pitch.

'Thought of a plan, have you?' said Siân.

Adie realised she was grinning. 'No.'

'Pleased to hear it. It'll save the heartache.'

'Are you two still hankering after the boss?' asked Matthew as he strode into the room. He was coated from head to foot in thick white dust. 'What's he done this time?'

'Nothing,' said Siân. 'Which you'd know if you hadn't just butted in on a conversation. You're back early. I thought you'd be gone for the day.'

'They sent me back once the spadework was over. Lucas probably couldn't wait to get rid of me.' He shrugged and began to ineffectually brush at the dust on his trousers. 'Like I care. The wind's up again. I feel like I've been sandblasted. And I've had Lucas breathing down my neck all morning.'

'Isn't he back?' Adie asked.

'No. Didn't you know *he* has specialist skills? I reckon they're trying to poach him.'

'And you don't – have specialist skills, that is?'

Matthew sauntered across to where Adie was leaning over the quad on her knees. 'Not any that Mark Leyham fancies using.' He pushed his tongue into his cheek. Adie ignored him, so he moved over to Siân. 'Hey, what do you think?' he asked.

Adie lifted her head and found him squinting at the incomplete figures in the mural. As she watched, he adopted the same posture as the pharaoh. 'Is he having his cock sucked, or what? Lucas reckons not. I've been arguing the toss with him for the last two hours.'

Siân put her tools aside and looked at him, then the mural. 'Maybe, but he's obviously not as desperate as you are.' She shuffled towards him on her knees, until she mirrored the position of the slave-girl. 'Give us an opinion, Adie.'

Adie rose, and took a step back to get a better view. Matthew's easy-going expression didn't really lend itself to the arrogance of the pharaoh, and Siân wasn't nearly servile enough. 'I don't know, there's something missing. You're not quite right,' she said hesitantly.

Matthew frowned then grinned. 'I've got it.' He unfastened his fly.

Adie gulped as she watched him hook his thumbs under the elastic of his designer underwear and push it down to expose his penis. He circled the shaft with fingers and thumb and gave himself a few strokes of encouragement to make it stand up straight.

'Now what do you think?'

It felt far more naughty seeing him fully clothed, with only his prick on show, than it had felt rolling around naked with him the previous night. She stared at the hot red tip, and unconsciously licked her lips. 'I don't know. Maybe if Siân was a fraction closer. You don't quite have the pose.'

A sense of erotic unreality seemed to infuse the chamber. Siân's mouth hovered just above the tip of Matthew's cock, teasing him with her nearness. Adie felt her heart racing. Just how far were her companions prepared to go? 'A little closer together,' she murmured in encouragement.

Siân leaned forwards as instructed, but jerked away at the last moment and gave a startled gasp. Adie followed her gaze and looked over her own shoulder to find Killian standing in the archway that led to the south corridor. His grey eyes glinted like splinters of glass.

'Fuck!' she heard Matthew hiss.

'What in god's name do you think you're doing?' Killian brought the steel ruler he was holding down into his open palm with a smack that must have smarted, but he didn't wince. Adie did that for him. She watched his nostrils flare and expected a string of expletives, but he seemed to master his anger, and his next phrase was delivered in a taut, icy tone. 'I thought this was an excavation, not a peepshow. Siân, go on lunch. Matthew, get some tools and start working.'

Adie heard Matthew zip up and risked a quick look at him. He was anxiously running his fingers through his dust-stiffened hair.

'Adie,' Killian said.

She stumbled forwards a few paces towards him, but didn't dare meet his eyes.

'Perhaps you'd like to explain to me why I don't put you on the next flight home.'

'It wasn't her fault,' said Siân.

'I told you to go on lunch,' Killian snapped at her, then turned back to Adie. 'Well?'

Adie dug her heel into the dirt floor. 'We were just trying to figure out...' She raised her head. 'I'm sorry. It won't happen again.'

'Correct. You're not a student any more. The same goes for you two.' They both nodded. 'Now get on with your work, unless you're more interested in Matthew's crotch than investigating your discovery?'

Adie worked through lunch, determined to prove her enthusiasm. If Killian noticed, he didn't comment on it. By mid-afternoon, the floor was clear, the fragments sorted into trays ready to take to the houseboat, and they were ready to investigate Adie's 'steps'.

'OK, you start,' Killian said, handing Adie a trowel.

She dug into the floor, and passed the sand to Siân to sieve. Killian watched her progress, which made the dirty, sweaty work that bit harder. She guessed he was checking her technique, or else making a point about trust.

They continued in silence.

When the trough was about a foot deep, Adie rubbed her brow with the cuff of her glove. She was following the lines of the carvings below the level of the floor. Killian was busy with something across the room.

'What is it?' asked Siân. She picked at something in the sieve, and added the splinter of pottery to the collection box.

'Nothing. Just adjusting my grip.' Adie glanced warily across at Killian.

'Next one,' prompted Siân.

Adie scraped back more loose earth and a dark sliver of space opened between the floor and the wall. She stared at it uncertainly, then tentatively reached forwards and pushed her fingers into the void. 'Siân . . . Killian!'

'What have you found?' he called.

Adie opened the hole a little wider. 'A tunnel, I think.'

'Are you sure?'

He came over and knelt beside her, then took the trowel from her, and enlarged the hole until it was large enough for him to stick his head into, before snatching up a baton-mounted torch to peer inside.

'Congratulations,' he said once he'd taken a good look. 'You've found something interesting. Clear the entrance, and then you can quit for the night.'

Adie glared at him. Was he really this underwhelmed? Sod him, she'd found something. Hooray! She allowed herself a grin.

'Nice one,' said Siân once he was out of earshot. 'Let me dig. You sieve for a while.' She lifted a shovel and stepped into the trough. 'Get some plastic to pile stuff on. You won't be able to sort fast enough, and this is going to take hours.'

It was after sundown by the time they'd finally uncovered a low, ragged tunnel. Adie rubbed at her aching muscles, too tired to be really excited about tomorrow's exploration. She wanted a long, bubbly soak, but she wouldn't get that on the *dahabiyya*; there wasn't a tub on board. She'd have to settle for her tube of Deep Heat.

Further north, Dareth Sadler was standing on the leafy roof terrace of a bar on the Pyramids Road. The night sky was clear and dark, the three stars of Orion's belt perfectly aligned with the pyramids of Khufu, Khafre and Menkaure, on the nearby Giza Plateau. He'd come here to discuss possible leads with antiquities dealers, but the interviews were dragging on and he was beginning to suspect that Jamāl was making a fool of him.

He turned and stared at the Egyptian, who had his nose buried in the chest of the dancer on his lap. Jamāl had been seduced by a traditional belly-dance, something Karima did with about as much grace as an amateur wrestler, although what she lacked in skill, she made up for in enthusiasm.

'I'm sick of this charade,' Dareth said. 'I know dressed-up tour guides when I see them.'

Jamāl briefly lifted his head and stared thoughtfully up into the striped canopy of the sun umbrella. 'I still don't understand why you can't just fake the missing piece of mural.'

'Because I don't construct plausible theories just to have an obvious flaw.' Dareth sipped his wine, and grimaced. It was undrinkable muck, locally produced table wine. He tipped it into the nearest flower box. 'I need to find the real thing to corroborate my theory, because we don't have any interior pictures. It wouldn't hurt the sales either.'

'Very well,' sighed Jamāl. He pushed Karima off his lap and leaned on the table. 'We've spoken to the dealers, let's see what they come up with.' He raised his hand to silence Dareth's snarl. 'I admit that they're the bottom of the pile, but they know people. Word will get around. Meanwhile, you need to investigate that journal.'

Dareth curled his fingers into his blond hair in frustration. 'Don't tell me my job.'

'I wasn't. But if I'd hacked a pharaoh's nuts off, I'd record what I'd done with them.' Jamāl reached for Karima and pulled her on to his lap again. She didn't speak, just leaned in and traced the curve of his scar with her tongue-tip.

'Yes, but he was an English gentleman, and you're just a sweaty pervert,' snarled Dareth.

'You're both. Look, you work on the journal and I'll speak to my source in the Antiquities Authority. He might be able to arrange a site visit.'

Dareth rose and slapped some *guinays* on the table. 'That would be helpful. I'm off. We'll talk later.'

6

The following morning, Adie awoke stiff but eager to get to work. She'd found the odd trinket before, Roman coins and Viking weapon shards, but nothing this major. She hoped the morning briefing would be over quickly, so they could get started on the tunnel.

Atypically, Killian was the last to arrive, and he was minus his customary cup of coffee. She wondered if he'd forgiven them yet.

'Good morning,' he opened, drawing them all around a map of the excavation laid out on the workroom's central table. 'Let's get started. Today's objectives are to explore the tunnel we unearthed last night and to start clearing the main passageway. Bill managed to secure the roof before he left, so there should be no problems. Let's see if there's a way through the rubble. Siân, you'll work on the tunnel with me. Lucas, you're in charge of the main passageway. Matthew and Adie, you're with Lucas. Any questions?'

Adie frowned. If it hadn't been for her, they would never have found the tunnel. And she'd done all that digging. It felt incredibly unfair. She glared across the table at Siân, who seemed equally nonplussed and uncomfortable over Killian's decision.

'Is there a problem?' he asked. It didn't sound like a question. He peered at Adie, who deliberately stared at the map to avoid his gaze. 'Well?'

She bit her thumbnail. 'I just wondered why Siân's working on the tunnel, when it was my find.'

Killian calmly placed both hands on the table. 'Because

you've no experience of potholing or working up a new area, and Siân has. We have no idea where that tunnel goes, and I'm not taking a novice down. You're a liability. You'll be of more use to Lucas.'

Adie felt a hot rush of blood to her cheeks. She couldn't argue with his logic. He was right; she was the least experienced member of the team, but she could still hate him for saying it. And it still wasn't fair. She turned away from the table and dug her teeth into her lower lip. He was being a prick. There was no reason why she couldn't have tagged along and helped. Experience had to come from somewhere.

Siân knelt on the lip of the pit, looking down at Killian. The rest of the team were in the descending passageway, and the echoes of their picks and shovels reverberated off the walls with a metallic ring. Lucas had virtually marched Adie and Matthew to their posts, Adie still scowling and dragging her heels. Siân remembered how forlorn Adie had looked gazing back towards the pit as she went. Killian either hadn't noticed, or he hadn't cared. He was showing his stubborn side, and Siân couldn't help thinking that he was being particularly hard on the newest member of their team.

'Come on down,' Killian said, peering up at her.

Siân put on a hard hat and carefully lowered herself into the pit beside him. It was cramped for them both, kneeling side by side at the tunnel entrance. The rough-cut channel extended beyond the range of their narrow torch beams, bearing left and down.

'You first,' Killian instructed her. Siân shuffled forwards into the oval space. The incline, barely noticeable for the first few feet, soon became an uncomfortably steep slope. Her hand slipped on a loose stone, nearly plunging her headfirst into the gloom. Shaken, she watched her torch roll away, its beam briefly lighting hidden crevices and supporting beams before it winked out near the bottom. Hell, she'd be happy to swap with Adie.

'Careful. Here, take mine,' said Killian, pressing in close behind her.

'Keep it for yourself,' she retorted. 'There are lots of loose stones. Anyway, I can manage. It hasn't rolled far.'

Now down to the light mounted on her helmet, Siân struggled onwards and downwards, aware only of the weight of the earth above her and her own loud breathing. After a sharp turn at the bottom where she reclaimed her torch, the tunnel opened out into a circular burrow, large enough for her to kneel upright. Hot and sticky, Siân shimmied in and turned to watch Killian do the same. He immediately flicked his torch over the rough-hewn walls, then mopped his brow and produced a flask of water.

Siân sipped from it gratefully. 'What is this passageway?'

Killian ran his hand over the wall as if he could read its history like Braille. 'A robber's tunnel, judging by the state of the stonework. If it was meant to be part of the tomb then the walls would be smooth. This was cut in a hurry.'

'Do you reckon they got caught? I'd hate to think we'd been beaten to the prize.'

Killian's brow knotted.

'I know,' she said, smiling and shaking her head. 'We probably won't find anything except a few broken pots, but a girl's gotta dream. After seven years in this business, it'd be nice to get a glimpse of gold. You can't always be a pessimist.'

'Realist,' corrected Killian, and continued his examination of the walls. 'Of course, if they were caught then the tunnel entrance would have to be concealed. Maybe that's why they raised the floor-level.'

'Makes sense.' Siân brushed the dust from her nose, where it was beginning to tickle. 'You know, you could have brought Adie with you. She's really excited about making a discovery, and she's capable.'

'It was the right decision.' Killian took a slow swig of water. 'Adie doesn't have your skills or knowledge.'

'You don't know that.'

Killian brushed the snowy strands of his hair back out of his eyes. 'I'm going on.' He crawled past her and shone a torch down the next stretch of tunnel. 'It looks like this will take us beyond the blockage in the main passageway. We might find a body yet. Go back and get some more batteries, then follow on. And hurry back.'

Adie was sitting on the bottom step of the main staircase when Siân pulled herself out of the pit. 'Find anything?' she asked glumly.

Siân shook her head. 'Nope, not yet. I came back for more batteries, and a decent lamp. Killian thinks it might access the burial area, so we'll be down there a while.' She opened one of the storage trunks and started to rummage through the contents.

Adie watched her enviously from the step. Maybe Joe had been right about Killian's team not being right for her, but not for the reasons he'd given. No, they were just out of her league. It made her feel like she was just there to make up the numbers. 'I suppose I'd better see if Lucas has a job for me yet,' she mumbled, and pushed herself to her feet. 'There's only space for two people to dig, so I'm not needed.'

Siân laid a hand on her shoulder as she passed. 'It's nothing personal, you know. It's just procedure. There'll be days when you'll kill for a moment of peace like this.'

'Maybe.' The attempt at reassurance just made her feel worse, and pulled the sickening knots of self-doubt in her stomach tighter. She'd been trying to convince herself that Killian was just being an arsehole, but it wasn't working.

Siân released her and turned back to the trunk to up-end a sack. Brushes and dental picks spilled everywhere. 'You'll get your turn,' she said.

Yeah, thought Adie, but only if someone else falls sick. She crossed to the edge of the pit and stared morosely at the tunnel entrance. Would it really hurt to go down there? Maybe once she was there he'd find her a job to do. Even something dirty and menial had to be better than watching Matthew and Lucas shovel sand. And it was her find. She had a right to be there. 'How far is it?' she asked.

Siân looked back over her shoulder. 'Not far. Why?'

Adie shook her head.

'Look, if you're planning on going down there, I haven't seen you. In fact –' Siân let the lid of the storage trunk drop, so that it closed with a thud '– there are no batteries here. So I'm going out to the car.'

Two minutes later, Adie shuffled into the circular chamber with her torch tucked down the front of her top, held in place by her bra. There was no sign of Killian yet, or of anything more interesting than the shingle-like floor which dug into her knees and palms, grazing skin and scuffing fabric. Not that it mattered. She'd dreamed of doing this ever since she was old enough to read about lost and buried treasure.

Pressing onwards, she crawled into the second half of the tunnel. Here the going was more difficult. First she had to arch her back uncomfortably to manoeuvre around a bend, and after that, the only way to move forwards was to wriggle on her stomach while pulling and pushing with her feet and hands. Thankfully, it was only half the length of the first section, and she soon pushed her head into the inky, airless space of a broad chamber.

'Siân.' Killian's soft voice echoed off the walls like the wind rushing across a desert lake.

Adie reached out for purchase on the floor below, for

she seemed to have entered the room at waist height. The chamber was strangely quiet, and she realised that she could no longer hear the constant, belligerent chatter of the *khamseen*. Presumably, this part of the tomb was a lot deeper than where she'd worked before.

A puddle of light bobbed towards her.

'Adie!' Killian's torch lit up her face. Adie squinted. 'What in god's name are you playing at? Where's Siân?'

'I don't know,' she lied. 'I came to help. Lucas doesn't need me.'

'And I told you that you're too great a risk to be down here. So you can about-turn and go back the way you came.'

'There must be something I can do.' Adie continued to wheelbarrow forwards out of the tunnel. 'Or maybe I can learn something.'

'You can learn to do as you're told. In fact, let me spell it out. I'm the boss, and you're new. Is there any part of that you don't understand?'

Adie's hopeful expression twisted into an equally disappointed one. She shifted her hand for balance.

Suddenly, there was a loud crack. Adie keeled forwards to her right as something gave way beneath her. A searing pain shot through her arm as her hand plunged into something slimy. She yelped in fear and agony.

Killian was immediately on his knees by her side, his torch lighting the shallow pit. Her hand had plunged straight through a large clay urn, leaving her arm elbow-deep in jagged shards.

Panicked by the damage she'd just caused, Adie gave an anguished moan and recoiled. Somehow, she managed to kick free of the tunnel and stagger to her feet, whereupon she collapsed against the nearby wall. Killian followed her, his expression flickering between concern and outrage.

'Keep your arm raised,' he instructed.

Adie peered hesitantly at her forearm where a series of scratches criss-crossed her skin. Sticky, red blood was running between her fingers, and her skin was coated in a yellowish viscous paste. Killian clasped her arm around the wrist and poured water from his bottle over the cuts, sending a spray of red droplets over the floor. None of the wounds were particularly deep. 'They seem clean,' he said. Adie watched him peel off his shirt and tear a strip from the bottom, which he bound around her arm. 'Not exactly sterile, but it'll have to do. I make rules for a reason, because this is what happens when you break them.'

Adie nodded, chastened, while staring at his naked chest. 'I just wanted to see what I'd found,' she tried to explain. His bare skin had a gentle golden sheen in the half-light 'Weren't you the same over your first big find?'

She thought she caught a smirk in response, but couldn't be sure, and when the dim light next allowed her to see his face, his expression was as stern as ever. He nodded towards the tunnel.

'We need to get that cut cleaned up properly. God knows what you've just put your hand in. Entrails, probably. You go ahead, I'll be right behind. And Adie, from now on you do it my way.'

Several minutes later Adie flinched as Siân swabbed stinging antiseptic across her grazes. 'It didn't go quite to plan, then,' said the blonde woman. She peeled the wrapper off a sterile dressing and positioned it over the largest wound. Thankfully, the viscous liquid appeared to have been honey and not ancient intestines.

Adie shook her head. The crawl back through the tunnel had been horrendous. Not only had the limestone chips and tight bends made scrambling forwards on her injured arm difficult, but she'd also been constantly aware of Killian behind her, and his air of brooding disapproval. Now he'd gone back down the tunnel, having first given her strict instructions not to do anything strenuous for the rest of the day. She almost resented the way he'd come to her aid. But at the same time, she still yearned for his approval.

'You're not thinking of going back down, are you?' said Siân.

'Not right now, but I don't see why the hell he can shut me out. It was my discovery.'

Siân tutted and swept cotton-wool swabs and sterile packaging into a sack. 'Do yourself a favour. Stop day-dreaming about your brilliant future as Mrs Golden Trowel and concentrate on your work. Killian doesn't let people in, and with good reason. He's had the sort of past you don't envy. And you have a job that most Egyptologists would kill for, so don't screw it up.'

'But –'

Siân waggled a warning finger, and Adie let her words peter out. She lolled her head back against the bench in the Land Rover and stared at the ceiling. She understood what Siân was getting at, but it didn't change anything. Then a thought struck her. 'Hang on,' she said, sitting up abruptly. 'What do you mean, a past you don't envy?'

'Nothing,' replied Siân. She leaped down from the back of the jeep.

'Siân!'

'Just dig where you're told.'

Too many people were keeping secrets, thought Adie that evening as she left the shower room. She'd spent the afternoon washing bits of pottery in the sunshine. The night air was cool against her damp skin as she padded along the deck. Around her, the flickering yellow lights of the *dahabiyya* were the only sign of life for miles, and the only sounds were the companionable roar of the *kham-seen* and the gentle lapping of the water around the hull.

Joe had been weird about her coming to work for

Killian, and now Siân was talking about dodgy secrets in his past. It was all rather clandestine, and completely intriguing. She considered confronting Killian about it, but she'd already pushed her luck enough today. Besides, she still had to clear the air first.

Adie patted the ends of her long hair dry then tossed the damp towel into her cabin. Standing on tiptoes, she leaned over the railing and looked down into the still black water. The night sky lay like a jewelled blanket across the river. An unbidden image shimmered in the dark, of Killian flat on his back, held down with thick manacles. Adie imagined herself astride his naked lap, teasing his erect cock with ice and feathers. From her position of power, she'd persuade him to tell all, and get his permission to work on the tunnel.

Adie laughed into the warm breeze. Who was she kidding? Even tied up she was sure he'd still be in charge.

She turned her head and stared along the deck. It was nearly eleven, but there was a light on in the workroom. She knew that both Siân and Matthew had retired, and Lucas had gone to Dashur for the weekend to meet friends. Which meant this was her chance to talk to Killian alone.

The door was open and the light, which had seemed so bright from the gangway, turned out to be a small desk lamp. It was illuminating the wall fragments she'd collected from the mural chamber. Killian was leaning against the work surface with his chin resting in his hands. The warm orange glow of the lamp made him appear less icy than normal, as if it had caused a temporary thaw, but she could see from his stiff shoulders that it was no more than an illusion. He lifted a piece from the table to study it, turning it between his forefinger and thumb. The other hand he drew through his hair, so that the snowy strands came together at the nape of his neck. Adie shifted uncomfortably in the doorway and wondered how to begin. The decking beneath her feet groaned. Killian looked up at her. She met his gaze and her breath seemed to melt away.

Adie blinked. The look in his eyes – it was uncanny. For a brief moment, she was a young girl again. The screech of the seagulls echoed in her ears. She was swinging a gaudy plastic bucket full of rocks and wearing a pink gingham sun-hat. Her two cousins and her aunt were playing by the water's edge, a game of catch with the incoming tide, while she helped her father fish treasures from rock pools.

'Look, Adie,' he said, holding out a dirt-encrusted, misshapen metal pin. 'A Saxon brooch.'

The memory was so vivid it rooted her to the spot. Her father, the amateur archaeologist, the man who'd encouraged her love of the past, and the only man who'd ever loved her unconditionally. It should have been a happy memory. Except two weeks later, she had stood in the rain at his funeral. A heart attack. She'd been twelve years old.

Killian straightened. 'What do you want?' he asked, as if her mere presence was likely to upset something.

Adie swallowed the lump in her throat. 'I didn't mean to interrupt,' she said. 'I just wanted to clear up what happened earlier.'

'An apology would be a good start.'

Adie bit her lip. She was sorry about the damage, but she wasn't sorry about trying to get involved, and the ghost he'd unintentionally raised made her feel even more determined. She was prepared to work hard and support the team, but as an equal, not a general dogsbody. 'I'm sorry about the urn, but I didn't come out here to sit around. I don't understand why you shut me out like that. If I'm not allowed to help, how am I supposed to learn?'

'If you want to be an archaeologist, you can start by

behaving like one,' he replied acidly, then returned to the task before him. Adie took a step forwards, and clasped the back of the chair next to him.

'What's that supposed to mean?'

Killian raised only his eyes. 'It means this isn't a porno shoot.'

Not the answer she'd anticipated.

Killian slotted the fragment between his fingers into the incomplete puzzle, and tapped it down twice. Adie's knuckles whitened on the chair back. So this wasn't just about a broken pot and a disobeyed order. She was still taking the blame for what happened in the mural chamber.

'It wasn't even me,' she said.

'You were offering plenty of encouragement.'

'They asked for an opinion.'

Killian stood, forcing his chair back abruptly. It scraped loudly on the wooden boards. 'Right. And I suppose your sordid little tryst with Matthew was all in the cause of archaeology as well?'

'I found the tunnel, didn't I?' she snapped, without considering what she was admitting to.

'So, I imagine, did he.'

Adie's mouth opened in retaliation, but the only sound that came out was an incredulous 'Aa!'

'I should have listened to Joe.' His voice was deeper than normal, but with a sharp inflection on each syllable. 'He tried to warn me that you were a tart with an overactive imagination. Frankly, I'm disappointed I didn't see it before.'

'Yes, well, I was under the impression that I'd be working for a gifted thinker, not an academic Nazi and a prude,' she snarled back. 'Do you expect everyone to be celibate in your little cult? It's my private life, and I'm a consenting adult. It has no bearing on my work.'

Killian's pupils widened, and his pulse showed clearly

at his temples. 'I think you've said enough,' he growled, and the restrained, cold inflections were gone, replaced by something infinitely more primitive and explosive. Adie realised as soon as he'd spoken that she'd hit a nerve.

Killian got to his feet and looked like he was heading for the door.

'Oh, shit!' she hissed, coming to her senses. All she'd wanted was a chance to work on her own find; she hadn't meant to start a row. 'Killian, please!'

'What?'

His mouth was drawn into a tight thin line, almost a grimace. Adie allowed her shoulders to slump, hoping that by backing down, she'd cool his strange temper, but the gesture had no obvious effect. He seemed to be barely controlling his rage.

She reached out and caressed the bare skin of his arm. Killian caught her wrist and held it.

'Are you trying to screw your way into my good books now?'

'No.' Adie tried to pull away, but Killian dragged her back. Suddenly, she was frightened. She hadn't expected an aggressive confrontation. Over-balanced, she fell against him and they both froze.

Adie hardly dared breathe. His fingers dug into her wrist and she winced at the pain, then her mouth fell open in shock as she felt the broom-handle hardness of his cock, pressing against her thigh through her bathrobe. She stared up into his inky pupils, half-expectant, half-afraid, just as he seemed to realise that his body had betrayed him. She'd fantasised about this – well, not quite like this. He seemed to make a decision. Then his hand clasped her bottom, drawing her closer.

Desire jolted through her core. A thumb rasped across her nipple.

'Killian!'

It was enough to make him pause, but only long

enough to grab the nearby chair and sit down, before pulling her astride his lap. His erection speared her through the cloth. Adie made a noise in her throat, somewhere between a whimper and a protest. It was all happening so fast.

Was he angry? Jealous? She raked her fingernails across his back, but that only prompted a retaliatory nip to her lower lip before his aggressive kiss moved to her mouth.

To Killian, everything felt blurred, confused. She'd been getting under his skin for days, ever since that dumb argument with Joe, and the first time he'd seen her in that damn semi-transparent dressing gown. She reminded him of something. A youthfulness and passion that he'd expunged, because it had led to all his biggest mistakes. He'd learned to temper his exuberance, and expected her to do the same. Yet her naïve enthusiasm enflamed him.

Their tongues sparred. Adie matched his fire with a dizzying fervour of her own. His attention moved from her lips to her throat and then to her breast. She smelled strongly of jasmine talc. The head of his cock pressed insistently between her cotton-covered sex lips, and she rolled her hips encouragingly. Killian grabbed the elastic between her legs and dragged her pants aside, then pushed in deep.

He had a sudden terrifying sensation of tunnel vision. He panted out his next breath. It was four years since he'd been this close to a woman, ever since he'd put a stop to the string of one-night stands that had left him feeling numb, and god help him, he wanted her.

Adie's hands were warm against his back; her breath was on his face. He hardly knew what he was doing. He was in free-fall, with only his instincts to guide him.

'Adie,' he tried to say, but no sound came out. The first spasm coursed along his shaft. She arched her back, thrusting her breasts towards his face. He cried out as his

orgasm s
wringing
Adie re
eyelashes b
pulse-point.
'Christ!' h
His knees
will power to
finger marks
roared out his
sweat-chilled f
situation? He n
avoided playing
a relationship.
He had to end
Without a wor
gered out on to th
dragged himself ov
He felt fucking a
Killian splashed
brow to the cold min
of him now. Probably
Now, no matter how
couldn't send her awa
How had he managed t

Back in the workroom,
bruises on her hips, the
tight. She didn't know wh
been nothing like how she
never expected it to start w
so aggressively. Or be over
there had been an emotion
mating of two wildcats, one
as it was over. And it still w
reached the solace of her cabi

7

'Run it by me aga
out of bed at six
said Siân sleepily.
the Land Rover sp
around them, an
into the sky.
'I told you, I w
herself into the
yawn from bein
Siân fished o
her mouth whi
tian Museum
don't give me
done to your li
Adie flicked
it was one of s
She squeezed
urgent feel of
him since sh
fused, insecu
soft word.
'I bit it,' s
'Yeah, rig
I'm not a c
to find ever
emphasise
stretch of g
driving, A
'I screw

'Again? What did you do this time, tip a tray of pottery overboard?'

'Far worse.'

Siân took her eyes off the track and frowned. 'You can do worse?' she said dubiously.

Adie let her chin drop. 'I had Killian.' She pressed her fingertips into her temples. 'Or maybe, he had me. Last night in the workroom.'

Siân snorted unsympathetically. 'So how was it – not what you expected? I did warn you not to mess.'

'I know. It wasn't the plan. I just wanted to know what the situation was regarding the tunnel, and we ended up arguing.'

'And then fucking ...'

'I think it was a choice between that or him murdering me.'

Siân briefly rolled her eyes into her head, before returning her attention to the road. 'So now you're running away. Like that'll help.'

'I'm trying to do something useful. I thought I could look at Jacob's journal like he suggested in order to track down the missing piece of mural. If I can prove myself, he might trust me a bit more. At least I might keep my job.'

'You're really hung up about that damn tunnel, aren't you? For heaven's sake, forget about it. You'll get your chance when Killian thinks you're ready, and that'll happen a lot sooner if you behave yourself. Meanwhile, life will be a lot easier if you forget what happened in the workroom.'

'Easy for you to say,' mumbled Adie into her hand. She'd spent most of the night trying to put it out of her mind, but something about the raw, bestial way he'd fucked her made her want to remember. Still, Siân was probably right; she figured she'd sparked enough fireworks for one season.

'You still want to go to the museum?'

Adie nodded. 'I still want to read that journal. How about I buy you breakfast to make up for the wake-up call?'

'It'll be a start,' said Siân. 'It'll be a start.'

Three hours later, after an Egyptian breakfast at the Ibis Café, Adie pushed her way through the crowded entrance hall of the Cairo Museum. The place was packed and hot sticky bodies pressed into her from all sides, their questing hands brushing against her clothing. Covering her pockets against thieves, Adie grasped her brand-new guidebook firmly and fought her way towards an empty space on the stairs. Halfway up, above the level of the crowd and the musky scent of their bodies, she looked back over the throng in amazement. Siân had warned her the place was a tourist trap and to stay clear of the main exhibits until late afternoon, but this was crazy. There wasn't a clear bit of floor between her and the exit in any direction.

Adie checked the map in her guidebook; she'd planned to look at Jacob's journal in the museum library, but that was where the crowd was converging. It would have to wait until later.

'Have you seen him yet?' screeched a voice behind her. The potent scent of patchouli infused the warm air. Adie turned to find a woman, her eyes heavily lined with kohl, peering excitedly at her.

'Seen who?'

'Dareth Sadler,' said the woman brightly. Adie noticed that she was wearing Egyptian ankh earrings. 'I've been waiting an hour, but it'll be worth it. I can't believe I'm finally going to meet him.'

Adie frowned. It seemed that she'd unwittingly arrived during the visit of some film star or rock god. 'Who did you say it was?' she asked.

'Dareth Sadler,' the girl repeated, starting another wave

of excited murmuring in the crowd. She squinted sceptically at Adie's blank expression. 'You must have heard of
him. He's the most famous archaeologist in the world.
He's written loads of books.' She flung her hands out wide
to emphasise her point.

'An archaeologist!' Adie gazed incredulously at the
crowd, then at the woman's outfit: half rock chick, half
New Age, with armfuls of jingling bangles. She wondered
if there was some mistake. It seemed incredible that an
Egyptologist could draw such crowds – of what appeared
to be adoring fans – particularly one she'd never heard of.
Obviously, the man either had twice Killian's stage presence or one very good publicist.

'Aren't you interested in ancient Egypt?' the woman
asked, her heavily shadowed eyes narrowing. 'Well, I
suppose you must be, but – everyone's heard of him. You
should pick up his books.' She pointed towards the gift
shop.

Adie left her in the disorderly queue and continued up
the stairs, looking for breathing space and maybe something of interest.

The crowd thinned to an intermittent trickle in the
upper galleries, where the air was less moist with sweat
and the stone floor echoed in a properly museum-like
way. Adie flicked through her guidebook, then arbitrarily
started with the nearby animal mummies. The battered,
dusty assortment of cats, birds and jackals stared back at
her accusingly. They made her shiver, so she turned on
her heel and retreated to the safety of room 45.

There were no ghosts here, only the memories evoked
by a board game with ivory pieces, which reminded her
of a draughts set she had at home. She stared through the
glass, thinking about Killian's hasty retreat, and how
things would be when she saw him again. Definitely
awkward. Their moment of passion had been a diversion,
but it hadn't resolved the issue. She still felt frustrated.

'Senet. The forerunner to backgammon. Do you play?' said a masculine voice.

Startled from her thoughts, Adie turned her head. A man was standing in the shadows to her right, between the casement of playing pieces and a figurine of Anubis. He was dressed in a traditional *galabeyya* and had long dark hair, which fell across a startlingly handsome face.

'Sadler's popularity must be waning. He'd be disappointed to know there was an attractive woman who's never heard of him,' he said dryly.

'Who are you, his publicist?' she replied, not sure if she found his comment creepy or flattering. She didn't appreciate the interruption either. Good-looking bloke or not, she wasn't looking for a conversation.

'Far from it. Can't stand the arrogant bastard. Anton Kelly,' he said and extended a hand, confirming that he was a westerner, despite his Egyptian mode of dress.

Adie accepted his hand reluctantly, not wanting to appear rude. 'Dr Hamilton.' His palm was warm but dry.

'I overheard you on the stairs,' he explained. 'I thought you might need a guide.'

'Did you?' she replied, convinced by now that he was a better-spoken and better-looking version of the pushy tourist guides that plagued Saqqara. 'Actually, I'm managing just fine.' She looked purposefully at the nearest display case, but the man was either persistent or just didn't take the hint.

'With this?' He pushed the guidebook away from her face with one finger and fixed her with his mocha-coloured eyes. 'It's good enough for tourists, but useless for a serious scholar. And it only covers a fraction of the exhibits.'

'No, really I'm fine.' Adie cautiously took a step back from him, perturbed by the way he invaded her personal space and the curious feeling of warmth it produced. She glanced around the upper gallery. The only other people in sight were an elderly couple. She clenched her fist and felt the fake wedding ring press into her palm. How much protection did it really offer?

'Perhaps you'd be better off asking them if they need any help,' she said, deliberately showing him the band of gold as she raised her hand to point.

Anton pursed his lips in response, and regarded her as coldly as his velvety brown eyes would allow. 'I'm not a tour guide. I was just trying to be of assistance. I guess I shouldn't have bothered. My mistake.' He turned his back on her and moved towards the exit.

Adie immediately felt embarrassed, and a little disappointed. Maybe he was someone important and she'd just insulted him. It was just about possible that he was an acquaintance of Killian's, or one of their sponsors. That wouldn't go down well at all.

She caught up with him at the next display case. 'Wait! I'm sorry, I didn't mean to be rude. I'm just sick of people trying to sell me things.'

He stopped. His loose clothing made a faint swish as he turned to face her. 'And you were waiting for the demand for baksheesh?'

'Yes. I'm sick to death of tipping.'

'That's understandable. What's your first name, Dr Hamilton?'

'Adie,' she conceded, and couldn't help adding a smile. After all, he was almost cinematically handsome, with his jet-black eyelashes, sensual mouth and cinnamon-coloured skin. He looked slightly wild too, and just a touch dangerous.

Anton gave a tiny nod. 'Apology accepted. The offer's still open.'

'All right,' she said, beginning to warm to the idea of company. 'I was trying to get into the library, but I guess that'll have to wait for another day. I'm interested in anything to do with Saqqara, since I'm working out there.'

'Then you started in the wrong place. Most of the early

dynasty stuff is downstairs.' Adie frowned at her mistake, while the laughter lines around his eyes deepened until he broke into an easy smile. 'Hey, it takes people months to navigate this place. Shall we start?' He offered her his arm, and Adie cautiously took it.

'Rahotep and Nofret,' he said 40 minutes later, as he encompassed the two seated figures with a sweeping gesture. 'Quite dull.'

Adie looked back and forth between Anton and the sculpture incredulously. Far from dull, it was an exemplary piece of craftsmanship, the details of the limestone figures picked out with precise skill, the colours still bold and vibrant. She wondered what Killian would say – something about the lives of the pair or about the master craftsman who'd captured their image.

Anton strode past the ostentatious display to some dusty half-hidden cases in the corner. 'Now these are interesting,' he said, pointing out some decorative but clearly functional objects. 'They tell us much more about society than that pompous pair.'

'What are those, some sort of weapon?' Adie asked, her brow pressed to the ancient glass. The tiny labels were written in an indecipherable spidery script, on yellowed card. She suspected that they were the original tags from when the place first opened in the 1890s.

'They're hunting boomerangs,' Anton said, and she felt his breath stir her hair.

Anton peered over her shoulder, causing the hem of his *galabeyya* to brush against her calf. An unexpected shiver of delight leaped up her spine in response. He was an attractive man, warm and easy to talk to. As they'd moved around the exhibits, she'd found herself looking at him appreciatively more than once. There was something feral about him, emphasised by the unmasked scent of his body. His attentive manner contrasted with her harsh, blunt treatment from Killian.

His shadowy reflection gazed from the dark glass beside her. Adie stared at it. She idly wondered what it would be like to run her finger along his upper lip, to knead the strong muscles of his shoulders, to dig her nails into his flanks and discover what lay beneath his linen robe. Adie unconsciously ran her tongue over the cut on her lip. Why not? She'd be able to distance herself from the memory of Killian's rough caresses. Perhaps it would even help her to face him again.

This was surely the moment to act if she wanted to, while she'd still be able to brush it off as a mistake if she didn't get the right reaction.

Adie stepped back a pace, so that her bottom nudged into his loins, half-expecting him to mutter a hasty apology and step away. But instead he held his ground.

'What are you doing, Dr Hamilton?' he asked, as she wiggled her bottom. Adie gazed at their reflection in the glass cabinet, and saw that her nipples were already distorting the line of her top. Anton put his hands upon her shoulders.

'I thought you were a professional,' he murmured against her cheek. 'Is the heat getting to you?'

Adie rocked backwards, and was gratified to feel his prick swell against her bottom. Anton moved his hands to the tops of her thighs. His lips hovered over the sensitive skin of her neck, his breath buffeting the hollow by her collarbone.

'Must be.' She lifted one of his hands up to her breast. Anton brushed her steepled nipple with his thumb, then turned her about to face him. Adie stared up into the black treacle swirl of his eyes, breathing hard through her nose, and parted her lips for a kiss.

'Come with me,' he whispered instead.

He led her through a staff door on to a staircase. A combination of anticipation, excitement and nerves had her panting by the time they crept into a dingy storage room, which smelled faintly of bleach. 'We'll be fine in here. Nobody comes down here much.' He pushed the door to.

She didn't question his knowledge. Instead, she pulled his mouth down on to her own. Anton's heart was beating hard; she could feel it where he pressed against her chest. Lower down, there was another pulse of life as his cock, caged by his underwear, appealed for release. Adie stroked it encouragingly through his *galabeyya*.

Anton guided her backwards into the room until she found herself pressed against a large solid display case. He lifted her so she perched on top. Adie bunched up his *galabeyya* as high as his chest and eagerly sought to release his cock with the other hand. He was circumcised, smooth and shiny at the tip, and warm in her hands.

'Lift up,' he instructed, as he tugged at the waistband of her clothing.

Adie pressed her palms to the glass surface of the cabinet and watched him pull off her trousers and pants. The cold press of the glass against her cheeks seemed to stoke the heat between her thighs. She rubbed her clit with her fingertips. Already her labia were plumped up and ripe. Anton brushed her hand aside. 'Let me,' he said, and brushed his thumb-pad over her ruby nub. He stroked downwards into the wet avenue between her lips, and then back up, a movement that turned her burning insides to jelly.

'Fuck me,' she said, wriggling forwards towards him, wanting the instant gratification of her desires. 'Now.' She hooked her legs around his waist, opening herself to receive him.

Obligingly, he allowed his cock to slide into her. Adie

sighed in rapture as her internal muscles gripped him tight, and pulled him deeper. She clawed at his shoulders as he made his first real thrust. Anton steadied himself, then bent at the waist and lowered her back to the glass.

The mingled scent of their bodies wiped out the sharp odour of disinfectant in the storeroom. Anton slid his hands inside her top and tugged her bra up over her breasts to play with her nipples. The black sheen in his eyes grew wider as urgent moans escaped her lips, his pinches and tweaks taking her to the heights of pleasure and pain.

'Hold that thought,' he murmured, as he stretched to lift an object from a nearby shelf. The cold press of a large bottle settled over her pubic curls. Its liquid contents sloshed in time with their thrusts as he rubbed the thick neck against her clitoris. The weird fusion of cold glass and hot cock made Adie catch her breath.

'More,' she demanded, throwing her arms out wide, and giving her body up to the rhythm. She turned her head and pressed one flaming cheek to the cool surface. Her eyelids fell open, and for a horrid second she glimpsed into the interior of the cabinet. 'Bloody hell!' she shrieked, and flexed into an involuntary abdominal crunch. She clutched at Anton's shoulders, fingers digging into his muscles. Within the glass case, a partially unwrapped mummy stared blindly up at her. Its teeth and the bridge of its nose poked through the crumbling bandages.

Anton swallowed noisily, then let out a harsh gasp. 'Careful!' His prick flexed eagerly in response to the sudden motion.

'It's a fucking mummy,' she hissed.

'It's not moving,' he soothed, and dug his fingers into her bum, until she eased her grip on his shoulders.

'You knew.'

'Course I knew, I'm looking at it.' He leaned into her, slid deep, lighting all the right nerves, reminding her how close she was to coming. 'Ignore it now.'

Too kinky, she thought, resisting the urge to look down. Warm waves of pleasure continued to lap at her insides, prickling and tormenting like an itch she couldn't scratch. They built rapidly, swelling with each clench of his muscular rear, until her senses lit like a flare.

Anton was still as he came, except for his cock, which pulsed inside her, sending her over the edge. As the moment shook a sigh from her, a morbid fascination also turned her head and dragged her eyes back to the corpse. Her orgasm shattered inside her head as she stared a 3000-year-old mummy in the face.

Their breaths mingled against their cheeks. Anton returned the bottle of embalming fluid, slick with her juices, to the glass case. 'A royal performance,' he quipped, nodding towards their silent spectator. 'We ought to take a bow.'

Adie shoved a hand against his chest and pushed him off. 'I suppose you think that's funny.' She slid to the floor and fished around for her trousers and pants. Anton lay a gentle hand to her shoulder.

'All right. I'm sorry. I should have told you. I noticed him after I lifted you up.'

'But it's a mummy,' she said squeamishly. 'Didn't it bother you?'

'No, and it didn't seem to bother you that much either.'

'It bothered me a lot. Yuck.' Adie's toes curled in her boots, and she turned her back to the cabinet feeling slightly queasy and rather sheepish.

'Surely you've seen one before,' said Anton. He traced his fingers along the join between the wooden frame and the glass casing, near to where her bum print had been left on the glass. Adie sucked her top lip. 'I've seen plenty, but I don't much care for sharing my sex life with them.'

'He's supposed to be in the Royal Mummy room. It says he's Seti I. They must have been working on him. Do you want to go there next?'

'No thanks.'

Anton's deep laugh filled the little chamber. 'Lighten up, Dr Hamilton, it's no different to doing it in a grave-yard, and every teenager has done that.'

'I haven't,' she said, then bit her lip, remembering that Saqqara was one huge necropolis and she hadn't thought twice about having her fun with Matthew there. 'OK, but you could have warned me.'

Anton shrugged. 'I think you might have had a sudden change of heart. At least you'll remember me now. I won't just be that man that you fucked in the museum.'

'I don't . . .' Adie protested. She took a deep breath and exhaled slowly. 'I don't normally go around picking up guys for sex, if that's what you think.' She wondered what he was basing his opinion on – the way in which she'd picked him up, or the bruises Killian had left. Before this week, she'd had no more than a handful of lovers. Now she'd just doubled that figure. Egypt was certainly having an effect on her sex life.

'What then, you just couldn't resist me?' He took her hand and rubbed it against his cheek, then drew her into the stairwell. Adie stalled him on the bottom step, and looked up into his brown eyes.

'Something like that, yes.'

He nodded, and shrugged. 'As you wish. Shall we continue your tour?'

'You never told me whereabouts at Saqqara you were working?' Anton commented later, as Adie sipped her drink. They'd just finished a late lunch. The museum café was nearly empty, but in the hallway beyond, the queue for the library still wound around the many towering pillars. Adie hesitated before answering. Killian had asked her to be cautious, but the man before her seemed educated, discreet, and thoroughly unlike a journalist.

'It's a new site, near Djoser's pyramid complex.'

He picked at the remains of his salad. 'Fascinating. There aren't many new sites these days; mostly people are just redoing what's been done before. Who are you working with?'

Again, Adie hesitated. 'Killian Carmichael.' She looked Anton in the eyes, but if he recognised the name, he gave no indication of it. However, speaking her boss's name made her feel uneasy. It seemed her misgivings about having sex with him weren't as easy to blot out as she'd hoped.

'Have you been working there long?'

'Two weeks. I'm still on probation.'

'I see.' Anton inclined his head a fraction.

'What about you? Who is this Dareth Sadler guy? You said you hated him.'

'I don't like what he stands for, and I don't like the damage his groupies cause.'

'Groupies?'

Anton tilted his head towards the table to their right where a group of women sat caressing hardback copies of Sadler's books. 'What else would you call them? They follow him about in the hopes of gratifying him sexually. Besides, enough crackpot theories come out of the establishment without his pseudo-academic drivel. It just astounds me that people actually believe that crap.'

'Maybe they just want to believe in something,' said Adie.

Anton speared a tomato with his fork. 'Maybe,' he said grumpily. 'I just wish they were more discerning. There's plenty of inspiration to be found in this world without settling for his phoney theories.'

Adie lowered her eyes to the table. Anton's outburst was beginning to draw attention from the other diners.

'If he's such a fraud, how come he's signing books in the Cairo Museum?' she overheard from one of the women on the next table. Her four companions were glaring daggers at Anton.

'Because he gave some official a walloping great back-hander,' Anton responded.

Slightly cowed, the woman turned away, grumbling under her breath.

'I'm beginning to wish I'd never asked,' said Adie. She reached across the table and ran a finger over his open palm. 'Don't cause a scene, please. It might cost me my job. I'm supposed to keep a low profile and I'm already on a warning.'

'Sorry. I should be going anyway. Whereabouts are you headed? We could share a taxi.'

'Back to the apartment on Gezira, I suppose. Did you want to leave right now?'

He turned her hand to look at her wristwatch, and nodded.

'Just let me see if I can get into the library yet.'

'You're joking, right? That's where Sadler's doing his signing.'

Sure enough, when she managed to push far enough through the crowd to see the library door, there was a large sign outside which read CLOSED. Underneath was a picture of an attractive blond-haired man, and the words DARETH SADLER. TODAY. 9.30 A.M.–4.15 P.M.

Back at the Gezira apartment they both got out. Anton asked the driver to wait. 'If you're in Cairo next weekend why don't you give me a call? I can show you some of the less salubrious parts or something.' He scrawled his number on a page from his pocket book and handed it to her. Adie stuffed it into her pocket with barely a glance. She hadn't bargained on actually seeing him again, despite having enjoyed his company. He hadn't once referred to their opportunistic shag in the storeroom, implying that there were no strings if she didn't want them.

'I don't know what's happening yet. Depends how work goes, I might be busy.'

'Of course,' Anton responded, apparently unperturbed by her negativity. He glanced back at the taxi driver, who was revving the engine. 'He looks a bit impatient, I'd better go.' He leaned over and planted a kiss on her cheek. Adie waved tentatively at the car until they were out of sight, then followed the drive up to the apartment.

Siân burst out of the front door, and sprinted across the gravel. 'Who was that?' she asked excitedly, as her neat plait of blonde hair settled over her shoulder.

Adie smiled at her infectious grin, and allowed Siân to link arms with her. 'His name's Anton. I met him at the museum. Why, do you think he's cute? Shall I arrange a date?'

Siân clucked. 'Cute is not the word I had in mind. He's bloody gorgeous.' She looked over her shoulder to the spot where the taxi had stopped.

'Uh, Siân.' Adie tugged her arm.

'Oh yeah, sorry. Samih and Jason phoned. I said we'd meet them for dinner this evening if they paid. I assume you don't have a problem with that?'

'Nope.'

They escaped from the overcrowded bus into the benzene-choked air at the Midan Tahrir. The early-evening traffic raced around them, buses and cars competing with donkey carts for lane space. Adie's nostrils flared at the greasy smell of burgers and the cloying aroma of spilled tomato ketchup.

'Fast-food avenue,' explained Siân, pointing out the line of take-aways facing the university buildings. They followed a group of students into the interior of the Aly

Baba Cafeteria, and found Samih and Jason by the window on the first floor.

'Ladies.' Samih rose and bowed in mock salute. 'We were beginning to think we'd been stood up. What took you so long?'

Siân dismissed the question with an eloquent shrug of her shoulders, and stole a mouthful of Jason's beer.

'I'll get a round,' he said.

Four tall glasses of icy Stella soon arrived at the table. Adie took a long draught and propped her elbows on the scuffed wooden table. 'Needed that, did you?' asked Jason. 'Boss working you too hard?'

'According to Adie, the boss isn't working her hard enough,' said Siân. Jason's look seemed to ask for clarification, but she shook her head in warning. 'She went to the museum to look for Jacob's journal.'

'I've heard it's been a bad day,' said Samih. 'Huge crowds for some signing or something.'

'Yeah,' sighed Adie around the rim of her glass. 'Dareth Sadler, apparently. I couldn't get near the library.'

'No sign of the missing piece on site, then?' asked Jason.

'Not so far.'

'Slim chance of that happening,' said Siân, as she picked up someone's discarded newspaper and began to flick through the pages. 'Lucas reckons that Jacob sold it to some collector to use as a paperweight.'

'What does Killian think?'

'He doesn't.' Siân shot a sly glance at Adie, then returned to the paper. 'Wannabes,' she added a moment later, tapping her finger to the print. 'You've gotta love 'em.' Adie leaned in to look at the blurred photo she was pointing at. Three enthusiastic amateurs had been captured posing before the Great Pyramid, holding a banner emblazoned with a grey-skinned alien.

'Does Killian really have no opinion?' Jason asked Siân.

Siân closed the paper and tossed it on to the neighbouring table. 'Who knows? If he does, he's keeping it to himself.'

Samih scratched his brow. 'I reckon it's probably in that damn museum.' They all turned to stare at him. Self-consciously, he gnawed his thumbnail. 'Well, it's the obvious place. I mean, how many boxes do they have stashed away? And they aren't exactly organised. If you went through all the stuff they've got you'd probably find most of the missing treasures of the art world.'

'That's true,' agreed Jason, and Adie nodded too. After the tour Anton had given her, she'd realised the place held enough material to furnish five museums.

'Is there any way to find out?' she asked.

Jason shook his head. 'You must have realised by now that labelling isn't exactly the museum's strong point. Add to that an incomplete, hopelessly out-of-date catalogue and believe me, it's a miracle they keep tabs on anything, let alone where you might find a bit of plaster with a hand and a willie on it.'

Colour flooded into Adie's cheeks as she recalled her earlier brush with a stray exhibit. 'But surely someone must know.' Anton had seemed intimately familiar with the layout. Maybe she should have asked him.

'Give it up,' said Siân. 'You're not going to find it. I admire your resolve, but I know how it is in this business. If there were any leads, Killian would have someone working on it.'

Adie pouted. 'I'll find it,' she said under her breath. 'Just you wait.'

Across town, Dareth Sadler peered out of his fourth-floor window at the Nile Hilton, as if he were searching for a single familiar face in the sprawling metropolis that was modern Cairo. His green-brown eyes shifted nervously from right to left, from the Andalusian Gardens across the river to the drab exterior of the Arab League Building. Behind him, the phone cable stretched out like a silver cord, pulled taut across the bed as he muttered affirmatives into the mouthpiece. 'Everything's cool,' he said, while his fingers traced the contours of a brown envelope marked 'freebies and publicity shots'. 'The signing went fine . . . Yeah, the public are really pepped up for this one. They're clamouring for a sequel. Have been for years.'

The firm rap of knuckles against the suite door pulled his attention from the window. 'Hold on a minute, will you, there's someone at the door.' He shoved the package into a drawer, then covered the receiver and yelled, 'It's open.'

A waiter wheeled in a coffee tray, and placed it on the small table by the window. He waited while Dareth pulled a few coins from his pocket and dropped them into his clammy hand.

'It's just my coffee,' he said into the phone, while he took up a spoon and stirred sugar into the steaming cup. 'What was I saying? Yes, I know, but *Six Steps to Heaven* started the whole thing, and once *Osiris Reborn* is out we're going to see sales rocket again. Forget the imitators, I'm the original and still the best.' He chuckled at the response, then drew his hand through his salon-styled hair and frowned at the amount of hairspray. 'Do you ever stop worrying?' He paused to take a sip of coffee. 'Look, I checked it out myself. It's him all right. I just need a few shots on location and we're away.'

'If you're sure,' the voice on the other end of the line sounded loudly, making the receiver screech and purr.

'I'm sure. I'll call you Wednesday and let you know how things are going, OK? Talk to you then. Bye.'

Dareth hung up on his agent in England and returned the telephone to the bedside cabinet. He reopened the drawer and upended the brown envelope, depositing Jacob's worn leather journal on to the bed with a satisfying thump.

8

Adie returned to the museum the following day, only to learn that the journal was missing, allegedly misplaced during an audit. She wasn't convinced, but the museum official she spoke to became rather aggressive when she persisted in her questions, so she gave up before he had her removed.

She was still trying to bury her disappointment on Monday when Lucas announced some changes in the work schedule. 'You're still with Killian in the tunnel,' he informed Siân. He waited until she'd gone, then handed Adie a pick and brush. 'You're moving into the right-hand corridor alongside Matthew.' Adie took off her sun-hat and followed him along the descending passage and into the branch to her new work space.

Work in the main passage was temporarily on hold. The cave-in was more extensive than they'd anticipated and would need some serious structural engineering before they could go any further. Instead, they were relying on the robber's tunnel she'd found to reach the remainder of the tomb. Still, she kept her mouth shut. Arguing hadn't got her anywhere and she didn't want another confrontation with Killian. She just hoped he wasn't avoiding her by handing her welfare over to Lucas on a permanent basis. She'd hardly seen him since her return from Cairo.

The hours passed slowly, and it was late afternoon before she even had any proof that Killian was actually on site. She was wedged into a tiny corner when the sound of raised voices echoed along the passageway towards her. 'What's happening?' she called to Matthew. The echo made it hard to pick out individual voices, but the fuss seemed to be coming from outside.

'I'm not sure. I think it's Killian. It sounds serious, but he's been acting weird ever since you went to Cairo.'

The voices grew louder. One of the aggressors was definitely Killian, and it unnerved Adie to hear his voice so loud. She remembered how she'd recently been the cause of such fury.

Adie dropped her tools into her hard hat and struggled out of the corner. 'I think I'll go and see what's happening.' The blood returning to her legs smarted like jellyfish stings, causing her to stumble into Matthew.

'You sure you want to go out there?' He apprehensively bit his lip.

Adie peered along the dingy corridor. She wanted to know what was winding Killian up so much.

Affectionately, she rubbed Matthew's head, sending a shower of dust into his face.

'Cheers, I needed that,' he moaned. 'Try and stay out of the firing line.'

'Sure. If it looks vicious I'll come straight back and hide behind you.'

Lucas was at the top of the stairs. He pressed a finger to his lips in warning as she drew level with him. Killian was standing just beyond the tomb entrance, framed by the brilliant blue backdrop of the desert sky, with every muscle of his six-foot-three frame drawn taut. Even from the antechamber, she could see the beads of perspiration on the back of his neck. However, she couldn't see past him to make anyone else out.

Killian's voice had dropped to a dangerous hiss. She heard what sounded like the snap of a lens shutter, then Killian drew back his fist. Everything slowed. The smack of a punch was followed half a second later by the heftier, muffled thump of a body hitting the sand.

'Killian! What are you doing? You can't do that,' Adie gasped as she pushed past Lucas, who made an ineffectual grab for her. She ran to Killian's side. His single assailant stared blankly up at them from the ground.

'Watch me.' His eyes never left the photographer's face as he opened the back of the fallen camera and exposed the film.

'Killian!' She grasped his arm in protest.

The man on the floor scrambled away from them several feet before rising. His left eye was watering, and already beginning to blacken. Adie wondered who he was. He looked like a tourist, or maybe a journalist.

'Get out of my sight!' Killian threw the empty camera at him. Two of Saqqara's tourist police were approaching from the north, obviously coming to investigate the disturbance. The man clearly didn't want any trouble, as he did as Killian instructed and hurried off towards the road. Killian scrunched up the exposed film and stuffed it into his trouser pocket.

'What was that all about?' Adie asked.

He turned sharply and glared at her.

Adie stepped back, cowed. She tried to meet his eyes. 'He's got a right to be here whether you like it or not, and he's allowed to take photos.'

'Not of me.'

'But . . .'

'But nothing,' he growled back.

Adie finally took the hint and shut her mouth.

'He's not a tourist. He was hired specifically to come here and make trouble. Photographs are just the first step on the agenda.' Killian had wound himself up from a cold fury into a burning rage, so that he was shouting at her. 'Now, stay out of my business and get back to what you're being paid for.'

Adie fled down the steps, past Lucas and away from her work pitch. She found a dark corner in one of the dingy magazines and curled into a tight ball to sob. She couldn't seem to get anything right, and if she didn't learn to shut up she was going to lose her job, as well as any chance with Killian.

Thirty minutes later Siân found her. 'I've been looking everywhere for you,' she said as she shuffled into the cramped storage space. 'I had to have my break with Lucas. Matthew's been sent into Cairo with a list of chores, and this arrived for you.' She held out a large package. Light from her torch beam flickered over Adie's face, illuminating the silvery streaks on her cheeks. 'Now what's the matter?' she asked.

Adie answered with a sniff. The well of tears in her eyes threatened to spill again. She wanted Siân's sympathy, but felt ashamed to admit it.

'Well?' Siân knelt and gently laid a hand on her shoulder.

'Killian shouted at me for being an idiot.' It sounded feeble and petulant.

'What kind of an idiot?'

Adie sniffed again; her face felt stiff with dried-on tears. 'He hit someone and I interfered.'

Siân raised her eyebrows. 'Oh dear.' She glanced over her shoulder to make sure nobody else was in earshot. 'Well, there's no point getting this upset. I'm sure he had his reasons.'

'Yeah, right.'

'He's a very private man, Adie, and he doesn't get riled about nothing. You just got in the way of his temper.'

Adie straightened out her legs. Siân was making sense. She'd lurched into the argument without knowing what it was about.

Siân clapped her on the back. 'Come on, girl, chin up, and I'll see if I can pump Lucas for information. And for heaven's sake, stay out of his way until he calms down.'

Adie gave a final sniff to clear her nose. 'All right, whatever you say.'

'Forget about it. Are you going to open this parcel or what?' Siân passed over the package. Adie carefully cut the outer string binding with her pocket knife and removed the lid. Beneath the fragile layers of tissue paper lay a dark-blue harem-girl outfit. She lifted it clear of the box to admire the delicate embroidered detailing of lilies in black and silver threads, and the sequinned waistband.

'Nice!' exclaimed Siân, her eyes widening. She reached across and caressed the silky fabric. 'What does the card say? I'll bet it's not from Killian.'

Adie read the elegantly lettered card. Nobody had ever sent her an exotic outfit before. She smiled. 'It's from Anton. The guy I met at the museum.'

'I remember. Go on.'

Adie chewed her lower lip thoughtfully, while caressing the fabric. 'He wants me to meet him tonight wearing this get-up.' She passed Siân the card, who scanned it quickly.

'Well, he has exquisite taste. You going?'

Adie shrugged her shoulders. 'I don't know. It's beautiful and sweet, but my head's messed up enough over Killian without this.' Adie realised that her friend wasn't listening. Siân had her cheek pressed to the diaphanous fabric.

'It reminds me of that old Turkish Delight ad. "Full of Eastern promise",' she mused, before closing her eyes and breathing in the scent of the fabric.

'He's English,' said Adie.

Siân gave her an admonishing frown. 'Don't you have any imagination?' She shrugged, and handed back the outfit. 'You're after the wrong man, Adie. Forget Killian, you should be out with this guy.'

Adie didn't reply. Maybe Siân was right. If she was less

emotionally involved with Killian, maybe their working relationship would improve. She'd have to think about it.

'So, what happened?'

Lucas shook his head. 'Keep your nose out of it, Siân.'

It was evening of the same day, and the mosquitoes were swarming by the thousands around the lights of the *dahabiyya*. He was sitting in a deckchair on the starboard side, having just mopped the wooden decking. Across the water, two birds were fishing among the reeds.

Siân flopped into another chair. 'Adie worked herself into a right state earlier. I think she's still brooding in her cabin now. Someone's got to sort it out.'

'There's nothing to sort out. She caught the sharp end of his tongue, that's all.'

'Is it true he hit someone?'

Lucas inclined his head a fraction.

'Who was it?'

He took off his glasses, blinked and rubbed his eyes. 'I'm not sure. Someone working for Dareth Sadler, I think. If that means anything to you.'

It was Siân's turn to hesitate. The answer wasn't unexpected, but she'd never thought she'd hear Lucas say it. 'I understand.' She apprehensively stroked her blonde plait. 'Adie mentioned he was at the Cairo Museum doing a book signing, and I saw an article in the *Middle East Times*. I thought there might be trouble then, but I didn't want to say anything. Why didn't you stop her going outside?'

Lucas replaced his glasses. 'I tried, but I wasn't going out after her. I know when to keep clear. And I'd already seen him fretting. He read the *Times* article on Saturday. Mind you, the fact that you two buggered off last weekend without telling anyone didn't help his mood.'

Siân nodded apologetically. 'Minor emergency. Do you know how he is?'

Lucas locked his hands behind his head and stretched. 'Killian? No idea, he stormed off. I expect he's driven somewhere to calm down, or else he's gone into town after the bastard's hide. Who can blame him? I'd probably do the same.'

The idea of scholarly Lucas pursuing someone in a rage struck Siân as rather comical. Sadly, the thought of Killian doing the same was not. He had more than enough reason to resent Sadler's interference, but she hoped he wasn't crazy enough to actually contemplate murder. 'How long have you known?' Sadler was a subject she'd avoided for years, and would never have brought up on her own.

Lucas shrugged. 'I've always known. It was big news when I first came out here. I was at Thebes at the time, but it was all anyone could talk about. A couple of my colleagues had worked with Killian before. They thought I was crazy when I took the job with him. Now of course they're a deep shade of green. What about you?'

'By accident. I read Sadler's book the term I spent lecturing between the projects at Dahshur and Lisht. It was doing the rounds at the university. It's all drivel, of course, but I got quite a shock when I saw my boss halfway through.'

'There's more than just the book,' said Lucas. 'But don't ask me for the details. Killian was more involved than even he cares to admit. And for god's sake don't ask him about it either.'

'I wasn't about to. I almost choked as it was, when he told me we were coming to Saqqara. I thought he'd want to avoid the place.'

'He came here to lay the ghosts to rest,' said Lucas.

'Except Sadler's back to raise them.'

'Perhaps.'

They stared thoughtfully at one another for several moments then let their eyes drift apart. Several large moths had joined the insects fluttering around the lights.

Lucas lit one of the potted citronella candles. Siân nervously tapped her soles against the decking. 'What should we tell Adie?'

'Nothing. Let him do his own explaining if he wants to. It's nothing to do with us. I don't intend to get involved and you'd be wise to do the same.'

Adie sat alone in her cabin. The room was dark except for a few shafts of moonlight that penetrated the open blinds to light the wooden floor with silver streaks. She stared at the box of gossamer fabric on her lap. Its dark contents tempted her to dress up and indulge her fantasies, but still she hesitated. If only the gift had been from Killian, then the choice would have been so much simpler. But that would never happen.

She brushed a finger along the sequinned waistband. Maybe Siân was right; she should forget Killian and his bizarre moods, and concentrate on Anton instead. That day at the museum had been one of the most enjoyable she'd had since she arrived in Egypt. The sex had been good too, even if it had nearly been a threesome. The thought of the ancient mummy even tweaked her lips into a wry smile. What the hell! Things weren't going anywhere with Killian, and she was keeping a handsome man waiting.

The decision made, she lifted the outfit from the box. The faint aroma of sandalwood and the richer, more exotic smell of myrrh wafted up from the fabric. She inhaled deeply, filling her nostrils with the spicy scent and letting its magic filter through to the pleasure centres in her brain. Full of eastern promise, Siân had said. If Anton lived up to that it was sure to be a good night.

Ten minutes later she was poised on the river's edge, admiring her reflection in the black water. The fabric sheathed her body in a sensuous film that emphasised her womanly curves. After weeks of seeing herself in shirts, vests and fatigues, coated in layers of sand and dust, it felt slightly shocking to be so underdressed. Her skin had come alive, and she could feel every tiny movement of the night air against her bare midriff. There was also a frisson of fear and danger to excite her. She just prayed that Anton hadn't given up on her after being kept waiting.

Adie paused beneath a date palm at the edge of the river where he'd arranged to meet her. Mirrored in the water's surface was a ghostly silk palace. She lifted her gaze to the shore, where the tent was pitched.

The soft rustle of fabric behind her made her turn her head. Anton was watching her from beneath a neighbouring palm. He was dressed in flowing midnight-blue robes that lapped against his body with each gust of the wind. She gasped in recognition. Here was her fantasy sheikh, the man she'd seen for a split second at Saqqara as she fled from the scorpion. Seeing him now, she was surprised she hadn't recognised him before. Questions about his motives and identity leaped into her head. Had their meeting at the museum really been such a coincidence? Was their current rendezvous simply about physical attraction, or was there some deeper, more sinister motive at play? Right now, did she really give a damn?

He stepped forwards, only to circle her slowly, first admiring her bosom clasped within the onyx sequinned cups, and then her barely concealed rear. His full lips twitched at the corners then elongated into a broad welcoming smile.

'I'm sorry I'm late,' she apologised. 'I got held up.' It was a half-truth, but she felt she owed him some kind of explanation and she didn't want to divulge the intricacies of the past few days. She was here to indulge in a bit of escapism, not to confess.

Anton said something in an imperious tone, but his words were Arabic. Then he appeared to ask her a question. Adie stared back at him in confusion. 'I don't speak Arabic.'

Anton merely repeated the phrase. When she still didn't respond he gestured towards the tent.

Adie opened her eyes a little wider and wondered what he had in mind. She let him take her hand and guide her towards the shelter. Anton pulled back the canvas tent flap and drew her inside. Her mouth fell open in astonishment. Truly, the place was a marvel. It was like no other tent she'd ever entered. The interior was on two levels, both carpeted with a heavily patterned fabric. The area nearest the door had a low table and was set with dishes of sweetmeats, fruits, and cinnamon-scented dainties. The back section was raised, and covered with a mountain of coloured cushions. Small coloured lamps cast multi-hued shadows, and a heavy, musky incense permeated the air, beckoning her inside.

Again, he spoke to her in Arabic. Adie shook her head. 'I don't understand,' she protested, then remembered Siân's comment on her lack of imagination. She looked down at her revealing outfit then coquettishly up at Anton. 'What is it you desire of me?' she asked, picturing herself as a harem girl to get into the fantasy.

Anton responded with his best Valentino stare. He pointed to the cushions and then to her. Adie licked her bottom lip, crossed over to the heaped cushions and reclined. She wanted to see what other marvels he had to show her besides the fabulous tent. Whatever they were, she was sure she wouldn't be disappointed.

Anton lifted a piece of fruit from a bowl. She watched him hold it aloft and let the juice in which it was soaked drip into his waiting mouth. He lifted another fruit, this time crossing to her. The first few drops fell on her tongue. The taste was both sweet and spicy, and made her taste-buds tingle with the delicious burn of alcohol. As she swallowed, the liquid dripped on to her chin, and rolled down her neck into the hollow between her breasts. Adie stared up into his eyes. The pupils were black, and glittered like the night sky reflected in the Nile. Anton lowered his lips to hers then drew his mouth to her chin, before following the trail of juices down her neck, and then to her bosom.

He offered a segment of orange next. This time the sticky sweet liquid pooled in her belly-button. Anton's lips followed the trail and lapped it out.

'It tickles,' she protested, while unconsciously lifting her hips in anticipation of the next lash of his tongue. The tip poked almost rudely into her navel, lighting rarely stimulated nerve endings and sending shivers out across her stomach. He took a black grape and placed it like a jewel in her navel. Then his mouth travelled lower. He skipped over the sequinned waistband and on to the silken fabric, which stuck to her skin as it grew wet from his kisses. The first touch of his tongue against her covered mound sent a wave of electrifying energy through her body. He probed at the fleshy lips with his tongue, wetting, patting and coaxing until her clitoris peeped from its hood, eager for his caress.

Adie lay back, lapping up the exquisite sensations. The Arabic phrases and endearments he was whispering blended with the music of the water outside and the heavy scent, making her relaxed and slightly drowsy. She became aware of other scents enveloping her, the sharp citrus zest of the fruit and the muggy, cloying smell of the oil lamps. These, coupled with the rising awareness of her own skin and the brush of the silk cushions, created a feeling of warmth and well-being.

'Anton,' she murmured, as his tongue-tip caught her clitoris through the fabric. He teased her mercilessly with short flicks and the occasional drawn-out stroke, each lap so irregular she couldn't predict when it would come or where it would land. Each touch was a surprise, each caress heightening her pleasure until she was writhing against the cushions, only dimly aware of her words as she begged him to take her.

Suddenly, he peeled away from her and lifted a knife that lay discarded by the fruit bowl. Adie's heartbeat pounded in her ears. A sense of trepidation and fear, combined with her body's sexually heightened responses, left her on the edge of a dangerous precipice. She didn't struggle as Anton lowered the blade and traced the tip down the side of her throat. Instead she screwed her eyelids tight, only to open them again immediately. She needed all her senses.

The knife point paused at the centre of her throat, then crept lower over her skin between the twin mounds of her breasts, followed in its course by Anton's lips. She felt the scratch of the tip as it dragged across her skin. Adie's breath seemed to freeze on her tongue.

His dark mocha-coloured eyes were hard to read. Suddenly, he angled the knife down again, this time between the apex of her thighs. Adie sucked in her next breath at the touch of the cold steel. With one quick slice, Anton cut away the stitching along the seam of her trousers, creating a large gash.

His breath was warm against her plumped, ruddy skin, but the sensation was fleeting, soon replaced by the tingling heat of a viscous oil. Adie nervously curled her fingers into a cushion as Anton claimed a dark curl from her pubis.

The oil tickled, and seemed to burn with some sort of spice, heightening her responses as his tongue lashed once against her clit, before being replaced by the hard warmth of his cock. It nuzzled through the newly made slit in her pants and pressed into her waiting core.

'Anton,' she hissed, clutching at his shoulders and seeking his lips. She was shivering. 'I think you delight in scaring me.'

She couldn't be sure of his response, but he seemed to be agreeing. And then it didn't matter, because he was filling her, kissing her, and biting at her nipples through the fabric of the costume.

The burning oil and myriad perfumes continued to drug her. Her senses seemed so sharpened from fear and overloaded with eroticism that the lines between fantasy and reality began to blur. She was a captive of the sheikh, a slave to his will, snatched from her lover while crossing the desert as part of a caravan. He'd brought her to his silken palace intent on ravishment and revenge. Yes, her lover had stolen a treasure from him, and now he was repaying the slight. Only she didn't want to be rescued any more. She'd come alive under his skilled touch.

The whole of her lower body felt as if it was on fire. She grasped Anton around the shoulders and clung to him, panting into his dark hair as his thrusts quickened. His lips closed over her ear lobe, and nipped her there. She felt him pulse inside her. He raised his head and roared out his climax. It was too much. Her orgasm broke in one exquisite shudder, from which she floated dreamily down into the silken nest between the cushions.

Adie sneaked back on to the *dahabiyya* in the quiet just before dawn, in time to meet Siân emerging from her cabin. The blonde woman took in Adie's extravagant costume and tousled hair at a single glance, before indulging her with a wistful smile. 'You took my advice, then,' she said.

Adie nodded, and sheepishly edged towards her cabin door, wishing she'd had the sense to take her coat the previous night. She was sure she looked a perfect fright in the cold light of dawn, with black kohl smudged around her eyes and her skin streaked with fruit juice and saliva. It was bad enough running into Siân, without the risk of anybody else seeing her.

Siân stretched out and prevented her escape by placing a hand on her shoulder. 'How was it?'

Adie clamped her legs together to hide the slit in the fabric. 'Full of eastern promise, as you said.'

Siân gave a thin smile, as if she wasn't surprised, but wasn't exactly pleased either. Adie began to wonder if Siân was getting just a little bit jealous.

'It's not serious, though,' she heard herself say. Why not? her mind seemed to query. Because of Killian, an inner voice replied. Suddenly, she felt a tightening across her brow as all the tension that had melted during her night with Anton returned. She glanced along the deck, fearing his imminent arrival, then wondered if she should go and see him once she'd cleaned herself up.

'He didn't come back,' said Siân. 'In case you're wondering. He's probably on site, so if you want to talk to him before work, we'll have to burn rubber.'

'I'm not sure I have anything to say. He's the one who's been acting strangely.' Did she really want to face him? Maybe it would be better for everyone if she stuck to indulging her fantasies with Anton.

'Nevertheless . . .' Siân let the seeds of doubt hang in the air.

'I'll be ready in five minutes,' said Adie. 'I'll meet you in the car.'

Killian wasn't on site when they arrived, so they walked over to the rest-house for breakfast. When they returned, Lucas had their tasks for the morning. He gave Adie another new pitch, in the bowels of the tomb near the storage caches, where she would be out of sight and mind when Killian returned. Matthew was still in Cairo.

Adie wondered at the turn of events that had led to her current position, and her mixed feelings about the night with Anton. She wondered if Killian was off somewhere doing the same. Was he the sort to go out and pick up a stranger? Or had he simply stayed the night in a dingy *ahwa*, drinking strong coffee and brooding?

The morning soon passed as she meticulously cleared away the debris in the corridor. It was only when her stomach began to growl that she realised that someone should have come and told her it was time for lunch. She paused to retie her ponytail, and sensed that someone was approaching.

She recognised Killian by the sound of his breathing – controlled, shallow inhalations. Adie turned her head a fraction, so that she could just see him out of the corner of her eye. He was still wearing the same outfit as yesterday and he hadn't shaved. His clothing was caked in dust, and the knees of his khaki trousers were discoloured and scuffed.

'How are you getting on?' he asked.

Adie shuffled around a little further on her knees so she could see him more clearly. His linen shirt was open to the breastbone and soaked. Not with sweat, but water, as if he'd just upended a canteen over himself. He looked rough and undeniably sexy, with the fabric hugging the contours of his skin. A hungry ache wakened between her thighs, despite everything that had happened.

'My knees are sore,' she snapped unreasonably. Her physical response to him made her feel irritable and brought home how little her night with Anton had changed things. She still craved a man who wasn't interested in her, and who'd clearly put their one foolish moment firmly behind him.

'So stand up and give them a rest,' he said amiably.

Adie stayed put, then changed her mind and stumbled to her feet. He offered her a hand but she shook her head, and ignored the pained expression that briefly flickered in his grey eyes.

'I expect I deserve that. I guess I owe you some kind of explanation ... And an apology.'

'No,' she said grumpily.

'Clearly I do.' His feet stirred up the sandy floor as he closed the gap between them, until he was standing right beside her. Adie could smell his body scent. He'd been working hard, and the fragrance excited her despite her feelings of resentment.

'I'm familiar with the photographer, and his employer. He got off lightly. I'd like to choke the life out of them both.' He seemed to check himself, then shrugged off his anger and smiled. 'You weren't to know.'

What about what happened on the boat? she wanted to ask, but refused to prompt him. Was he going to explain that away too?

'Adie.' She looked up at him and saw that he was choosing his words carefully. 'I have to go to town tonight. Our chief sponsor's invited me to dinner. Matthew's already at the apartment, but I'd rather take you along. If you're interested, that is?'

Adie's mouth dropped open and she stared at him, unsure she'd heard him correctly. 'Repeat that.'

'I'm asking you to accompany me to dinner. Would you like to come?'

'Yes! I mean, I think.' The photographer's face briefly swam through her head, as did the image of Killian stalking out of the workroom.

'Well?' Killian leaned forwards and touched her hair. A rush of colour immediately flushed her skin.

'Yes,' she said, and nervously licked her lips.

Killian nodded. 'Good. Have you anything formal to wear? Otherwise, see if Siân can loan you something. We have to be there for eight.'

9

Dareth Sadler sank into the bubbling Jacuzzi in his hotel room, his brow covered by a cool flannel. Pre-publication promo aside, his book was now on hold until he could get some interior photos of the excavation. With the mural as a central theme, his eloquently reasoned theory just wouldn't cut it without at least one picture. Plus he wanted to use a detail of the defaced pharaoh as cover art.

Dareth grimaced. He hadn't expected Carmichael to deck his photographer. Consequently, he'd been forced to pay the guy double without gaining a single shot. Even worse, the Egyptian authorities had actually snubbed Jamāl and his bribe, informing him that the excavation wasn't open for viewing.

Dareth tore off the dripping flannel and flung it across the room. Short of burglary or blackmail, he was flat out of ideas.

The patter of footsteps made him look up from the sunken bathtub just as a tall woman plucked the cloth from the floor and wrung it out in the sink. Although nude, a leather choker and vampish make-up made her seem anything but vulnerable.

'Jamāl called again,' she said. Dareth closed his eyes and listened to the water spray over the tiled floor as she stepped into the tub and kneeled before him. 'He wants to arrange a meeting. He says he's got a lead to the fragment, but he wants more money.'

'Hmm. There's a surprise.'

He'd expected this. Jamāl had probably already got

wind of the incident with the photographer, and had decided to add danger money to his extensive list of fees. Providing he came up with the pharaoh's missing penis, Dareth could afford a little extra.

'I'll call him later,' he said.

He gazed at the dark-haired sylph beside him. Lana wasn't most people's idea of a perfect PA, but she had other, more unique talents. 'I've something else for you to do.'

He touched her shoulder where a tiny ankh, the symbol of rebirth, had been tattooed, and then followed the caress with a kiss. His lips traced the line of her jugular, teasing the sensitive bare flesh, while warm jets of water nuzzled around his groin.

He captured a nipple between his thumb and forefinger.

'I thought you were abstaining until the ceremony,' she said.

Dareth allowed a smile to tweak his lips. 'Well, that's the thing about being a god, you can change your mind,' he said into her hair. Already her nipples were crinkling beneath his fingertips. Pleased with this result, he tugged a little harder, making her groan. 'Besides, I'm only abstaining from fucking you. I didn't say anything about relieving myself.'

The thought of her rubbing his seed into her honey-coloured skin made his cock jump. He twisted his hips so that the spray of bubbles played more firmly against his shaft, and took a breast in each hand. Pressed together, they'd make a slippery passage, but it would mean lifting himself virtually clear of the heated water. He let them fall again and cupped the fleshy globes of her bottom instead.

His cock flexed at the prospect of her plump derrière and wept pre-come into the water. Above him, steam swirled in the air, and tiny rivulets streaked the tiles and mirror. Dareth moved his hand to the apex of her thighs. Last night he'd partially shaved her; now he stroked a digit along the narrow remaining line of hair and into the wet heat of her. She whimpered and opened her legs wider to the penetration, accepting two fingers, then three, as his thumb found and worked her clit.

Dareth speared his erection between her thighs and forced her against the side of the sunken tub. 'Close your legs,' he instructed.

Off balance and straining against the rim, Lana obeyed.

'Tighter,' he demanded. 'Cross your ankles.'

Dareth felt her warm slippery thighs clamp together around his needy cock, and let himself go. Riding her, he welcomed the rushing sensation in his head that spread down his spine and ran into his shaft. So what if Carmichael and the other academics hated him? His methods had their own rewards. His theories had practical applications for modern life. There was nothing dead and dull about them.

He stared at the ankh on Lana's shoulder. He was about to be reborn.

The warm jets nuzzled against his cock-tip. He slid between her thighs again and a charged pulse of energy streamed down the shaft to the tip, making him jerk violently, repetitively.

'Dareth,' he heard her protest as he pulled away. He smacked her rump in reply and climbed out of the tub, away from the milky strands forming in the water.

'I need you eager.' He picked up a towel and drew it about himself. 'I told you, I've got a job for you.'

From the concrete driveway, Adie gazed at the rest of Masud Al-Saddiq's home in awe. Its opulent Mamluk design of banded red and white stone, with stalactite-like stone carvings, rivalled many of the mosques she'd seen dotted across the city skyline. Flame trees shielded the building from the road, and bedded plants provided small islands of colour. Adie smoothed her outfit with damp palms. She felt nervous. Killian had barely spoken on the drive over, other than to approve her outfit. It was a blue satin sheath-dress with tiny shoelace straps, borrowed from Siân, along with matching shoes. Why Siân kept the outfit on the boat eluded her, but she wasn't complaining. The most glamorous thing she'd brought with her to Egypt was a glizty black thong. Wishful thinking while she was packing, she supposed, although it had come in useful this evening.

Killian had dressed all in black except for a pair of antique emerald cufflinks, and the glossy silk of his shirt rippled like dark water as he walked towards the arched front doorway. For once, Adie didn't feel underdressed beside him.

'Killian! How lovely to see you.' A slender Egyptian woman in a vibrant red dress greeted them in the airy hallway. Adie felt a pang of jealousy at the way she draped herself over him. Her dress – more like a handkerchief held together with ribbons – shimmered against his dark suit and gaped intentionally around the bust and thighs. Killian, however, appeared completely unmoved by the show of affection and flesh.

'Safiyya,' he said, and dutifully pecked the cheek she offered.

'And you must be Bill's replacement.' She turned to Adie, and pressed a kiss to each of her cheeks. 'Adina, isn't it?' Adie didn't bother to correct her. Only her maternal grandmother called her Adina. 'Let's go through. Masud is waiting.'

After exchanging their shoes for Persian-style slippers, she led them into an immense dinning room, overlooking a shaded courtyard and a well. Masud was at least twenty years Safiyya's senior, and alone, much to Adie's surprise. She'd thought Killian had invited her to some dry, academic dinner party, not a candlelit supper for four.

The conversation was hard going at first, although Adie had started to relax by the second course, helped by two glasses of spicy wine. She listened to Killian and Masud discussing the project, hoping to add a useful comment.

'I think it's time we released a few photographs,' Masud said. 'I'd like to see that mural intact, and a photograph might jog someone's memory. There are fragments all over the world. The object we're looking for might just be sitting on someone's desk.'

Killian frowned and set down his fork. 'We have enough unsavoury interest in the site already, without advertising. I'm not sacrificing the whole project over one mystery. Besides, I'm more interested in whose tomb it is.'

'I wasn't thinking of the nationals, Killian. Just a quiet release in the academic press.'

Killian straightened his cufflinks, then lifted his fork again. 'That'll only delay things for twenty-four hours. I've had the press descend on me before. They're worse than the tourists; no, actually, they're worse than jackals.'

It was Masud's turn to frown. 'May I remind you that I'm making the investment here? The rest of the board approve.'

'Surely there are other options we could try?' said Adie, cutting in quickly to prevent an argument. 'Couldn't we check museum catalogues, and aren't there experts on erotic art?'

'Museum catalogues rarely list the entire inventory,' replied Masud. He leaned over and topped up her wineglass. 'As for experts, you're already working for the foremost scholar on early dynasty erotic art.'

Adie glanced at Killian. He was chewing his food thoughtfully. 'What about at the Cairo Museum?' she asked, thinking of Samih's suggestion. 'Could they help? I mean, maybe the fragment is actually in there. They have the journal, and the place opened around the time of Jacob's excavation.'

Masud stroked his chin. 'I suppose it's possible, but finding it in that building could prove more difficult than digging it out of the sand. I have an idea. Some years ago, there was an attempt to catalogue the erotic treasures hidden in various museums. I sometimes correspond with the man who worked in Cairo. I can give you his address, though he isn't working any more. What do you think, Killian?'

Killian finished the last mouthful of his meal and sat back in his chair. 'I think it's a wild goose chase, only marginally preferable to releasing photographs.'

Masud wasn't listening. 'I'm sure Adie will be happy to pursue the fragment, while you're busy with more important things.' He turned to Adie, and smiled. 'I'll get you the address after dinner, and we'll review things in a fortnight.'

Killian rose abruptly and stalked over to the window. 'She's got better things to be doing with her time.'

'You'll barely know that she's working on it. Now –' he said, following Killian to the window, where he lit a cigar. 'What's this I hear about you thumping a man? A photographer, wasn't it?'

Adie saw his scowl reflected in the glass. She wondered if he'd give Masud a better account than the one he'd given her. She watched him brush a hand back through his white hair. 'I was protecting the project,' he said.

'Sadler?' Masud placed a hand on Killian's shoulder. The gesture was almost paternal. 'I understand he's in town and his minions are sniffing for information, but I'm surprised you let him bait you.'

Startled by the mention of a name she recognised, Adie turned a fraction more in her seat, wanting to join them by the window, but she didn't dare interrupt. Dareth Sadler – the man who'd been signing books in the museum. What had he to do with Killian? She tried to remember what Anton had said. Something about him being an academic leech with a cult following, but that hardly explained Killian's reaction.

The two men opened a door on to the courtyard and stepped outside. Adie rose to follow them, but Safiyya caught her arm. 'Leave them,' she coaxed. Adie reluctantly resumed her seat. 'Everyone knows Killian never stops working, but you're allowed to take a break. Now, I'll make some coffee and we will talk. Next door.'

Adie hesitantly let herself be led through the hallway and into a comfortable den with squashy brown armchairs. She browsed the rows of black and white photographs while Safiyya disappeared, and wondered what the men were talking about now.

Safiyya returned a moment later with a tray. 'Masud's parents,' she explained, nodding towards the photos. 'His mother was an English aristocrat. His father is the man on the extreme right.' She pointed to the end figure in the picture Adie was staring at, and then to a portrait-style photograph above. 'Handsome devil, isn't he?'

Adie nodded. 'Yeah, quite the dandy.'

'Masud has more of his mother in him. That's probably a good thing, considering his father was a gigolo.' She handed Adie a thimble-sized cup of steaming coffee, before kicking off her shoes and curling up in one of the armchairs. 'We use his old boudoir as a guestroom. People think it's a throwback to my past.' She took a sip of steaming coffee. 'I used to be a professional belly-dancer. It's how Killian and I met. He came to see me perform at the Sheraton.'

Reading between the lines from Safiyya's wistful expression, Adie suspected he'd done more than just come to see her. Well, if she was an ex, at least it explained the overly familiar greeting earlier. 'Is that where you met Masud, as well?'

'He came with Killian one evening.'

'Did I?' said Masud, as he entered the room.

Adie peered beyond him into the hall, expecting Killian to follow him in, but there was no sign of her boss.

'He's turned in,' Masud explained, as he slipped into a chair beside his wife. 'He intends to make an early start tomorrow.'

'Then I'd better do the same.'

'Don't feel you have to,' said Masud, bringing Adie to a halt in the doorway. 'He's just sulking. He doesn't like it when I exert my authority.'

'I think I'll turn in anyway,' said Adie. Knowing Killian, he probably thought she'd sided against him. She'd better go and talk to him. Having just settled one dispute, she didn't want to start another feud immediately.

Masud raised his palms in surrender and shrugged. 'Very well. I'll escort you to your room. But give me a moment and I'll get you that address.'

He caught up with her at the bottom of the sweeping marble staircase and handed over a carefully folded piece of paper. 'Dr David Franks. Email only, I'm afraid, but it should mean you get a quicker response, assuming it's still valid.'

He showed her to her room, and wished her goodnight. Adie stowed the paper in her overnight bag, which had been brought up, then went in search of Killian. His room turned out to be the next one along, at the end of the gently curved corridor. The door was ajar when she reached it, as if he'd been expecting her.

Killian's room was clearly the former boudoir. It was twice the size of hers, and the lavish decorations were both gaudy and sumptuous. He was on the far side of the huge bed, standing by the second of the two lattice-screened windows. He regarded her entry impassively as he slid the knot down his tie, then cast the silk over a brocade-covered stool.

'Was there something?' he asked.

Adie crossed the threshold. 'Masud gave me the information,' she said. 'Dr David Franks.'

'Fascinating.' Killian turned his back on her, and removed his shirt while facing the mirror.

Adie sucked her tongue, then inched her way across the thick pile carpet until she too appeared in the mirror. 'What does Dareth Sadler have to do with the project? Who is he?' she asked. She saw no reason to mince her words.

'Nobody,' he snarled. He lifted a bottle, and began vigorously rubbing moisturiser into his skin. Adie let the echo of the word lapse into silence, and watched his fingers working for a moment. 'So why did he want pictures of the site – and of you? And why has he taken Jacob's journal from the museum?'

'He's what?'

'It's missing. It disappeared just after his signing at the museum. It seemed like a coincidence before, but now . . .' She watched his expression carefully, but the only indication that he'd even heard her was in the slight tensing of his jaw. Adie wondered what to do next. Her instincts told her that knowing about Sadler was important. 'Shouldn't I know if there's a threat to the project?' she said.

'There isn't.' Killian replaced the cap on the moisturiser.

Adie closed in behind him. Apparently, this called for desperate measures. She traced a single digit over the right cheek of his bum, where the fabric had pulled tight, and felt his back stiffen.

'What do you think you're doing?' he said, fixing her with his gaze in the mirror.

Adie smiled sweetly. This would only work if she kept her nerve. She stroked a course around his hip. 'Getting your attention, because I'm not sure if you're listening to me.'

'I heard you perfectly well.' He turned abruptly.

Adie drew her hand back. If he was being this stubborn it had to be important. 'So why did you punch the photographer?'

'Drop it, Adie.' His voice became low and gravelly. 'And I'm not interested in your treasure hunt, even if Masud is forcing it on me.'

'Is this what Joe tried to warn me about?' Adie placed a hand on one hip and held her ground. She meant to get something out of him, even if it was just the truth about an old controversy. Although, as she glanced slyly at his naked torso, another part of her wondered what he'd do if she pushed him hard enough. Their last encounter had been more thrilling than she cared to admit, and she hadn't forgotten the feel of his skin sliding against her own. Her sex liquefied at the thought of repeating the experience.

'You can leave now,' Killian said. He crossed to the open door and held it wide for her. 'I need some sleep. I didn't get any last night.'

Adie resolutely sat down on the bed. 'When you've explained.'

Killian left his position by the door, and grabbed her arm. Adie tore at his grip in retaliation.

'Now stop that,' he snarled. He stared at her a moment, and his eyes darkened. Then he hooked his arm beneath her legs and hoisted her upwards.

'Hey! Let go!' Adie beat and scratched at his bare chest, only to have Killian suddenly drop her. She hit the carpet with a muffled thud; the thick pile cushioned her landing, but the impact still stung. 'Bastard!' She snatched at his trouser leg, bringing him crashing to his knees beside her.

Killian glared at her, his nostrils flaring with every breath. Adie glared back. She watched the hard muscles of his torso rise and fall, and felt a strange desire to bite him. Her gaze dropped lower. Beneath his zip, his cock had stiffened. They stared at one another, locked in a wary impasse, torn between anger and desire.

'Killian,' she said, forcing the words out. 'The workroom that night. If you won't explain Sadler, at least explain that.'

'It was a mistake,' he said flatly.

'Is that so?' Her hand snaked forwards and traced the length of his cock through the fabric, at the same time as she craned upwards to kiss him.

He was just out of reach.

'Do I have to tie you up to get some peace?'

Adie smiled. It was time to call his bluff. 'Maybe. I think I might enjoy that.'

Killian sighed wearily, then turned and tugged the sheet from the bed. Adie's eyes narrowed, only to widen immediately as he tore a long strip from the linen. What would their host make of the wreckage and, more importantly, what the hell did Killian have in mind? All of a sudden, her mouth felt dry. Images of herself trussed up and helpless sprang into her thoughts.

'Sure you'd rather not go to bed?' Killian asked, and there was a gleam in his eyes.

Adie mutely shook her head. Not unless he was coming too. She watched as he scooped up the hem of her borrowed dress and pulled it over her head, then discarded it. He began by binding her ankles and feet. Soon her torso and limbs were covered in strips of bed-linen, and the only movement she could make was an undignified wiggle.

Killian pulled a pillow off the disarrayed bed and rolled her over so that it was beneath her hips. 'I wish I'd thought of this before. It might have stopped you breaking that urn.'

'Do you think I'd have kept still for you then?'

Killian playfully tapped her bum. 'That would depend on what you thought you'd be getting out of it.'

'I'm not sure I know what I'm getting out of it now, except a nice view of the carpet.'

'Patience,' he whispered into her ear, and she realised that he was now straddling her thighs, leaning over her up-thrust bottom. 'And you might just get what you came for.'

'You'll tell me about Sadler?'

His lips alighted on her wrapped shoulder, then again midway down her back. 'No, not that.' His breath stirred the linen stretched across her back, then his tongue poked rudely between the strips and into the channel between her cheeks.

Adie's bottom tingled in response, and her cunt began to plump. She wriggled when the wicked intrusion dabbed closer and closer to her anus, and felt her bonds grow somehow tighter. 'Killian,' she gasped as his tongue finally poked beneath her thong.

His response was to lick her so intimately that it brought two hot spots of colour to her face. Adie rubbed herself against the soft carpet. This certainly wasn't what she'd anticipated from him.

Killian looped his fingers into the bandaging and pulled her cheeks further apart. She felt his breath, and then his tongue-tip dipping inside her puckered whorl. The sensation was intoxicating, and so rude that it forced her next breath to come out as an excited gasp. She gave a second whimper when she heard the slide of his zip. Where his tongue had been she felt a more insistent pressure. His fingertip wormed its way inside. She tried to squeeze her cheeks together, but two fingers from his other hand found a path through the bandaging to stroke her clit, and threads of fire streaked through her body in response.

'What are you going to do to me?' she managed to gasp.

'Watch the shadows and tell me what you think.'

Adie turned her head. The low lighting from the lamp cast their entangled silhouettes upon the wall. She caught a glimpse of his erection. It looked impossibly big. She turned her face back to the soft pile of the carpet and hid, nervous and more than a little embarrassed, but something about the shadowplay was strangely riveting and she soon turned back to watch.

His fingers circled the head of his cock, and his thumb pressed into the sensitive spot beneath the eye. Adie's mouth fell open and she slowly licked her lips. She'd never expected him to be like this, so relaxed, so uninhibited. He was so distant normally, and private.

He reached across to the dressing table and retrieved something from the surface. A moment later, Adie recognised the faint smell of cocoa butter. She watched him squeeze some moisturiser into the channel between her cheeks and rub it in with languid teasing strokes, which darted around the whorl of her anus. She stiffened slightly, unable to relax as she anticipated the further intrusion of his fingers. For a fearful moment, she wondered if that was where he intended to slide his cock.

The bonds around the tops of her thighs tightened as he drew them down to expose her bum. Yet the movement of his fingers was lulling, and strangely seductive. When his cock brushed her inner thigh, her heart jumped.

'I think this is what you really came for, isn't it?' he said, holding his cock against her clit.

Adie only managed an affirmative whimper. He was poised and ready to slip inside, and she wanted him to impale her, to fill her swollen cunt. With his next breath, he did just that. When he moved inside her, she bucked her hips as much as the restraints and the cushion would allow. Killian groaned approvingly. Then his finger was back again, dabbing persuasively, insistently, against her anus. When he slipped it inside up to the knuckle, it seemed to scorch her like the tip of a firebrand. Nerves lit up that she never knew she had, making her light-headed. Despite her bonds, the broken taboos made her feel free and open as her initial tension dissolved.

Adie lifted her hips again, desperate to take a more active role. The angle made his next thrust go deep, and combine with the teasing of his finger to flood her senses with dark ecstasy. She grunted into the carpet, and realised that she was drooling slightly. His next thrust drew another guttural sigh.

'Oh!' His exclamation matched her own.

'Touch me,' she pleaded.

His hand slipped beneath the bandaging, where his middle finger caught her clit. Adie's back arched in response. All the uncertainties and strife of the last few days flashed across her mind's eye then faded into insignificance. The extent of her world became the beat of their motion, the rub of the carpet and the tingling of her nerve endings. Her orgasm came on fast, and hit her hard, shredding her last vestige of control. She thought she screamed; then she went limp. She was only dimly aware of Killian gently laying her on the bed, and removing the mummy wrappings and her underwear.

When she finally opened her eyes, Killian was sitting naked on the bed beside her. He'd left two long pieces of linen bound around each of her wrists.

'You OK?' he asked.

Adie gazed up at him. 'What do you do for an encore?' she croaked.

Killian kissed her brow. Then his lips found her mouth, and Adie realised that it was the first time he'd actually kissed her. These weren't the savage bites they'd shared on the houseboat; this was different – personal.

When he drew away and rolled on to his back, she followed him and rested her head against his stomach. She hardly dared ask what was going on, just in case he suddenly stalked off again, but she had to know. 'The night in the workroom,' she said, repeating her earlier question. 'I don't understand. What was that about?'

Killian propped himself on his elbow and looked along the length of his body towards her. 'It's that dressing gown,' he said, smiling. 'It should come with a warning.'

'And now?'

He shrugged. 'Quit asking questions and come here.' He tugged on the linen bound to her wrist, and pulled her astride his torso.

10

Downtown, Matthew fought his away across the dance-floor, up the basement steps and into the cool night air. The heaving disco, packed with bodies writhing in airless confinement, had left him gasping for breath and space. Maybe he was just feeling jaded with the Egyptian club scene. When he'd first come to Cairo he'd loved it for its vibrancy, but this evening that intensity was finally starting to grate.

He crossed the road, weaving between the lines of parked cars and the odd donkey cart, strode on past KFC and turned into an adjacent street. Halfway along he found himself an outside table at an all-night *ahwa* and ordered coffee and a *sheesha*. The smoke from the water pipe quickly calmed his thoughts, making him light-headed into the bargain. It wasn't often he felt such claustrophobia away from the houseboat, but tonight he couldn't seem to shake it off. If only Siân could have come into town with him.

As he turned his attention away from the pipe and back to his coffee, he noticed the woman. She was watching him, sitting one table down and along, already drawing stares. Matthew took in the silky black hair that spilled loosely around her shoulders, the long-lashed eyes the colour of the desert sky, her serene oval face, and immediately wanted her. It had to be worth a shot, he thought. There was no other action likely to come his way that night. Abandoning his coffee, he moved across to her table. '*Salam 'alekum. Ismi Matthew,*' he introduced himself, cringing inwardly at his accent. Suddenly he wished he had Killian's talent for the language.

'Is your English as bad?' she asked, in a North American accent.

Matthew grinned sheepishly. 'May I join you?'

She pushed the chair opposite out with her foot. 'If you like.'

He sat and watched her brush her fingers through her long hair, imagining its silky length brushing against his skin. He loved the way long hair tickled, and the way it framed a woman's face when she sat astride him. Matthew enjoyed the give and take of sex, but most of all he liked a woman who could take control, and this woman seemed more than capable of doing just that.

'Are you here on holiday?' she asked, gazing past his shoulder.

'No, I live here. Well, some of the time. I work out at Saqqara.'

'Must be lonely.'

'It can be.'

She lowered her eyelashes, and then stared back up at him. 'Is that why you came over here?' She let the question hang in the air for a moment. 'For company?'

Her forthrightness startled him. He gaped at her. Then his gaze slid downwards to her curvy bosom. Even covered up by a high-necked top, the promising swell of her breasts made his cock thicken and press uncomfortably against his fly.

'Is it?' she prompted.

Matthew jerked his gaze back up to her face and met her eyes.

'Because,' she said, 'I came out looking to scratch an itch, and if you're not the man to do it there are several other cute guys over there.'

Matthew grinned. It seemed his luck was changing. 'What's your name?' he asked.

She reached forwards and ran her finger across his

lower lip. 'You don't need to know, but I'll tell you if you're a good enough fuck.'

Adie lay with her cheek pressed against the mattress; the room around her came into focus slowly. Her limbs felt heavy and stiff, and it took a moment to realise where she was. The skin between her breasts had dried shiny, and the air reeked of sex. Killian was asleep beside her. His bare chest rose and fell with each gentle breath. She watched him for a moment in fascination; rays of light streaked through the lattice screens lighting his sleeping face. Age lines had begun to soften his eyes, and there was a pale shadow of stubble around his jaw. He had come out of himself last night, but now she sensed his defences would be back in place, and she dared not touch him.

She sat up. The improvised mummy wrappings were gone, apart from a single strip still tied around her left wrist. She struggled with the knot but it resisted her attempts, so she wound up the loose end and tucked it in.

Adie left the bed as quietly as she could. She wasn't sure where the boundaries of their relationship had been drawn, and she didn't want to deal with any messy aftermath.

The fact that he was kinky had come as a surprise. He'd clearly enjoyed tying her up, and had shown more than a passing interest in anal play. Was he planning more than just a finger next time? She wasn't sure how to feel about that – intrigued and a bit apprehensive, mostly, considering where their relationship was taking her.

Curious, how he could be so unconventional in bed and yet so orthodox an Egyptologist. Did his turbulence hint at something deeper, something buried? She remembered Sadler's name cropping up in the conversation between

Killian and Masud, when they thought she wasn't listening. Maybe Joe had some answers. Then there was Franks to contact. She could make a start on that and forget about the strange dissonance of Killian's psyche until she felt ready to deal with it. She was going to have to find a balance between their personal and professional lives, even if Killian couldn't.

She slipped Siân's evening dress on over her head and padded back to her own room, where she quickly showered and changed into her ordinary clothes. First task was to email Dr Franks, then she'd think about contacting Joe Levine and maybe tracking down Anton, to see what they could tell her about Dareth Sadler.

'Off already?' Masud called to her from the dining room as she crossed the tiled entrance hall. 'Come and join me for breakfast.'

Adie waved her hand. 'No, I'm fine. Really,' she insisted when he raised an eyebrow. 'I've got some things to do, then I want to get this email sent before we go back to Saqqara.' She realised that she could have asked to use his computer, but she wanted to escape before Killian woke.

Masud left the table and caught up with her by the front door. 'There's a good place in the basement of the Nile Hilton Shopping Centre. Keep me informed of how things go through Killian. He's interested, he just won't admit it.'

'Mm. OK.'

Masud unlocked the door for her. 'Does he know that you're leaving?'

Adie shook her head. 'Would you tell him that I'll meet him at the apartment?' She stepped out on to the wide circular steps, wondering if she should apologise for the ruined sheets. 'Thanks for dinner,' she said, leaving Killian to explain.

'My pleasure. Good luck with your quest.'

Adie strode down the drive in her comfortable work boots, and managed to flag an empty cab. It was only as they sped towards Gezira that she thought of asking Masud about Sadler, but by then it was too late.

Thirty minutes later, she managed to secure a computer terminal at the cybercafé Masud had recommended. The email to David Franks was polite and to the point: a simple request for his assistance in tracking down the lost section of mural. The message to Joe was more difficult. It was hard to phrase her questions without sounding accusatory, and she had to rewrite them several times. She just hoped that Joe would give her some straight answers, assuming he ever read it. Joe didn't like technology; he still preferred letters and memos.

As Adie logged out, a figure reeking of patchouli took the seat next to her. The new arrival had heavily kohl-lined eyes and seemed vaguely familiar. She recognised her as the woman she'd spoken to at the Cairo Museum, who'd first mentioned Dareth Sadler. This had to be more than luck.

'Hi,' said Adie. The woman gave her a vague nod in response, without any sign of recognition. 'Did you get your books signed in the end?'

The blank look in the woman's eyes melted away. She smiled conspiratorially. 'Yes,' she confided. 'I did. It was a long wait, but worth it. How about you?'

Adie shook her head in feigned regret. 'I couldn't stick around that long.'

The woman nodded sympathetically, and patted Adie on the knee. 'It was a long queue. I guess that means you missed out on your invitation too.'

'What invitation?' said Adie.

'There's a promo party out at Saqqara. They were handing out special invites along with the signed photos, but if you wanted to go I don't think there'd be a problem.

It's all over the Internet. I guess someone leaked it, as usual, and there are loads of people planning to gatecrash.'

Adie stared at her, feeling sick. 'At Saqqara,' she said meekly. Who'd authorised this? Their entire excavation could be at risk; treasures might be stolen or damaged. She grabbed the woman's arm above her shimmering array of metal bangles. 'Whereabouts?' she demanded. The necropolis covered a large area.

'Djoser's step pyramid, of course,' replied the woman, eyeing her suspiciously. 'You know, the one in *Six Steps to Heaven.*'

'Right.' Adie nodded dumbly. The Stepped Pyramid was too close for comfort. She had to get back, to warn everyone. If any of Sadler's groupies got into the site, they'd have more to worry about than a few photos. Killian – he'd be able to stop it, wouldn't he?

Adie stood abruptly.

'Hey, you all right?'

'Eh? Oh, yeah. Fine.' She returned to her seat. 'What time did you say it started?'

'I didn't. Are you sure you're interested? Because you don't exactly look the type, and it'll spoil it for the rest of us if you're just gonna hang about looking straight.'

Adie peered down at her faded-green cargo pants and then across at the woman's tasselled skirt and collection of silk scarves. She had a point; Adie didn't really fit the image of one of Sadler's fans. Come to think of it, she'd never worn much in the way of eye make-up either. As a teenager, she'd always been too busy gluing Airfix dinosaurs to worry about mastering the art of liquid eyeliner.

'I have to tone it down for work,' she bluffed.

'Bummer.'

'Yeah. Look, I really am interested.' She forced some enthusiasm into her voice. 'It'll be great to hang out for a change. I don't know many people outside work, and I guess I'm starting to look a bit normal as a result.'

'Just a bit,' said the girl, although she was smiling again now. 'I'm going with some mates. You can tag along if you want...'

'OK,' said Adie, wondering how it had got this far. 'I'll meet you there. Djoser's pyramid...'

'About half eight, Friday.'

'See you there.' Adie waited until her new friend's attention had returned to the computer screen, then scuttled off to find the nearest taxi rank.

Killian's four-by-four was parked on the gravel driveway when she arrived at the apartment. Samih had his work spread over the kitchen table. 'He's in the shower,' he said in response to her questioning gaze. 'Came in fifteen minutes ago looking a bit rough. He asked where you were.'

Adie ran up the corridor and rapped loudly on the bathroom door.

'Nearly finished.'

'Killian, it's me. Can I come in?' The latch opened with a sharp click. Adie turned the handle and let herself into the steam-filled interior. Despite the open window, the blue tiles were slick with condensation. Killian stood over the sink brushing his teeth, dressed in a white bath towel. His skin was glowing slightly where he'd scrubbed too hard with the loofah, making Adie wonder if he'd been trying to remove the evidence of last night.

'Where's the fire? Don't I even get to brush my teeth in peace?' He spat out the toothpaste and rinsed his mouth. 'You can't have found the fragment already.'

'Sadler's having a party inside Djoser's pyramid,' she blurted.

Killian's eyes narrowed. He snatched up another towel

from the rack and slowly dried his face. 'And that concerns you how?'

'Can't you stop it or something? I mean, isn't it a bit close to us?'

'You overestimate my influence, Adie,' he replied. 'Besides, it's probably all cleared with the authorities. Right forms filled, right palms greased. Just remind me to bolt the doors on Friday, and hire a really vicious guard dog in case the bastard tries to get in.'

'But –'

The bathroom door swung against her, knocking her into Killian. They both turned to find Matthew on the threshold. He looked blankly at Adie, then at Killian.

'You might like to try knocking,' Killian said. Matthew merely grunted and staggered between them towards the sink. He ran the cold water tap, splashed his face, and then peered blearily into the streaky mirror. His skin was dark and puffy around the eyes and he was swaying on his feet.

'God, I look wasted,' he said.

'Where have you been?' asked Adie.

Matthew shrugged his shoulders. 'Heaven and hell.' He grabbed the towel Killian held out to him and wiped his face. 'I've just had my brains fucked out. I need to sleep.'

'Then you'll have to do it in the car. You're due back on site in an hour.' Killian retrieved his watch from the shelf above the sink and strapped it on. 'Get yourself in the shower and you can drive back with us. It'll save you the taxi fare.'

'Mercy,' gasped Matthew.

'Shower,' said Killian and walked out. Adie watched him pad across the hall, and then turned to Matthew.

'Son of a bitch,' he cursed and sat down on top of the toilet seat.

Adie kicked the bathroom door closed with her toe and

turned the lock. 'You all right?' He looked like something out of a zombie flick. His skin was sallow and – her nose wrinkled – he reeked of incense and pussy.

'Fine, except for my back.' He winced as he rolled his shoulders.

'What's up with it?'

'Been whipped.'

'Who by?' Adie carefully leaned over him and tried to pull up his shirt. 'Stand up.' Matthew yawned. He held on to the sink and pulled himself up, then shrugged off his rumpled shirt. The skin on his back was unbroken, but etched with a latticework of fine red lines. It looked painful, but she didn't dare touch it to find out if it was. 'Who did this?'

Matthew shuffled round on the spot. 'Don't worry,' he said. 'I liked it.'

'And what's this?' continued Adie, not listening. She traced a finger over a circular red mark below his pierced nipple. Matthew scratched at the shiny blotch.

'Candle wax. There's more lower down if you want to look.' He tugged at the button fly of his jeans, but Adie backed off.

'No, I believe you.'

Matthew shrugged and stumbled towards the shower while shimmying out of his jeans. 'How was your evening?' he asked slyly. He kicked off his boots, which landed by the side of the bath, closely followed by his black socks.

'All right.'

'Would that be, all right we talked shop all night, or all right it turned into an orgy but I'm not imparting the details?'

'Just all right. I've been asked to work on finding the missing fragment.'

Matthew turned on the spray and stuck his hand under

the water to gauge the temperature. A mischievous sparkle had returned to his eyes. 'So what happened to your wrist?'

'Nothing,' she began to say. She hadn't done anything to her wrist. Adie looked down at her hands in confusion, to find the strip of bed-linen still bound around her arm. 'Oh, I . . .'

Matthew sniggered. 'Is he as good as Siân reckons?'

Adie pursed her lips. All of a sudden, she felt rather vexed. Sadler was holding a party at Saqqara. She felt sure that something bad would come of it, and Matthew was baiting her.

'Oh, shut up.'

'Chill out.' Matthew hooked his thumbs into the waistband of his shorts. 'Tell him I'll be ready in twenty, OK? And get Samih to make me a coffee. And Adie,' he said, bringing her to a halt at the door.

'What?' She glanced back at him over her shoulder.

'Don't look.' And he dropped his shorts.

They drove back to Saqqara in an uncomfortable silence. Five minutes out of Cairo, Matthew fell asleep with his head against the window. Adie fixed her gaze on the world rolling by outside. As the dust of the city turned to the verdant green of the river-bank, then gave way to the pockmarked landscape of the necropolis, she reflected that maybe things hadn't gone as smoothly as they could. Maybe she should have woken Killian with a kiss or even a blow job, instead of sneaking off. Maybe in her eagerness to contact Franks, she'd made a serious error of judgement, because now Killian seemed distant and unresponsive.

'What's the big secret about Killian and Dareth Sadler?' she demanded of Siân once they were back on site. Siân was in the mural room putting on a hard hat. In answer to the question she lifted her boot on to a storage crate and eyed Adie thoughtfully.

'Have you asked Killian?'

Adie nodded. 'And he won't tell me a thing.'

'I'll tell you over lunch, away from here, all right?'

They eventually found a table in a shady corner of the rest-house, out of sight of the large and loud group of American tourists who were bargaining furiously with the hustlers for camel rides to Giza. Adie looked down at the black syrupy liquid before her. Steam curled from the surface of the thimble-sized cup, and sugar granules clung to the rim.

'Let's start with what you know,' said Siân. 'Then I'll tell you what I know.'

'Not a lot.' Adie took a tiny sip of coffee and set it back down. 'He's a writer, sensationalist stuff I guess, since he has a cult following, and for some reason Killian hates him enough to punch the photographer he sent sniffing round here. Your turn.'

'OK,' said Siân thoughtfully. 'What he writes is pseudo-archaeological bullshit, which is offensive enough, but about eight years ago he somehow managed to sell himself to Killian as a pro, and listed him as a contributor to the book he was writing. Then he twisted Killian's words, used them completely out of context, and nearly destroyed his career.'

'What was the book?' asked Adie.

'Six Steps to Heaven. It claims that the Egyptian gods are space-travelling aliens who seed planets and set up pyramids as huge transmitting devices to beam into space. Killian was a lot more free with his opinions in those days, and he's quoted extensively on Egyptian magic and ritual.'

'Right. Beam what into space, exactly?'

'The pharaoh's ba, so he can join the space-travelling gods on their journey. What else?' Siân smirked. 'It sounds just about plausible while you're reading it. Certainly, it's no wackier than the Ani Papyrus.'

Adie drew her eyebrows together. 'Yeah, whatever.' It sounded completely crazy, but there were enough addled New Agers around who believed it, considering the crowd he'd drawn at the museum. That still didn't explain Killian's reaction. 'OK, I can see why he'd be upset by the guy sniffing around again, but thumping someone seems a bit extreme. Why do I get the impression there's more to it?'

'Because there probably is. I don't know what. Lucas does, but he's keeping shtum.'

Adie sighed into her coffee cup. Maybe Joe would fill in the blanks, but she wasn't hopeful. He'd probably write back and say he didn't know what she was talking about, assuming he actually wrote back. 'Do you think Sadler's planning a sequel and someone's tipped him off about the mural?'

'Maybe,' replied Siân. 'I've heard that he's into sex magic these days, so an erotic mural would interest him. The blurb probably reads something like, "Learn how to attain immortality by reciting from the Book of the Dead while standing in a pyramid having your cock sucked."'

Adie grinned at Siân's deadpan delivery. It sounded ludicrous, but it probably wasn't that far-fetched. She lifted her hand and rubbed her brow, unsure whether to be amused or worried.

'Sprained your wrist?' asked Siân. She was staring at the bandage around Adie's wrist, and her bright-green eyes seemed uncannily knowing. 'Got more than you bargained for again, did you?'

Adie swallowed the last of her coffee and pretended that she hadn't heard. The linen strip seemed to be attracting an awful lot of attention and she couldn't get the knot undone.

He'd tied it damn tight, she cursed to herself, once she was back at her work pitch. Adie tugged at the stubborn knot but only managed to draw it tighter. She was going to have to cut herself loose.

'You're not that desperate to forget last night, are you?' said Killian.

Adie spun abruptly on her heels in response to his voice, nicking her wrist with the pocket-knife in the process. A single drop of dark-red blood beaded over the cut. Adie licked at it in irritation, then stared at Killian. 'How long have you been there?'

'A while.'

Adie picked up her brush and turned her attention back to the wall carving she was working on. 'Am I doing something wrong?' she was forced to ask after a few more minutes of scrutiny.

'No.'

'Then why are you watching me?'

'I'm assessing your skills. I don't want to let you loose down the robbers' tunnel without first seeing what you're good at.'

'You're going to let me work on my find?' she said, surprise and delight showing in her face.

'Less of the mine. I'm thinking about it. Your technique could benefit from some practice, though.' He moved forwards so that his breath whispered against her hair. Then his fingers curled over her shoulder. She waited for him to turn her, her lips tingling in anticipation of his kiss, but he left her facing the wall.

'Why the hurry this morning?' he asked.

'You said you wanted to start early, and I had that email to send.'

He drew a fingertip down to her hip, where he began to trace concentric circles over the bone. The memory of their night together came fresh and sharp to her mind, and her body awakened at the images of their shadows moving as one. All of a sudden, it wasn't just her lips that were awaiting his touch.

Killian clasped her hips with both hands. 'So eager you didn't have five minutes for a good morning?' His loins pressed against her bottom, the way they had the previous night. He was hard again now. His solid erection was branding her through her clothing. His lips grazed her shoulder, further sharpening Adie's lust. 'Lift up your top.'

Adie gasped. 'Right now?'

'Nobody will look twice if they think you're working.'

Excitement fluttered in her chest. Did she dare? What if he was testing her? Was she supposed to swat him away in the name of professionalism? Was it worth the risk? The pleasant jittery feeling inside her suggested it was. Adie took a chance, grabbed the bottom of her figure-hugging vest, and hitched it to above her breasts.

There was no hiss of outrage. Instead, Killian released the catch on her bra. He cupped one breast in each hand and began to roll her nipples between his fingers and thumbs. They perked up immediately. Adie rubbed back against him, savouring each subtle and not so subtle squeeze. She was sure she could excel at this test.

'Keep working,' Killian prompted when the brush she was holding glanced against the wall, sending down a shower of dust.

Adie straightened her wrist and flicked at the debris. It was hard to concentrate, especially when he released one breast and slid his free hand down the warm plane of her stomach to slip open the button fastening of her trousers. 'I wanted you on your first morning in Egypt.' His finger wormed its way inside her knickers and found her hot spot. 'What a vision, all tousled, warm and sleepy. I wanted to take you right there.'

Adie fought not to close her eyes, to keep working. She remembered the desire she'd felt that morning too, and the dream she'd woken from. 'Let's make up for it now,' she whispered, wanting him closer.

She thought she sensed him smiling, but he didn't say anything. His fingers kept working, though, and soon there were tremors running all over her body. Between her thighs she was moist and aching, desperate to feel the firm press of his cock, but somehow she managed to keep moving the brush.

Footsteps echoed in the adjoining passageway. The sound of Siân's voice made Adie jump, and she only just managed to stifle a squeak.

'Killian, we need your help. Lucas thinks he might have found something.'

Adie felt her friend's eyes boring into her and her cheeks began to burn. Surely it was obvious what Killian was doing to her. It was all she could do not to roll her hips in time with the rhythm of his hand, and Siân was no fool. Still, Killian seemed determined to bring her off while the other woman watched. Adie bit her lip until it hurt, and willed her mind and body to be still, but a rough piece of skin on his fingertip kept grazing a certain sensitive spot.

'I'll be up in a moment,' said Killian. His cock twitched against her cheeks. 'I'm just helping Adie finish off.'

Adie suppressed a whimper. She didn't know how she managed to keep the brush working, except that she was sure that Siân could see them quite clearly and there was security in the repetitious motion. Still, it seemed a lifetime before she left. By then, Adie was bathed in sweat. She released the breath she'd been holding, and it erupted like a cough. 'Jesus!' she gasped, and pressed her hands to the wall to steady her trembling limbs. Killian released her other breast and drew her vest over her shoulders and head, then twisted it to capture her wrists. Her trousers and pants were next; they slithered down her thighs to her ankles. Warm air caressed her bare bottom before his cock nuzzled between her cheeks. Adie's breath caught.

For a long uncertain moment, she thought he'd penetrate her anus the way his finger had the previous night, but then his cock glanced away from her back entrance.

Adie let the brush fall from her stiff fingers. His penis slid back and forth between her cheeks while sliding, kneading fingers teased her clit. Hot breath buffeted her neck and ear. He caught the lobe between his teeth and nipped at it. 'You're not working,' he whispered.

'I can't work,' she gasped. 'I can't concentrate while you're doing that.'

Adie pushed back against his thrusts and he began moving her to a more urgent rhythm. 'We'd better finish this quickly, then, so you can get back to it.'

'Not too quickly.'

His teeth grazed her ear lobe again, as she rode against his hand, their bodies sliding together, growing increasingly sticky with sweat. Adie was almost there, her mind and body slightly disconnected, one moving spasmodically, the other dazed and dreamy. Then, just as the buzz started in the back of her brain, he gave an abrupt jerk and came.

'Oh!' she whimpered.

A moment passed in silence.

'Killian.'

'Sorry. Too much,' he said, breathlessly. He touched her with two fingers where she'd received his ejaculate and began to rub it into her skin. Too surprised to be shocked, she didn't stop him.

'Are you marking your territory?'

'Giving you a keepsake. One a little less obvious than this.' He cut through the linen around her wrist with her discarded pocket-knife.

Adie turned to face him. His white hair was damp with perspiration, while his eyes were so dilated that only a tiny circle of grey bordered his pupils. His mouth locked on to hers in a deep satisfying kiss. Then he dropped to his knees.

'Aren't you going to see what they've found?' She'd expected him to drop everything and run. Hell, she was tempted to do it herself, except there was a frustrating prickle between her thighs that desperately needed attention.

'In a moment. It's waited three thousand years, it'll wait another five minutes.' The warm moist lap of his tongue darted around the sensitive opening of her slit and dipped inside like a miniature penis. Already highly aroused, her senses soared. Adie stretched out her arms above her head and arched her back. 'Just a bit more,' she encouraged. His tongue moved in long quick strokes over the whole of her bud, touching her in just the right place with just the right pressure. Even as her heart fluttered like a caged bird, her climax flowed out from his tongue and through her body in waves.

He continued to lick until she slowly came down. Only then did he rise to his feet and seek her lips again. Finally, he pulled away and rested with his back against the opposite wall.

'Now I'd better go see what got Lucas so excited.'

Adie nodded, then reached down and tugged up her trousers. 'Mind if I come?'

Killian strode along the dingy corridor, following the line of fluorescent-yellow tape that marked the cables of the lighting rig. He hadn't hurried because he didn't expect to find anything particularly special, certainly nothing worth pulling himself away from the warmth of Adie's body. Lucas, despite his staid manner, was a bit of an attention-grabber when it came to finds, and prone to giving them inflated importance. What he'd found might be anything from a golden sarcophagus to a piece of pharaonic dental floss. Not that dental floss wouldn't be interesting on a domestic level, just not actually all that riveting. Still, he felt a gut-level tingle of excitement, and he didn't think it was just down to the endorphin rush of his recent orgasm. Perhaps it was Adie's simple enthusiasm washing off on him. He hadn't felt this agitated in a long time.

He smiled in the gloom, picturing the pearly skin of her bottom bedewed with his seed. She had slightly plump rounded cheeks, soft, glorious, and just perfect to press up against.

Killian glanced back over his shoulder at her. He was probably crazy for getting involved right now, and with Sadler lurking he could do without the distraction. But it felt so good to hold her, to slide deep inside her and meld with her into one being. It had been a long time since he'd felt such a connection to another living person.

She smiled at him, and he thought he saw unguarded affection in her eyes. Killian's jitters increased. Maybe it wasn't the find that was so exciting after all. Maybe it was just her, and the possibilities that existed at this moment.

He reached the mural chamber and found Siân, Lucas and Matthew all gathered around a tray of pottery fragments, lit by a bright heavy-duty lamp. 'Anything, then?' he asked.

'A cartouche,' replied Lucas, as he moved back to allow Killian to reach the tray. 'It was among the potsherds left over from when Adie smashed that urn.'

Killian gave him a hard stare. He didn't quite catch his meaning but, regardless, projects were down to teamwork. It didn't matter who found what. Adie, he noticed, was hanging back from the group. She was probably cursing Lucas for reminding everyone of her clumsiness. No matter, he'd already decided to increase her responsibilities. He had to if he didn't want her getting side-tracked by frivolous treasure hunts.

Killian knelt and brought his lamp a fraction closer to the tray. The fragments appeared to be part of a larger piece, but the oval cartouche was perfectly clear. 'Huni!' He stared at the reassembled pieces in disbelief.

Siân bent down beside him, so that her long shorts rode up her thighs. 'Do you think he could be here?' Her voice sounded slightly shaky.

Killian lovingly traced a finger over the name of the third dynasty king and father of Sneferu, trying to maintain his own outward calm when he wanted to whoop in delight. There were a couple of other pyramids tentatively accredited to Huni, one at Abu Roash and another at Seila, but no one had found a body in either tomb. There was a distinct possibility that they might find him, and that would make this tomb particularly special. It already boasted an unusual and magnificent mural. He raised his head, to gaze at the vibrant colours of the gods and courtiers depicted on the eastern wall. This could be the most important discovery since the reopening of KV5.

'Killian?' Siân's voice intruded on his thoughts.

He pressed his fingertips together and splayed his fingers. OK, time for a reality check. The main descending passage was still blocked, and only a specialist mining team would get through that. Too expensive, plus it would generate far too much publicity. But how else could they reach the burial chamber?

He thoughtfully tapped his index fingers to his lips. Of course, there was the robbers' tunnel and the chamber beyond. Maybe there was an alternative route. Other tombs had them . . .

'We need to take another look at room three,' he said suddenly. 'Lucas, Matthew.' They both looked up. 'Get to work on the rest of those fragments. Take them back to the boat if you need better lighting. See if there are any other references to Huni. Siân, Adie, you're with me. There shas to be a way past that rubble in the corridor.'

Jubilation flooded into Adie's face in response to his words. Killian stepped back. She looked as if she was about to hug him, and he wasn't quite ready for public displays of affection just yet. Meanwhile, Siân dipped her head in acknowledgement. She caught Adie's arm and pulled her close. 'Try to stay calm and focused,' Killian heard her whisper.

They tooled up and headed down the robbers' tunnel. Room three still had only minimal lighting, some battery-powered lamps and a few hurricane lanterns. There was no quick and safe way of running cables along the tunnel, although they had widened the exit to make it easier to emerge into the chamber, and put boards across the pit.

Killian lit the last of the lanterns. He had a good feeling that there was a logical solution, and licked his dry lips as Adie circled the perimeter of the chamber. She hadn't been down here since that first fateful visit. Now she was taking it all in, absorbing all the details of the painted borders and the stelae – the carved false doors through which the *ka* of the deceased could pass in order to find sustenance, which were a feature of this kind of tomb.

'What exactly are we looking for?' she asked.

Killian shook his head, then joined her by the stelae. 'A flaw in the plaster, something out of place.'

'You mean a secret door.' Siân flashed him a smile. 'Let's not mince words.'

Killian dragged his hand through his dust-stiffened hair. 'Fine,' he snarled. 'A secret door. Call it what you like. Just find it.'

11

Adie stretched painfully and winced. It was 24 hours since Lucas had found the cartouche, and Killian had made them search room three systematically, from one corner to the next. They still hadn't found anything. She sat on an upturned bucket and rested her chin in her sweaty, dirty palms.

Killian had gone outside to get some air. Hell, she needed some air, and a cup of Samih's extra-strong coffee. She'd had eight hours' sleep last night, but it felt like eight minutes.

Siân, on the other hand, seemed energised by the whole desperate search. She was using her rest break to investigate the rubble that blocked the main passageway. Adie watched her pick over some loose rocks. Killian had refused to bring in a mining specialist for that job. Adie rubbed her nose. She'd never known anyone to be so secretive about their work.

She stared gloomily at the ornamental stelae. The stone had an almost pinkish tint in the dim light. She'd always wondered why the Egyptians had buried their best works underground, where no one would ever see them. The carving before her was good example: it showed Huni, presumably, performing the ceremonial Heb-Sed run while holding the deeds to upper and lower Egypt. She wondered if he'd appreciate an offering. That's what the stelae had traditionally been for.

Adie placed her water bottle on the ground before the image, then remembered the dried figs in her shirt pocket.

They were a bit squashed, but she figured he wouldn't mind.

'What are you doing?' asked Siân. She took off her work gloves and crossed the dingy chamber. She reached down for the water bottle, but Adie stopped her.

'Maybe if we're nice to him, he'll invite us in.'

Siân patted her on the shoulder. 'Enjoy your picnic. I doubt that Killian will be impressed if he sees you, though. Anyway, I'm thirsty.'

'Drink your own water, then. And he will be impressed, if I find a way through.'

They stared at the tiny offering for a moment, until a noise from the tunnel warned them of Killian's imminent return. Siân picked up the figs and popped one in her mouth.

'Hey!' Adie complained. She slapped Siân across the bum. 'They're not for you.'

'Well, I don't think he was about to eat them.'

Killian slid out of the tunnel, and stared frostily at them. 'Well?'

'Adie's resorted to making sacrifices.'

'Have not.'

'I'm pleased to hear it.' He moved her water bottle away from the false door.

Adie sucked her lip. 'What if it's not false?' she said.

'It is. We've looked,' Siân said, between bites of fig.

'No, we haven't. We just assumed the join around the edges was decorative.'

'Right, quit arguing,' said Killian. He picked up work gloves and flung a pair at each of them. 'Let's see if it moves.'

'Left a bit. Steady,' said Killian as they eased the stone slab out of the wall with a block and tackle. She'd been right about the door. The wooden splints they'd wedged into the widening gap creaked, then one splintered. 'Carefully!' Adie felt her muscles strain as she tightened the rope.

Siân slotted in another wedge. 'That's it,' she said. 'Ease it forwards now.' Adie tugged harder and watched Killian do the same. There were fat beads of perspiration rolling down his back. He was naked from the waist up, and streaked with dust. Adie's vest stuck to her, dark patches of sweat making a camo pattern on the khaki.

Suddenly, the stone gave a grating sigh, then slid on to the rollers they'd carefully positioned. Once it was balanced, they pushed it aside and laid it flat.

Killian picked up a torch and shone it into the void behind, which breathed cool air at them. The stone they'd removed was quite large, but the passage was only a squat square shaft about a metre wide. 'Siân, you first,' he said, the golden light of the lamp dancing in his pupils. 'This is your speciality.'

'So I'm the tunnel rat,' she replied. 'Suits me.'

Adie peered into the crawlspace as Siân pulled on a head torch. It didn't feel real. She thought of Lord Carnarvon asking Howard Carter what he could see as they opened the tomb of Tutankhamun, in the Valley of the Kings. 'Wonderful things,' Carter had replied. All Adie could see were shadows clinging like cobwebs beyond the range of the beam.

'Ready?' said Killian, beckoning Siân forwards. He squeezed her hand for luck, passed her another light, then he and Adie knelt either side of her as she wriggled into the shaft on her belly. After a brief false start, she slid forwards quickly, so that the inky shadows lapped around her and finally swallowed her completely.

There was a dull thud.

'She's through,' Killian muttered. He was lying flat, straining to see her progress.

'Where are you?' he called more loudly.

Siân's torches flashed at the end of the tunnel. The dual pinpoints of light swept left, then right.

'I'm in some sort of gallery,' she replied, her voice brisk and slightly shrill. 'There are statues ahead. I can't make out what from here. Hang on.' She vanished from view to the left of the hole, leaving them staring into the darkness, ears straining to pick up the soft scurry of her footsteps. 'They're missing their heads. Oh! They're bound. Naked and bound.'

'Like the prisoner statues from the Pepi I mortuary temple?' asked Killian. He snatched up another flashlight and strained forwards into the crawlspace.

'Similar,' replied Siân, her voice echoing. 'But these are completely nude. I think there are four of them. Two facing each other where I am now and another pair further on, past what looks like a portcullis slab.'

'Blocking the entrance from the main passageway?'

'Yes, almost certainly. Which means behind me should be . . .' She fell silent.

'Should be what?' asked Adie, in the space of her pause.

'The burial chamber,' said Killian and Siân simultaneously.

'I'm coming in,' Killian announced. He scrambled through the tunnel, bare-chested. 'Stay there, Adie, in case we need any help.'

'But!' she protested.

'Two in, one out, for safety. You'll get your turn soon.' Then he was gone.

'Bastard!' This was the second time she'd made a discovery and he'd left her behind. She slapped the wall, hard enough to make her palm smart beneath the protective layer of her glove. The sound echoed with a watery tone.

Ten minutes later, Adie was sitting on the floor staring morosely into the tunnel when Siân shimmied out.

'Go for it,' she said, grinning like a lunatic. She found new batteries for the torch and passed it to Adie. 'Go on.'

Adie slid stiffly into the crawlspace. Her body wouldn't work as fast as she wanted it to. She brought her knee down on a loose stone, winced, and emerged into the darkness of the gallery, limping and rubbing her leg while her torch beam bounced off the walls.

She straightened herself up. She was in a broad aisle. Many of the wall facings were fractured and broken, but the remnants were covered in painted images. One depicted the fertility god Min with an erect phallus the colour of ox blood. In another section, hunters had cornered two hippopotamuses.

Adie carefully traced the contours of one design in the air above the carving, then suddenly found herself laughing. It didn't matter that she wasn't the first in. This was her moment, just what her father had encouraged her to seek, and dreamed of doing himself. She wished he was here. He *was here*, in her memory. It was magical, sacred. She was seeing what no one was meant to see, a tomb sealed for all eternity. This was the pharaoh's private domain, his space between the mortal world and afterlife with the gods.

She found Killian in the centre of the burial chamber. Here the smooth walls were undecorated, although the ceiling was painted blue and embossed with stars to resemble the night sky. The sarcophagus was in the centre of the room. Adie hurried over to the granite sepulchre to run her palms over the stone. The sides were carved, the top stone etched with hieroglyphs. Adie pressed her cheek to the lid. It was icy cold.

'It's empty.'

For a moment, his words didn't register.

'There's a crack in the bottom corner. You can see right to the head. There's no mummy.'

Adie stepped back. All of a sudden, she felt cold and her chest was tight. She didn't know what she'd expected. Not treasures as such, but a body, definitely a body. Without one, it was just a hollow vault. She swallowed hard over the lump forming in her throat. Suddenly she felt tired and dirty. She wanted a bath and a whole huge bar of chocolate.

'Stolen?' she asked. She stared at Killian, finally noticing just how still and withdrawn he seemed. He'd grazed his shoulder-blade crawling through the tunnel, and now the skin around it was mottled with dried blood. Tentatively, she reached out and touched him.

'We can check the casket for traces,' he said. 'But it was probably never used. We already know the earthworks above ground were never completed. Maybe it was only intended as a cenotaph.'

'So what now?'

'We photograph everything, and then learn what we can.'

'And right now?'

'We call it a day. We'll come back tomorrow with fresh eyes.' He pressed a gloved hand to her shoulder. 'It's a great find, and after a night's sleep we'll all appreciate that, mummy or no mummy.'

They packed up early and headed back to the *dahabiyya*. Killian seemed withdrawn, while Adie felt like she'd reached Eden only to be told to keep off the grass. She realised that it was just a matter of perspective. What they'd found was precious and important, but they'd all hoped for something greater. The site would still inspire future generations, but with the murals rather than a pharaoh. In fact, by the time she'd showered and eaten, she almost felt relieved that the sarcophagus was empty. At least she wasn't going to be responsible for removing somebody from their path among the stars to eternity in a glass box being gawped at by tourists.

'Find yourself a perch,' Siân said as she ushered Adie into her cabin. They were supposed to be getting an early night, Killian's orders, but they both needed to unwind a little. 'Sorry about the mess.' There were clothes everywhere. 'I couldn't find my boots this morning.'

Adie moved a pair of baggy shorts and several scrunched vests to the floor and dropped into Siân's ethnic armchair, a weird construction built out of driftwood, clearly made by someone with a vivid imagination. It turned out to be surprisingly comfortable.

'Ha, stowed booze.' Siân produced a bottle of gin from inside a hiking sock and deposited it on the bed. 'And somewhere around here there's some tonic and a lemon.'

'I have the ice,' said Adie and she rattled the bag of ice cubes she'd just brought from the freezer. 'But it's melting fast.'

Siân poured the drinks into two tall glasses and then found herself a comfortable space on the bed. 'To Huni,' she said, and took a generous sip. 'Wherever he is.'

'Huni.' Adie raised her glass. The tonic bubbled on her tongue. If only Killian had joined them. He'd turned a blind eye when she'd taken the ice from the freezer. She wondered if he was moping alone in his cabin, or if he'd already got over it. 'Where's Matthew? Isn't he joining us?'

Siân shrugged. 'If he ever turns up. Dozy sod left his cabin keys on site and went back for them. Killian wasn't too pleased about him going back alone. I thought he was going to make him sleep on deck. He said something like, "The site's too precious for fools to be locking up."'

'Shouldn't he be back by now?'

Siân glanced down at her watch, removed it and gave it a shake. 'Damn thing's stopped. The battery's probably dead again. I keep forgetting to get a wind-up one.'

'It's nearly ten.'

She suddenly looked worried. 'He left while you were in the shower.'

'That was over an hour ago.'

'Shit!' Siân stood up and kicked the bed. 'Damn. That idiot's good at getting himself into trouble.'

'Want to go look for him?'

'No.' She swallowed another mouthful of gin, then sucked in her upper lip. 'But I suppose we should. Except he took my car.'

'We could borrow Killian's. He won't know. I think he's gone to bed.'

Siân eyed her sceptically a moment. 'You're a bad girl, you know.' She swallowed the rest of her drink in two long gulps and slammed down the empty glass. 'All right. Let's go, but you're driving.'

Matthew gripped the wheel of Siân's Land Rover moodily as he drove back to Saqqara. The jolts from the ruts in the road punctuated his cursing. He'd been looking forward to a drink and a chance to relax with the girls. Two days working with Lucas on the hieroglyphs had left him desperate for company with a sense of humour, except he'd managed to leave his cabin keys on site. At least he hoped they were on site. Otherwise, he'd left them in Cairo. While he was sure Siân would offer him bed space for the night, he badly needed a change of clothes. So here he was, black night surrounding him, still out in the desert.

He parked up close to the excavation, and a moment later, the chunky padlock slid easily from the hasp. Matthew gave the door a hefty shove. If he made this quick, he might get back before Siân and Adie called it a night.

The dark had never bothered Matthew before, but now he found himself pausing before the black maw of the entrance. He'd often worked late to emerge into starlight, but going down into the gloom made him feel inexplicably nervous. He hesitated for a moment, then ducked under the doorway, feeling slightly foolish.

A scraping sound behind him gave him a start, but he had no time to turn before a hand smacked his bottom. He wheeled in surprise and found the curvy outline of a woman framed in the doorway by the night sky. He blinked. 'Lana! What the hell are you doing here?'

'Looking for adventure. Looks like I found it. Oh, and I thought you might need these.' She lifted her hand so that he could see his keys dangling from her index finger.

'Thank god.' He regained his balance. 'You surprised me. I'm not normally here this late.'

'We figured you'd look here first. Oh, I brought a friend.' A second figure appeared in the narrow entrance. 'Matthew, Karima.'

Matthew dipped his head in acknowledgement, his gaze quickly returning to Lana. He had no idea how she'd found him, but she'd certainly dressed for excess. Matthew was just glad Killian wasn't around. Their costumes – for they were dressed almost identically – were little more than scraps of silk, secured with thick brass clasps. Matthew thought of the houris, pleasure slaves of the Hashisheen, and wondered if he'd been drugged.

'What's down there, anyway?' asked Lana, pushing past him.

'The rest of the pyramid,' Matthew mumbled warily. He wondered what they were planning. He knew from experience that you refused Lana at your peril.

'This is a pyramid?' Karima sounded dubious. 'It doesn't look much like one.'

169

'It's buried like Sekhemkhet's pyramid. They stopped building before it was complete.'

'How interesting. Mind if I take a look?' said Lana as she picked up one of the electric lanterns, and began to descend the stairs.

'Yes, actually,' said Matthew. He hurried to catch up with her. Killian would have his guts if he found out about this.

'Oh, come on. Just to the bottom of the stairs and back.'

Matthew reluctantly let Lana take his hand and continue down. 'OK, but no further,' he growled as they reached the bottom. Unfortunately, he'd forgotten about the mural.

'Mm. Inspiring.' Lana's comment turned all their heads towards the ancient mural. Matthew silently cursed. This was getting out of control.

'Don't touch,' he said, pulling them both away from the delicate surface. 'You should leave.'

'Oh, don't be such a spoilsport,' purred Lana. She turned to him and drew one of her long fingernails across his chest. 'This is just perfect ... too perfect ...' Her fingertips reached his throat, then the pad of her thumb rubbed suggestively over his bottom lip. Matthew swallowed slowly. The azure blue of her eyes was inky in the dim light. She lowered her eyelashes flirtatiously. 'You don't want us to go yet, do you? Just think what you'll miss out on. And we've got all dressed up for you.'

The soft brush of her thumb against his lip continued. He heard a soft thump next to his feet and realised that she'd dropped the bag she was carrying. With her free hand, she found his zip, then cupped the bulge of his cock and balls. Matthew's breath caught in his throat. A pair of hands alighted on his bottom, where they began to trace languorous circles.

Lana tilted his head and drew him into her kiss. He felt the waist of his trousers go slack and seconds later the tough cotton slid down his thighs. Two hot hands pushed inside his shorts and his cock reared as Karima's fingers tangled in his pubic hair. This definitely beat drinks on the boat with Siân and Adie.

He felt the nip of Lana's eye-teeth against his tongue and pressed eagerly against her. Karima urged him out of his trousers. Then between them they lifted his T-shirt and sent it sailing off into the gloom. There was something about the mural, he decided, that just made people want to fuck.

Suddenly, Lana dropped to her knees and her tongue swished across the head of his cock, there, then gone. They spun him around, and Karima tugged at his nipple ring with her teeth. Another dizzying turn and his cock was in Lana's mouth again, her tongue swirling about the tip.

Karima's lips alighted between his shoulder-blades, then danced playfully down his spine to his tailbone. Her wet, eager tongue pushed into the crack between his cheeks, wakening sensitive nerves. 'Whoa!' he gasped, as they switched again, and Lana tongued up his spine.

Matthew caught Karima in his embrace. He tore at her inadequate halter and buried his face in her bosom. She fell away from him and stretched out on top of one of the large equipment crates, her nipples steepled in the cool air. She parted her legs and swept aside her loincloth. The glimpse of her plump pink slit was both shocking and lewd.

'What are you waiting for?' she mouthed.

Matthew didn't need a second invitation. He rolled the condom she offered over his cock and pressed inside.

For several moments, as their bodies found a rhythm, he wasn't aware of anything beyond the immediate feel of his skin and the heat in his cock. Then Lana raked her tapered fingernails down his back, and appeared before him, dropping a kiss on his nose. She caught up Karima's ripe breasts and moulded them in her hands, squeezing and tugging until the brown nipples stood like two crooked towers. Matthew groaned at the display. Lana stepped back, bringing her crotch level with his gaze. Black leather straps fastened with shiny silver buckles ran across her upper thighs and hips, supporting a thick black dildo.

'Want to give it a kiss for luck?' she asked, thrusting it towards his mouth. Matthew, slack-jawed and unthinking, accepted the press of the latex. He felt sweat form above his lip, on his brow and across his back. This was unreal; he'd wake in a moment and find himself on the houseboat.

Lana poured oil over the dildo, dropped the vial into her bag, then positioned herself behind him. Anal play wasn't anything new to him, but he'd never had anything bigger than a girlfriend's finger. This thing was huge.

Lana grasped his hips. His anus stretched around the slippery, bulbous tip, leaving him shocked and breathless. His own cock throbbed and bucked inside Karima's hot core. For a moment, he feared he'd come right away, but one of them tugged on his balls and stopped him.

They began to rock together, Lana dictating the rhythm. He felt the cool press of a silver buckle against his cheek as the dildo slid in, and the rasp of her stocking-tops against his thigh as it slid out. The rubber cock in his bottom felt like it was impaling him all the way to the tip of his own cock. He closed his eyes, unable to help himself. Red vision and pumping heat shook his body. He felt a buzzing in his head like a swarm of angry bees. He was being stung repeatedly. There was sweat in his eyes, between his fingers. His penis felt too tight. White light blinded him as he shouted out his orgasm.

Matthew shook his head groggily. Normally he recovered quickly, but he seemed to have had all his strength knocked out of him. He couldn't even lift his hands. He gazed blearily at his fingers and found his wrists cuffed to the handles either side of the chest.

Karima slithered out from beneath him to land in an ungainly heap on the earth floor. She stood up at once. 'You're fucked,' she said, hand on hip, and he didn't think she meant it in a literal sense. There was another blinding flash. The light hadn't been anything to do with his orgasm. It was Lana. She turned the camera on him and he realised to his horror that the dildo was still protruding from his arse.

'Smile, please.'

Matthew grimaced as the flash strobed. Horrified, he watched her return to her main objective. They'd used him to get to the mural and he'd fallen for it. 'Oh, shit!' he cursed.

'Shut him up,' said Lana, without breaking concentration.

Karima scooped up Matthew's discarded shorts, stuffed them into his mouth and smoothed a piece of silver gaffer tape over the top. Matthew beat the sides of the trunk and tugged against his bonds. There was no give. He grunted unintelligibly through the gag.

Lana reached over and pulled the plug from his butt. 'See you around, pretty boy. It's been fun.' She dropped his key and the handcuff key on to the floor before him.

Matthew tugged futilely at his leather bonds as he listened to their departing footsteps, but, with a feeling of disgrace and degradation, he realised how helpless he was. He'd still be here at dawn when Killian arrived, and then all hell would break loose.

Siân's battered Land Rover had been driven right up to the dune beside the excavation. Adie pulled up alongside in Killian's four-by-four. Guilt had stopped her long enough to leave a note when she'd taken his car keys.

The padlock was hanging loose on the iron ring,

although the door was closed. Adie shoved it open and ran her torch beam over to the top of the stairs.

'There's someone down there. I can see a lamp.' Siân pushed in alongside her, and they both edged forwards.

'Hello.' Adie's voice echoed off the stone walls. There was no reply. 'Grave robbers,' she said, airing her worst fear.

'I doubt it,' said Siân. 'What are they gonna steal? More likely it's Matthew playing silly buggers.' She crept down the first few steps. 'Anyone down there? Matthew?'

They heard a thump. 'Clown,' said Siân. She jogged down the remaining steps. Adie followed more cautiously. They entered the mural chamber, their gazes drawn to the lantern in the south-east corner, but a loud thump immediately turned their heads. Matthew was cuffed face-down on a work trunk and was thumping at the sides as vigorously as his bound position would allow.

'What happened here?' Adie asked. She pulled the tape from his mouth and Matthew spat out his saliva-soaked pants.

'About sodding time,' he blurted.

Siân unlocked the handcuffs. 'What happened?'

Matthew grunted and tugged his trousers on. Adie handed him his T-shirt. 'Are you going to tell us what's going on?'

'Later,' he snarled. 'The bitches are still around here somewhere.'

Siân's eyes narrowed. 'Forget it. There's nobody out there. The place is deserted. How long ago did they leave?'

'I don't know.' He dragged a hand through his brown hair. 'A while, I guess.'

'I guess?' Siân shook her head wearily, as if she could barely credit the stupidity of those around her. 'OK, sit down and tell Adie what you've done. I'm going to scout around outside for your missing women, and I'm optimistically going to assume they haven't taken anything.'

'Just pictures.'

Siân left, and Matthew slumped on to the chest. Adie pressed a hand to his shoulder, and watched him push the balls of his hands into his eyes.

'OK, I'm a fool,' he said, red heat flooding into his cheeks. 'They were here when I arrived. I should have realised they were after something but at least it was just a few photos.'

'Photos!' Adie shook him. 'Jesus, Matthew. Have you forgotten what Killian did to that photographer? He's gonna roast you. This could bring down the whole project.'

'Don't be stupid. It's just a few pictures of a fractured painting.'

'Yeah, that Dareth Sadler has an unhealthy interest in.'

Matthew looked blank, but Adie didn't feel like explaining. She was already wondering what to do. 'We're telling Killian, is what we're going to do,' said Siân when she returned. 'Unless you have any bright ideas about how to get their camera before they upload the images. I take it the camera was ditigal?'

Matthew nodded. 'I don't even know why they'd want them. Who's Dareth Sadler, anyway?' he asked.

Siân shook her head in dismay.

'We might be able to intercept them tomorrow,' said Adie thoughtfully. 'He's holding some kind of promo event at the step pyramid. They might pass the pictures to him there. We could hold off telling Killian until then.'

'I don't know, Adie.'

'Come on, Siân. Don't you want to know what Sadler's up to?'

'I do,' said Matthew.

'Oh no. You're not coming,' they both snapped.

Matthew opened his mouth to protest, but Siân stayed his tongue with an uncompromising glare. 'You've done enough damage already. You're spending the weekend out of trouble on the boat, and don't argue.' She paced the length of the chamber and back again. 'This probably won't achieve anything, but OK, we'll give it until tomorrow night.'

12

Dareth lay on the hotel bed. Staring up, he could just make out the hairline crack on the ceiling that he was focusing on in order to ignore the chilli-like burn of the weird concoction he'd rubbed into his cock. This time tomorrow he'd be out at the centre of a ritual he'd dubbed the 'Coming of Horus', which was also the title of one of the key chapters of his new book. His head was still swimming with all the ideas he'd pulled together to make it work. Luckily, he had Lana to deal with the boring logistics of publicity and other preparatory details. He could have lived without a few of them, though, such as the potion, and the six raw egg-whites she'd convinced him to swallow in order to achieve a truly godlike spurt.

The click of the latch announced her return. He waited for her to close the door. 'What have you got for me?' he asked.

'Thirty-two interior shots and a few happy snaps.' She dumped her bag on the bed beside him. 'Karima's taken them to Jamāl to upload and print them. We should have them back tomorrow.'

Dareth propped himself up on one elbow and watched her unpack the contents of her bag: camera, leather straps and buckles, an assortment of dildos, hairbrush, stuffed asp. He raised an eyebrow quizzically. 'What the hell's that for?'

'Security. It keeps the wankers out. Speaking of which, how's your cock? Still smarting?'

Dareth let the insult go. He was too pleased at the thought of filling out his book with all those glossy prints, and he knew he wouldn't have got them without her. 'In need of a kiss? Care to oblige?' He wondered if he could coax her into bed for a ritual warm-up. Sod abstinence. He needed to temper the heat of his cock.

Lana shook her head and laughed. 'The only person I'm getting off tonight is me. In private.' She whipped off her bra and dropped it over his crotch, where it hung on his erection. Dareth groaned and slumped back into the pillows. 'You could at least let me watch.'

'Think of tomorrow night. You don't want to disappoint anyone, do you?' She kicked off her knickers, blew him a kiss and with a graceful swagger disappeared into the bathroom.

Dareth watched her go, admiring the jiggle of her bottom until she moved out of view, then he rolled on to his side and watched her reflection straddle the bidet and direct the jet towards her clit. If she wanted privacy, she should have closed the door.

The following evening Killian locked up early and disguised the site entrance with sand and dirt, to Adie's immense relief. She was worried enough over the camera, without the risk of trespassers from Sadler's party. They hadn't mentioned last night to Killian, and luckily he'd never noticed their absence.

'So you two are heading back into Cairo for the weekend,' he said.

'I want to concentrate on tracking down the mural fragment. Masud thinks it's worth my time, and since the tomb is empty . . .' She let her words trail off.

'Well, don't wear yourself out. There's still lots to do. It's going to take weeks just to photograph, draw and record everything inside the gallery and burial chamber. We've barely started.'

'Don't worry, we'll come back raring to go.'

Siân and Adie drove up the road, then doubled back

and parked by the deserted ticket office, well away from the excavation and Djoser's pyramid.

'Whose crazy idea was this?' asked Siân as they hurriedly changed into their party gear of short shorts and crop tops in the shadow of the Land Rover. The light was already starting to fade, and the sky had turned a vivid shade of magenta. 'We're going to bloody freeze later.'

Adie peered over the top of the wing mirror, wielding a heavily laden mascara brush. 'If this doesn't work, we'll switch to plan B and tell Killian everything. At least this way we might limit the damage.'

'Hmm!' Siân snapped her compact shut and threw it on to the driver's seat. 'You ready?' She perched her penny-shades on her nose. Adie nodded. 'OK, let's mingle.'

There was a steady stream of arrivals at the colonnade entrance as they sauntered up. The thumping Egyptian dance music, amplified by the pyramid, almost knocked them off their feet. 'It's a bit loud,' shouted Siân, pulling a face. It wasn't really Adie's taste either, she preferred something she could sing along to, and she knew from hitching lifts that Siân preferred either classical music or techno.

'Over here,' called Adie. She grabbed Siân's arm and dragged her over to a group of three women dressed in a collage of black velvet, PVC and fishnet stockings. 'This is –'

'Nadine,' the woman helpfully inserted.

'Nadine. We met at the museum. She's the one who told me about the party.'

'Glad you made it. Michelle and Simone.' She nodded towards her companions. All three were done up in extravagant Cleopatra-style make-up, with arms full of bangles, a popular image amongst many of the predominantly female guests.

'It's quite a crowd,' said Siân, glancing around, 'plus the usual glitterati, literati and professional liggers, I suppose.'

Adie was thinking the same. Right now they had no chance of spotting the two women Matthew had described, even if they were dressed in the same clothes as last night.

'Afraid you won't make it as one of the chosen ones?' drawled Simone between drags on her clove-scented cigarette. Adie was about to ask what she meant when Nadine jumped to their defence.

'And you're not?' she sniped at Simone, who smirked and puffed a white smoke ring into the air.

'I'm here for the free booze. My mum hung out with Sadler back in the eighties. He could be my dad for all I know. I wouldn't mind his PA, though.'

'Liar. Dareth's not that old.' Nadine's bangles tinkled as she balled her hands into fists.

Simone dropped her cigarette butt and stubbed it out with the pointy toe of her boot. 'No chance. He's definitely the wrong side of forty.'

Nadine gave her an evil glare, emphasised by the thick kohl lines around her eyes. Simone shrugged, and retouched her bottom lip with a black lipstick from her shirt pocket.

'Let's go in,' said Nadine, turning to Adie and Siân with a theatrical flounce.

Leaving Simone and Michelle to follow, they made their way between the towering stone columns to emerge into the south court of the pyramid complex. Adie let her hand graze against the ribbed stones as they passed. The structure had been the first of its kind, and a model for future generations of tomb builders. She wished she had more time to admire it, but she had to concentrate on Sadler.

The sunlight was rapidly fading, but Dareth's people had erected a huge open-sided marquee in the Heb-Sed court. From one end, the music was blaring, and flashing disco lights strobed the faces of the dancers. At the other end, there was a trestle-table bar serving local wine and chilled beer, and several buffet tables, around which a group of the local press were networking.

'So where's the star?' said Siân, helping herself to the hors d'œuvres.

'Oh, he won't show up till later,' said Nadine. She handed them each a bottle, and they stood in silence for a while, sipping the amber liquid and watching the other guests.

'Who's that?' Siân eventually broke the silence. She pointed towards a woman in a white organza dress with a basket of white flowers. 'It looks like the woman Matthew described.'

'She's Dareth's PA,' said Nadine. 'The one Simone says she fancies. She thinks pretending to be bisexual makes her look cool.'

'What's with the flowers?' asked Siân.

'Privilege tickets. Dareth chooses women from the crowd to join him in the inner sanctum. It's a huge honour. They only pick people who are enlightened enough to perform in the ritual.'

'Sounds like a quick and easy way of pulling,' Siân whispered to Adie.

Adie nodded, but her mind was still absorbing the fact that Matthew's seductress was Sadler's personal assistant. Presumably, he'd orchestrated the whole episode just to get those pictures. They'd have to be on their guard in case he had any other schemes in motion.

'We need to get ourselves an invite,' she said to Siân. 'I don't think the camera's going to show up, so we'd better find out what his angle is before we go to Killian with the news.'

Sian nodded. 'I'm just glad he's still on the boat, too far away to hear this.'

Over the next two hours, they watched Lana approach several women and present them with lotus blooms.

Eventually Nadine joined her friends on the dancefloor, allowing them to drop the pretence of enjoyment. At ten to midnight the chosen women left one by one and disappeared into the shadows on the far side of the step pyramid. There'd been no sign of Sadler all night.

'We need a flower,' said Adie. 'If we want to get into the VIP area.'

'Leave it to me,' replied Siân. She drew Adie away from the multi-hued lights of the Heb-Sed court and moved into the deep shadows around the base of the pyramid. After a few moments, she pressed a finger to Adie's lips as a woman carrying a single white bloom approached their position. Siân tucked her shades into her top pocket. When the young woman was almost level with them, she sprang at her. 'Bitch! You stole my boyfriend!' She clawed at the bewildered woman's clothing, and they fell to the floor. In the confusion, she snatched the flower and thrust it at Adie, who took off as fast as she could. She sincerely hoped that Siân had a suitable apology lined up.

Adie stopped by the entrance to the inner chamber to catch her breath. Amazingly, there didn't appear to be a guard. She plucked a micro flashlight from inside her bra and shone it into the dark tunnel. The stolen lotus flower she tucked into the strap of her vest. Who knew what kind of debauchery she'd find down there, but she was out of options.

The passageway led into a broad gallery and from there into the bedrock via a long flight of stairs. Her feet scuffed against debris, forcing her to step carefully for fear of losing her balance. She continued down, her torch beam flickering ghostlike off the glassy walls, until she reached a junction with more stairs.

The torch beam wavered as she reached the bottom steps, then blinked out. The darkness was absolute. Adie shook it, but the tiny battery was dead, and she didn't have a spare. Suddenly, the trappings of ancient civilisation were oppressive. The air in the base of the pyramid was stale and heavy. Still, she reasoned, she was in a corridor, and it had to lead somewhere. She edged forwards, letting her instincts guide her. They felt a little rusty after weeks of suppressing them for Killian's benefit, but they'd still helped her find the robbers' tunnel and the secret door.

When she next stopped, there was cold stone against her right arm. The sound of footsteps echoed through the open space to her left. 'Is somebody there?' she hissed.

'Adie, is that you? Where are you?'

'Nadine? Just here.' Adie felt the brush of fingers against her back and then a hand clasped her arm. 'You came to find Sadler, didn't you? I want to take part too. I have a flower.'

Adie didn't want to think about how this particular blossom had been obtained. She just knew that there were now two furious groupies above ground.

Just then, a wavering light licked across the blue-tiled walls of the room, followed by the sound of light footsteps. A procession of five women appeared, dressed in identical semi-transparent white robes to the ones that Lana had been wearing earlier, as well as elaborate eye-masks.

'What are you doing here?' asked the woman at the head of the line.

'Lana sent us,' bluffed Adie. She offered her lotus bloom to the woman, who matched Matthew's description of his second assailant, Karima.

The woman pushed the flower away from her face. 'You're late.'

'We got lost.'

'Never mind.' With a gesture she sent one of the parade members back along the corridor. The woman reappeared a moment later carrying two sets of robes and more of the ornate masks. 'Get changed, quickly.'

Adie made to slip the organza dress over her head, but Karima stopped her. 'Clothes off first.'

Indeed, all the women were naked beneath their gowns. Adie apprehensively stripped and let the light robe fall over her head. It floated over her body on a cushion of air, barely touching her skin. In the dim light, the dark circles of her nipples were still visible through the cloth, as was the V of her pubic curls. It concealed nothing, yet caressed everything.

Karima placed a feline mask over Nadine's eyes. Adie's was plainer, but with a large horned solar disc. They had jewelled bangles pushed over their sleeved wrists, and were instructed to carry the lotus flowers before them like an offering. Finally, they were pushed to the back of the line.

A moment later they entered the central shaft above the burial vault. A man, presumably Dareth Sadler, was standing by the granite plug that sealed the vault below, at the centre of a circle of white candles. He was dressed in sheer black satin, his face hidden by a large falcon mask. Kneeling beside him was Lana.

'Horus,' Adie mouthed to herself, recognising Sadler's persona for the evening. The mural immediately came to mind. The guy clearly had an ego the size of Africa.

Once they'd taken up the eight compass points, he swept open the front of his robe, revealing his naked body. There was a large ankh drawn on his chest, and his impressively erect cock had been painted an obscene Nile blue. An apprehensive gasp escaped Adie's lips, as she realised that she hadn't really thought this out properly. To avoid discovery, she'd have to be a participant, not an observer.

In the background, a drum began to beat slowly, and the heavy smoke of incense permeated the air. Dareth turned slowly on the spot, appraising each of the women in turn. Most bowed their heads. One or two met his gaze,

that the way to really pleasure a
age her imagination. Did he exploit
. He was only giving them what they
being taken by a god made flesh.
cross his face beneath the mask. He
e slow burn of Lana's poultice last
ying off now, keeping him hard and
he was good for at least two more
reward Lana by spilling his last one

gods had ever existed, then they were
ts in masks getting what they wanted
ggestion. He had no more or less power
y what his followers bestowed. He just
that more of them would get the joke,
He felt like laughing. His cock was
few more strokes and he was going to

w Adie enter the pyramid, she climbed
oman, mumbled something about mis-
nd made a hasty retreat. Skirting the
ers outside the marquee, she left the
ded back towards the ticket office to

d Rover, she noticed another car parked,
sleep over the wheel. The plate was
was a small figurine of Sadler hanging
nd a sheaf of promo bookmarks above
gnised his image from the dust-jacket
lled a bit closer. There was more promo
s the back seat and, curiously out of
er book.
g, she thought. She tried the hand
wly, quietly, she eased open t
e book from the seat.

before dropping to their knees as instructed. A goblet of
sacramental wine was passed around. Adie only took a
sip, but she still felt the heat of some aphrodisiac slowly
infuse her senses. She shook off the dreamy lethargy it
induced, but had to admit that his set-up was good. It
would be easy to get drawn in by the theatrics and mock
ritual.

Once the cup had completed the circle, Dareth dropped
his robe and stepped over the shimmering puddle of cloth
to cross to the woman at the north point, who wore an
elaborate black-feathered mask.

Lana, in the north-east position, began to intone the
words of a spell. Before her was a decorative faience cup
from which the aromatic scent was pouring, and beside
that was a small white urn.

'Rise, oh Horus, come into your inheritance as possessor
of wisdom, vanquisher of fools. Receive the blessings of
your sister goddesses, to magnify your potency as you
make your way among the stars to the table of Osiris.'

'Mut, consort of Amun, receive the offering of Horus,
and bestow with your kiss the gift of your wisdom.'

The woman obligingly opened her mouth, accepted
Sadler's cock, and sucked it blissfully for a few moments.
Adie clenched her fists. She wondered if Siân had seen
this coming, and chose to act as the diversion for that
reason. She wasn't sure sucking Sadler's cock was something she was prepared to do in pursuit of knowledge.
But she couldn't just walk out either.

Sadler stood before Lana, whose mask was decorated
with a single, gorgeous ostrich plume.

'Maat, daughter of Ra,' intoned Lana. 'Bestow with your
kiss the gift of truth.' She paused in her litany to briefly
close her lips around the phallus.

He was moving far too quickly around the ring. Nut,
Sekhmet, Hathor, all mouthed Sadler's cock. Then
Nephthys, and suddenly Nadine was next. She took Adie's

hand and gave it an excited squeeze. Adie felt like things had gone completely beyond her control. She hoped nobody ever found out she'd taken part in this hopeless charade. The embarrassment would kill her.

'Bastet, daughter of Atum, receive the offering of Horus.' Nadine gratefully fellated Sadler. He seemed to stay with her only a few seconds, before his blue cock was level with Adie's nose.

'Isis, consort of Osiris, bestow with a kiss the power of your magic.'

This was it. The potent incense filled her nostrils and the chanting grew louder in encouragement. She couldn't believe she was doing this. This was the man who could wreck her career, who had come so close to destroying Killian. She closed her eyes and waited for the intrusive thrust, tempted to keep her mouth shut. Instead gentle, persuasive fingers stroked down her cheeks and lifted her jaw. She looked up into his face. Behind the beautiful feathered mask, green-brown eyes seemed to plead with her for only a moment of indulgence. Her jaw fell slack. Dareth lifted her hands, releasing the lotus bloom, and laid them to rest on his thighs. Mesmerised, Adie allowed his hot cock to fill her mouth and throat, and found herself, instead of gagging, enjoying the salty and yet sweet taste of him. He tasted of butterscotch. She heard him groan, very quietly but audibly, and lashed at his cock-tip with her tongue. He was clearly close to orgasm, and she was bringing him closer. She wondered if he would last long enough to complete the circle. Suddenly, she wanted to be the one to make him come, and she worked her mouth harder.

Sadler pushed gently on her shoulders and withdrew. He was breathing hard through his nose, and there was a glassy sheen to his eyes as he moved on to Adie's right. He did close the circle, reaching Lana as his blue cock bucked. Lana captured the long jet of his seed in the white

alabaster
substance.
drying blac
room and p
giant grani

What it
the shatteri
everyone. Th
Sadler selec
relief, he cho
Sadler's still-
by the other
of the drum.

Adie backe
thing, but taki
to get out.

Dareth Sadler
the scene. He
problem was? N
chosen. At least
was only a little dis
trix in the circle was
get eight adoring w
mouths? Only in
chosen badly.

There were
Someone's brea
moved rhythm
as Bastet, allow
wasn't going t
the best part.

He met the
seemed slight
while the oth
at tedious

you, and he knew
woman was to eng
them? Definitely no
wanted, the idea of

A smile spread
may have cursed
night, but it was p
horny. He reckone
encores. Maybe he
over her breasts.

If the Egyptian
just like him, pries
by the power of su
than they had, on
wished sometime
share the fantas
starting to throb.
come.

As soon as Siân
of the mocked v
en identity,
kets of strag
plex and he
ait.

Close to her La
with the driver
Egyptian, but the
from the mirror,
the dash. She rec
of his book. Siân s
stuff spread acro
place, a worn leat
That's interesti
was unlocked. Sl
door and slipped t

Siân lovingly stroked the aged spine. The leather was cracked and scuffed, and smelled of musty libraries. William Jacob's journal: Sadler had obviously lifted it from the museum, which meant she wasn't technically stealing.

The driver snored. Siân pushed the door over, but left it open a fraction to avoid making a noise. She stepped carefully back.

'Tut, tut.'

Siân froze. The driver was still snoring. She turned her head. Seated astride a horse was a man in Bedouin dress.

'Did nobody ever tell you that stealing is wrong?' he said.

Siân pursed her lips and met his gaze. 'It belongs in a museum. I'm taking it back.'

'Fair enough. You'd be wise to leave before that brute wakes up.'

'No introduction?' said Siân. The wind had lifted his long dark hair as he'd spoken, and the moonlight now revealed him as the man whom she'd glimpsed on the driveway of the Gezira apartment with Adie. This was the man who'd sent a beautiful outfit to a woman he hardly knew, and clearly knew how to engage the senses.

'Anton Kelly,' he said, bowing his head to her. She felt he should have been called Hāsim or Ismāil. 'And you're Siân Lawrence. See that it gets home, won't you.' He reached into his robe, and held out a papyrus to her. 'And since you're closest, would you mind putting this on the back seat?'

'What is it?'

'The weight of his sins.'

Siân took the papyrus and inched open the door again. She placed it carefully in the space the journal had occupied then eased the door closed. Anton nodded, then nudged his horse forwards.

'Good night.'

'See you around,' mouthed Siân, hugging the journal to her chest. Adie had all the luck. Maybe she could be persuaded to part with Anton's phone number.

Siân was dozing over the dashboard, wrapped up in a battered old flight jacket, when Adie slipped into the passenger seat. 'Hey!' Adie jabbed her in the ribs.

'Oh, hi.' Siân rubbed her face and stretched. 'Learn anything useful?'

'Not really.' Adie slammed the door and fastened her seat-belt. 'Just helped elevate Sadler to godhood, that's all. What have you been doing?'

Siân shrugged nonchalantly. 'I found this.' She passed over a worn leather book, with several index tabs sticking out.

'Jacob's journal!'

'Correct. It was in Sadler's car. Looks like he's found all the good stuff.'

'So combined with his Horus outfit and the ritual I've just seen, we can be pretty certain that his new book is about our mural.'

'That's not all,' said Siân. 'I had a flick through the pages. He's looking for our missing fragment.'

'Gets better, doesn't it? I suppose there are notes on all these tabs. Does it look like he's ahead of us?'

'He's been more systematic.'

Adie groaned and banged her head against the dash. 'Well, what are we waiting for? Let's get to Cairo and see if Dr Franks has written back yet.'

'Get up, you lazy sod!' Siân bellowed as she pulled the bedclothes off Samih. Olive skin flushed with sleep, he whimpered in response to the sudden exposure, grasped ineffectually at the covers, and finally curled into a tight defensive ball. Adie gave him an apologetic smile from her position in the doorway. Siân had already moved next door to inflict the same torture on Jason, who, by the sounds of it, was putting up more of a fight for his duvet.

Samih yawned, and wrestled a T-shirt over his head. 'Coffee,' he muttered.

'Coming up,' replied Adie. She stepped sideways to allow Siân, who was dragging Jason by the tie on his shorts, to pass.

'What do you want?' he complained wearily. 'I've only been in bed an hour.'

'To check email,' said Siân.

'You need us for that?' He collapsed on to the denuded bed next to Samih. 'Man, I know you're stuck in the dark ages out there on that boat, but I'd figured you'd learned how to switch on a computer by now.'

'It's urgent, you dope, and the cybercafés are all closed. I know you've got keys to the university department, so quit complaining and get dressed.' She opened Samih's wardrobe and chucked clothes at them.

Jason shook his head in disbelief and handed Samih his clothes. 'We do have Internet here, you know. Thoroughly modern of us, don't you think? It's all set up in the living room, think you can find the button?'

Siân sniffed. 'Since when?'

'Start of term.'

'Well, no one told me.' She strode off towards the lounge.

Samih got to his feet. 'Well, I'm awake now.' He pulled on some jeans and trudged past Adie into the kitchen. 'Anyone not want coffee?'

Several minutes later, they all sat huddled around the screen, nursing mugs of syrupy ground coffee. Adie yawned despite the caffeine, and dug her knuckles into her eyes; the text on the screen looked blurry. There was nothing from Joe yet, but David Franks had written back.

'OK,' she said. 'Franks can't be sure if he catalogued our missing fragment, but he says that all the depictions of male genitalia are boxed up in the Cairo Museum.'

'I told you that,' said Samih.

'He also reckons that there are loads of them, and his old assistant, Ihsān Fuād, might be more help. Apparently, he did most of the cataloguing. Only they lost touch because Fuād was dismissed on suspicion of theft. He thinks he's still in Cairo, though.'

Siân clucked her tongue. 'Dead end.'

The two men each took large swigs of coffee.

'We've got a name.'

'Come off it, Adie, how many Ihsāns do you think there are in Cairo, in a population of sixteen million?' Siân rose and paced impatiently towards the window. 'Matthew's screwed things right up. We're gonna have to tell Killian. In fact, we should have told him straight away.'

'Told him what, exactly?' asked Jason. He and Samih turned their chairs towards Siân, who sighed, then began to explain. Adie turned back to the screen, feeling sick in her stomach. There was a horrid taste in her mouth, a bit like out-of-date dolly mixtures, which she guessed was the aftertaste of Sadler's cock. What had she been thinking of?

'So Sadler's causing grief again,' Adie heard Samih say, as she deleted her junk mail. 'We'd heard he was in town. And it's been in all the papers. They haven't dredged Killian's murky past yet, but give them time.'

'What murky past?' Adie spun around on the swivel chair to face him. She'd never thought to ask Jason or Samih.

'You know about Sadler's first book, *Six Steps to Heaven*, right?' said Samih.

Adie nodded. 'Siân mentioned it.'

'The misquotes were only the beginning. There were five mysterious deaths linked to the rituals described in the text. Sadler immediately left on a promotional tour of the Far East, so the press went for the next best person.'

'Killian,' said Adie.

'Exactly. He was quoted extensively and he was working on Djoser's complex.'

Adie leaned forwards to hear more. This explained why Killian always avoided the subject. She was glad now that she'd backed down when she had, but she was still surprised that Joe hadn't told her more. Then again, he'd never approved of idle gossip.

'What sort of mysterious deaths?'

'I don't know the exact details. Some sort of weird ritual suicide involving mummy wrappings and auto-asphyxiation, I think.'

'I thought it was something to do with asps and meat-hooks,' said Jason.

Samih's brows wrinkled, and he gave his head a slight shake. 'You're thinking of something else. This was a few gullible wannabes who wanted to hitch a ride with the gods.'

Siân, who had her forehead pressed to the glass window-pane, drummed her fingers against the window-sill. 'But what about means and motive?'

Jason chuckled. 'The media were on a witch-hunt. Killian was an easy target, especially when he was already trying to distance himself from the book.'

'What happened?' Adie asked. Samih's casual mention of mummification was making her feel distinctly uneasy, despite her firm belief in Killian's innocence.

'The final verdict was death by misadventure, but the damage was already done. Academically, Killian was a joke. His project had collapsed and his work partner walked out on him. It's amazing he ever managed to recover.'

'And Sadler?'

'Instant bestseller. Any publicity is good publicity in

the entertainment business. They couldn't print them fast enough.'

'You mean he didn't show any signs of remorse?'

'Don't be daft,' said Jason. 'It elevated him to cult status. He's been doing his best to maintain that ever since.'

'Hence tonight's little ritual,' muttered Siân into the glass.

Adie clamped her hand to her mouth, feeling a sudden wave of nausea. 'Scumbag!' she blurted.

'Rich scumbag, with friends in high places,' said Jason. 'So what is it we're supposed to be doing to stop him from wrecking our careers?'

'Letting Killian know what's going on,' advised Siân.

'Finding Ihsān Fuād,' said Adie resolutely. 'Without the fragment it's just Sadler's crazy theory against our imperfect one, just like the situation Killian was in before, and we know who came off best that time. We need to know what the mural depicts. Anyway, I still have one lead – Anton. He knows the museum pretty well; he might be able to help.'

'Hang on a moment,' said Samih. He sounded rather incredulous. 'Anton who? Not Anton Kelly, surely?'

Both women's eyes narrowed. 'Yes. Why?' said Adie.

Samih and Jason exchanged worried looks.

'Better spit it out,' said Siân. 'She's only been fucking both of them.'

Jason hid his face in his hands.

'Anton Kelly,' said Samih meekly. 'Oh shit!'

'What the hell is all this about?' demanded Adie.

'Anton Kelly,' Samih replied. 'The partner who walked out on Killian, just when he needed a friend.'

'So what happened next?' asked Siân.

'He turned to the dark side.' Jason took a large gulp of coffee. 'He's in with the grave robbers now.'

Adie stared at the computer screen.

'He knew.' She shivered. 'He knew who I was from the start. It's why he introduced himself.'

Siân nodded. 'Makes sense. I bumped into him by Sadler's car. Adie, you realise that if he knows the grave robbers, he might know Ihsān Fuād. Just be careful how you ask him.'

13

The next morning, Siân still didn't rate Adie's chances of success. It was unlikely that Anton would know Ihsān Fuād, or that the disgraced Egyptologist would remember one piece among hundreds.

If she'd been on the houseboat, she'd have told Killian the truth there and then. He'd find out eventually, and the sooner he knew, the more time they had to come up with a way to save the project. However, she'd agreed to wait until they'd spoken to Anton, as Adie was convinced that Killian would stop her search if he found out that they'd been compromised.

Now she was waiting patiently in the lobby of the Nile Hilton, armed with a Dictaphone and a reporter's note-book. After Adie left the apartment, she'd decided on a whim to meet Sadler face to face, and she figured that, being a complete fame junkie, he wouldn't pass up the chance to talk about himself to a journalist.

The receptionist at the Nile Hilton buzzed through to his suite on request and he met her a few minutes later in the hotel lounge. She'd expected a sweaty geek wearing an army pullover with patched elbows, but the reality was very different. He'd dressed in a white linen suit, and his blond hair had been gelled and sculpted to perfection.

Lana also presented a very different image. No longer the devoted priestess, she'd pulled her long dark hair into a high ponytail and adopted a dark, feminine-cut business suit, which emphasised her hips, breasts and tiny waist. Siân knew immediately how she'd got to Matthew. He was a sucker for the whole boardroom bitch, scratch-you-while-they-fuck-you look.

Lana adopted a protective position three feet behind Sadler, and gave Siân an unfriendly stare.

'Miss Lewis.' Sadler greeted her by the false name she'd given the receptionist, and offered his hand. 'You're lucky to catch me. I normally spend the mornings out on research, but I was working late last night.'

'How fortunate. It's an honour to meet you, Mr Sadler.' Siân accepted his hand, only for him to press his thumb into her palm and bring her knuckles to his lips. Creep, she thought. Then his lips brushed the sensitive skin between her first two fingers, stimulating rarely touched nerves and sending a tiny shiver of pleasure along her arm and into her chest. Make that a dangerous creep. She waited for him to release her hand.

'Dareth, please,' he said, maintaining eye contact along the length of her outstretched arm. 'Shall we sit?' He guided her into one of the armchairs.

Siân smoothed her skirt, then pressed record on the Dictaphone. 'Your new book. Can you slip us a few details for the readers?'

Lana leaned forwards. 'What magazine did you say you were from?'

Siân resisted the urge to fidget with the few stray hairs that had escaped her French pleat. 'The *Astral Times*.'

'Hardly a quality paper to give an exclusive to.'

'We're not asking for an exclusive, just a few teasers.'

Dareth reclined in his seat, clearly amused by the interplay. 'Refreshment?' he asked, defusing the conflict. 'Lana, *ahwa mazboot* for two, please.'

'Perhaps you could give us the title and a synopsis?' suggested Siân, once the other woman had left the room.

Sadler pressed his fingertips together. 'Of course. The title is *Osiris Reborn*, and I build on the themes first introduced in *Six Steps to Heaven*. This book expands on the sacred rituals and preparations undertaken by the pharaohs in their quest to join their ancestors among the stars.'

'And could you give us an example?'

'Ah!' He brought his fingertips to his chin. 'No. There must be some surprises. You must allow me my secrets, Miss Lewis.'

Siân nodded. It was uncanny, that gesture, the way he thoughtfully splayed his fingers. It was pure Killian. She stared at him. There was a faint physical similarity too, and the same presence. Given different choices, she wondered if Killian could have turned out like this.

'How about a location, then? Is there a particular site central to this book in the way that the Step Pyramid was to *Six Steps*?'

The muscles of his cheek twitched as he smiled. 'The Step Pyramid is still of immense importance, but I have also drawn on relevant material from other sites in the area.'

'Any we may have heard of?'

'I really don't want to give too much away at present, but one recently discovered site is of particular relevance. I suspect you'll hear more of it soon.'

Siân brought her pencil down hard on the pad. Well, that was a confession of sorts. She wondered if he was any closer than they were to finding the missing fragment, but she couldn't ask him straight out.

'Aren't you concerned about past allegations?' she asked, changing tack. 'After all, there were several deaths connected to your previous work on the Step Pyramid.'

Dareth rubbed the side of his nose. 'The rumours of suicide pacts connected with my work are totally unsubstantiated. Additionally, before you print anything libellous, I'd like to point out that it's been eight years since *Six Steps to Heaven* first saw print. In the five books since,

I've covered an enormous amount of material which could be loosely associated with unfortunate cases around the globe. People need to take responsibility for their own actions, and stop seeking scapegoats.'

He was leaning towards her as he finished. 'OK,' said Siân, somewhat abashed, and he abruptly sat back. He began drumming his fingers along the arm of the chair in a light rhythm. The question had clearly irritated him. She looked about, half-hoping to find Lana returning with the milky coffee. The patter of his fingers was strangely lulling, momentarily causing her to lose her concentration. She shook her head to clear it. 'Will you be collaborating with Dr Carmichael again?' she asked determinedly.

Dareth abruptly stopped drumming, but remained silent.

'Shall I take that as a no?'

'No comment.'

Finally, the coffee arrived. Dareth ignored it. 'I'm afraid I'm going to have to cut this short. I've matters to attend to.'

'One last question, then,' said Siân as he rose. 'Suppose someone does follow the magical formulae you describe in your book. What waits for them? Do they really get to meet Anubis?'

Dareth managed a smile. 'I don't purport to be a medium, Miss Lewis. Despite popular opinion, the afterlife is beyond my experience. I record only what is plain to anybody who not only looks, but also *sees*. Now I'm afraid I must be getting back to my work. Goodbye, Miss Lewis.'

Siân stopped the tape and watched him go. She'd learned very little, but at least she knew their enemy now. She didn't doubt he was dangerous. It wasn't that he was amoral. He was just out for himself. Quoting bona fide Egyptologists presumably lent credibility to his work and sold more books, regardless of whether it also destroyed careers.

'Journalist my arse,' said Lana, as the lift doors closed. '*Astral Times*, what's that, a fanzine? Why did you even bother to talk to her?'

Dareth cupped his hand around the back of her neck. 'Because you don't build a following without meeting your public.'

Lana turned and rested against the grey metal wall. 'Is that why you attend all those horrid conventions? I always thought it was for the freebies and the sex. How silly of me.'

'Don't sneer, darling. Those conventions help pay your salary.' He grasped her upper arms, forcing them straight by her sides. She pursed her lips in response and snapped her teeth at him when he drew in close for a kiss.

Dareth laughed, and forced his mouth down on hers. 'What's the problem?' he whispered on to her tongue. 'She'll probably stretch the few titbits I've given her to a five-page spread. We're hot news again, baby. Enjoy it.'

'I don't trust her. I've seen her somewhere before.'

'Yeah, probably at one of those cons.' He sucked at her lower lip, stealing her pout.

'Maybe,' she said, as the lift doors opened. 'But I doubt it.'

Thirty minutes later, it was Lana's turn to feel smug. 'Sneaky bitch. I knew she wasn't a journalist. She's one of Carmichael's lackeys. Siân Lawrence, BA, PhD from Durham University, etcetera.'

Sadler looked up from a selection of large-scale prints of the mural photographs, and cocked an eyebrow. 'Interesting. Not here on his instruction, I'll bet. Bring the laptop over here. We'd better check out the rest of them, just in case they're planning any more surprise visits.'

They scrolled through the Cairo University web pages detailing Killian's research team, and came to the recent additions link. The new page contained only a veiled reference to a project at Saqqara and a mug shot of the team's newest member.

'Now then.' Dareth tapped the screen. 'There's another familiar face.'

'Adina Hamilton,' read Lana. 'Brought in a few weeks ago as a last-minute replacement.'

'And I bet I know how she got the job. That lady gives terrific head.'

Lana stared at the picture, her oval face clouded with scepticism. 'Are you suggesting she took part in the ritual? Because I didn't invite her, and you only saw them with their masks on. I've certainly never spoken to her.'

'Eyes are my speciality. Didn't you mention that there was a little incident over the flowers?'

Lana smoothed her sleek ponytail. 'It's a bit unlikely that someone on Carmichael's team would go to all that trouble just to suck your dick, but you've always attracted the freaks. What do you think they're up to?'

'Maybe they've heard I'm after Horus's missing cock, and they're sussing me out?' Dareth crossed to the bed and stretched out on the mattress. 'Or maybe they just wanted to see how the other half lives.'

'Maybe.' Lana joined him on the bed, and straddled his thighs. 'What are you going to do about it?'

'Talk to them, of course. I think we'll start with Ms Hamilton. I can't imagine her boss would be pleased to learn that his new recruit has been drinking at the fountain of my wisdom.'

Lana drew her fingernail down the seam of his trousers. 'Jamāl should have no problem tracking her down; he's been keeping tabs on their movements anyway. I'll call him.'

'Yes, do that. I've work to do.' He pushed her off, so

that she lay sprawled on the bed. 'And ask him if he's found that damn journal yet. I don't care if he's lost it, sold it, or whatever. I want it back.'

'I've already spoken to him about it. He said he only has one clue.' Lana crossed to the night-stand and returned with a piece of papyrus. 'This. It's a convincing fake.'

'Behold the man who has broken faith, he who is a friend to vipers. His tongue shall be cut out and his mouth stopped with bitumen; that he may speak no more lies, nor receive cakes and ale at the table of Osiris,' read Dareth. 'It's not bad.'

'Maybe you should hire the author. It's better than the drivel I have to recite.'

'Watch your tongue,' he snapped. 'And tell Jamāl I'll stopper his mouth with bitumen if he doesn't bring that book back.'

Adie took another sip of her iced *limoon*. She'd arranged to meet Anton at Fishwari's, hoping that the crowd would help her act naturally. It wasn't working. The last time she'd seen Anton he'd covered her in fruit syrup and opened her clothing with a knife. Now he was sitting across the table from her as if awaiting the punchline of a bad joke.

It had seemed so simple at the apartment. All she had to do was ask him why he was interested in the mural, then ask for his help finding Ihsān Fuād. Except now she couldn't think of a way of opening that didn't sound like an accusation.

'You don't look pleased to be here. Why did you want to meet me?' Anton asked, when the mistrustful silence had grown to the point that they could hear each click of the domino contest on the adjacent table.

'Why didn't you tell me that you knew my boss? Why are you interested in the mural?'

'What mural? What does Killian have to do with it?' he challenged her.

'So he didn't have anything to do with why you introduced yourself?'

'No.'

'So why did you?'

Anton gripped the wooden table. 'You really want to know? I saw you cavorting topless amongst the sand dunes, and I fancied you. I didn't even know you were working for Killian until you told me, because I don't keep up with his work. It's ancient history, just the way he likes it.' Anton stretched across the table to take her hand. 'Look, what's this about?'

Adie moved her hands to her lap. 'You're not a grave robber?'

'No more than you are.' Anton's mocha-coloured eyes turned hostile. 'You thought I was going to rob you? I was only ever interested in you.'

'What about last night? Siân told me she'd seen you.'

He folded his arms across his chest. 'My business is with Sadler's hired thug. What about you?'

Fellating him, she wanted to snap. Instead she turned away and glared at the snake of dominoes on the next table. This wasn't going at all to plan. She took a deep breath. 'I'm sorry. Can we start again? I'm trying to find someone who used to work at the Cairo Museum and I thought you might be able to help me.'

'Because of my underworld connections?' growled Anton. 'You know, I don't think I'll bother.' He jerked his chair backwards and rose.

'Anton. Please. His name is Ihsān Fuād, and I need to find him before Dareth Sadler does.' She dug into her money belt and pulled out several Egyptian notes. 'I can pay you for your time, it doesn't have to be a favour.'

'Keep your damned bribe. Baksheesh might drive the

economy, but you can't buy me. We were lovers, Adie. What happened?'

'Anton, wait.'

Adie frantically stuffed the banknotes back into her pocket, but Anton was already out of the café. She searched the crowd, but he'd vanished into the confusing sprawl of the Khan al-Khalili.

Not sure what to do next, she wandered aimlessly among the stalls of the great bazaar. It was everything she'd imagined the east would be: labyrinthine alleyways, narrow shop fronts and overloaded market stalls, boxes of lamps and brass kettles, alembics and spell books, spices, snakes and gold. Hot sticky bodies pressed against her; the air was thick and muggy, heavy with the composite smell of humans, animals, rotten fruit and spices.

The variety of goods was bewildering, the layout completely disorientating. In the heart of the market, she lost all sense of direction, and even the sun was a feeble marker, its rays filtered through heavily patterned fabrics.

She'd blown it with Anton, her only solid lead, and she'd already checked if the museum had any contact details without success on her way here. She had no idea what to do. Realistically, her only option was to head back to Gezira and start trawling the phone book, terminator-style.

'Hey lady, look for free.'

A small boy of about eight grabbed her hand and pulled her past a trough of snake skins, into the dim confines of a fuchsia-coloured stand. Adie managed to extract her hand from the boy's grubby palm, and rubbed it irritably against her trousers. She gazed disinterestedly at the stall's collection of stuffed camels, plastic 'magic razor pyramids' and 'real genuine mummified hands'.

'Buy gifts,' he announced jovially, and began thrusting items at her. 'You like. Good prices. Very cheap,' he said emphasising the 'ver' in very. He gave her a dazzling smile that showed off his teeth. 'Many relatives?'

'No thank you,' said Adie. She replaced the sphinx money-boxes on the table-cloth.

'Tell Nagubi what you like. Nagubi has lots of friends. He can get you what you want.' The boy determinedly grabbed her sleeve.

'I'm fine, really,' Adie insisted, trying to shake him off. 'I don't need any gifts.'

The boy chuckled. 'Why come to bazaar if you don't need anything?'

'I was meeting someone.' Adie paused. The light was a murky pink under the canvas, giving everything a peculiar rosy glow, but there was something familiar about the collection of figurines in the old Sprite crate. She lifted one of the moulded figures. 'Sadler!' she said, staring at his tiny replica.

'Three hundred *irsh*,' said the boy, holding out his hand.

Adie sighed. 'One hundred, no more.' She held the miniature up, letting it dance on its key chain.

'Two hundred.' The boy nodded. 'Very reasonable. You like.'

'Nagubi! *Imshi!*' shouted a raspy male voice.

The boy backed off immediately, and dived beneath the lurid raspberry table-cloth. Adie watched him scramble away under the row of stalls. She shivered. Suddenly the day felt cold and she longed to be back out in the open sunlight.

She dropped the figurine in the crate, determined to leave, but when she turned her head, the raspy-throated man was just inches away. Unlike Nagubi, there was nothing endearing about this man's smile; it creased the skin around his shadowed eyes, emphasising the semi-circular scar on his cheek.

'There's someone who'd like a word,' he said, leaning so close that she could smell the foul tobacco on his breath. Adie recoiled, but he grabbed her wrist and twisted it painfully. She drew breath for a scream, only for him to press a stained finger to her lips. 'Don't be foolish, Dr Hamilton, and I won't have to hurt you.' Her scream died in her throat, as he transferred his grip to her upper arm. Adie numbly allowed herself to be guided through a cloth-covered doorway into a room stacked with boxes.

'Who are you?' she demanded. Her pulse felt so rapid there was almost a red haze to her vision, and there was no comfort in the warm bite of the fake wedding band. 'Who wants to see me?'

He didn't reply, just shoved her forwards, and they emerged into the filtered daylight of another canvas-covered alleyway. The air was heavy with the chemical smells of dyes and spray paint. Clothing and banners hung from every available surface. 'Help!' she mouthed at several onlookers. They watched her struggle with blank eyes, but nobody interfered with the scarred man.

Finally, several turns later, he pushed her through a set of double doors into the cool foyer of a dingy hotel. 'Upstairs,' he said to the man on reception. Adie took advantage of his momentary lack of attention and kicked at his shins. Her heavy boots connected with the bone, making him stumble and curse. He reached out to grab her again, caught her hair and dragged her into the lift.

'Let go of me,' she snarled as he tugged several dark strands from her scalp.

He laughed and slammed her head into the side of the lift. 'I warned you not to be foolish.'

Adie squealed in protest as the pain jabbed behind her eyes.

Two floors up, he led her along a corridor, then pushed

her through a doorway into a dismal little room. Adie stumbled, crashing to her knees on the tiled floor.

'Good afternoon, Dr Hamilton. Lovely to see you again. I hope Jamāl has treated you with courtesy.'

The voice was low and melodic. Adie lifted her head. She recognised it, although it took her a second to place it.

The plaster walls were crumbling, and the only light came from a tiny skylight, at the top of a narrow shaft. There were no escape routes, and the man who'd brought her here guarded the door.

Dareth Sadler was seated half in shadow.

'What do you want?' she demanded.

'You didn't stay for the party, and I missed you. You have quite a talent, Dr Hamilton, or may I call you Adina?' With a nod, he offered her a chair. Adie hesitated, then took it. Once she was seated, Dareth leaned forwards out of the shadows, revealing his face. Adie met his gaze. She remembered his appealing green-brown eyes. They seemed oddly contracted now, for such a dimly lit room.

'Cut to the chase.'

Dareth gave her a thin smile. 'I believe we're both hunting the same thing. A missing piece of an unusual third-dynasty mural.'

'Really!'

'Yes. Perhaps we might discuss a mutual arrangement.'

'Oh, no.' Adie's heart was racing faster now. She wondered how to get out. 'You're not selling any books off my back.' How had Killian ever fallen for this? Overconfidence, inexperience, or had the approach been far more subtle?

She saw Jamāl recline against the wall, and carefully braced herself. Any second now.

'Your loss,' said Dareth, reclining in the chair. 'I'm sure Dr Carmichael would be interested in the fact that you attended my costume party.'

'I'll tell him myself,' said Adie.

'And risk your job?'

'Better than making a deal with the devil.'

Sadler laughed, genuinely amused. 'You flatter me. You obviously have more imagination than your boss. What do you think we should do with her, Jamāl?'

Adie didn't wait to find out. 'You can kiss my arse!' she spat, and abruptly leaped from her seat, catching them both off guard.

Jamāl lurched forwards as she ran for the door. Adie dived under his flailing arms and out of the room. She rushed towards the stairs and took them three at a time. At the bottom, she fled across the foyer and out into the alleyway. With no landmarks to guide her, she headed towards the sound of traffic, aware of the heavy footfalls of pursuit. She didn't look back. Instead, she raced past a row of buildings with aged medieval façades, until the sweet aromas of turmeric and cumin mixed with the odour of petrol, and she was out into the whirr of the traffic.

'Hey, watch out!' A strong arm circled her waist and snatched her backwards out of the road. 'Do you have a death wish?' Adie choked on a lungful of benzene exhaust as a bus sped past just inches in front of her face.

She turned in the man's embrace. 'Anton!' Relief tugged her lips into a smile. There was no sign of Jamāl or Sadler. She let her head rest on his shoulder, then stiffened. 'What are you doing here? Were you following me? Why didn't you intervene?'

'Nothing, no, and with what?' he said, drawing her away from the road and back into the street of spice merchants. 'Who were you running from?'

'Sadler,' she said warily. 'What's going on? Why are you always about when he is?'

Anton clasped her hand, and they stopped in the shrouded doorway of a tiny incense shop. 'I'm not. My business is with Jamāl, not Sadler. Not everything revolves around you and your dig, Adie.'

He tenderly rubbed his thumb across the lump on her forehead. 'Jamāl did that,' she said.

Anton's dark eyes narrowed, while his pupils dilated with sudden anger. 'Bastard! He'll pay for that.'

'Maybe we should just go to the police?'

His fingers traced over her lips. 'That wouldn't help me.'

Adie caught hold of his wrist. 'Why not? Anton, are you involved in antiquities trafficking?'

There was a fierce light in his dark eyes when he answered. 'There you go again with your accusations!' His hand rested on her shoulder. 'Not everything in this world is black and white, Adie. I tell you again, I'm not a thief.'

'You are connected to the underworld, though, aren't you?'

He inclined his head. 'There are families in Cairo who've been grave robbers for centuries, who know secrets we might never discover. And they are no more thieves than us. Maybe they even have more right to the treasures than most of the people who end up with them.'

Adie couldn't believe what she was hearing. 'But so much is lost forever to grave robbers.'

'Bones and baubles, Adie. If you can't feed your children, and dead men have put gold in the ground, wouldn't you dig for it? At least this way, I can save the really interesting items.'

Adie nodded impatiently. This wasn't the time to discuss Egyptian social history. She couldn't approve of Anton's stance, but she could understand where he was coming from. And she could see it was a unique opportunity to learn history from the descendants of the people who'd created the monuments.

'Can you help me find Ihsān Fuād, then?' she asked.

Anton sighed. 'I could. But what's in it for me?'

Adie gasped. She hadn't actually expected Anton to know him. 'You didn't want my money.'

'There are other things of value besides money.' Against her back, she felt the cool press of the wall. He cupped her cheeks again and lowered his lips to her brow. 'Tempt me a little.'

Adie's body responded instantly, turning the adrenaline shock of fear to desire, and making her ache between her thighs. But she held back from touching him. Her relationship with Killian was still uneasy, and she didn't want to jeopardise it. Still, she didn't turn away. And when he lowered his mouth for a kiss, her lips parted, allowing his tongue to dart inside with a hot jab that seemed to strike straight to her core. His upper lip tasted of salty perspiration while his erection pressed into her abdomen, starting a crazy percussive beat in her chest like a little bird trying to escape.

'Anton,' she said, clawing at him. 'The shopkeeper.' They were blocking his doorway, but the thick muggy scents seemed to be acting on her pleasure centres, making her feel sluttish, more wanton, unable to push him away.

'Shhh,' he hissed and nudged her legs wider apart with his thigh. He loosened the zip of her trousers and slid his hand inside. Adie clutched at his shoulders, conscious of the people passing only yards away, and the risk of being caught. Two of his fingers worked their way into her slit, and sent a ricochet of fireworks through her sex. The flush, which started in her cheeks, quickly spread to her breasts. She tangled her fingers in the dark strands of his long hair and pulled him closer.

'We'll be seen,' she whispered as she rocked against his hand, seeking the release he offered.

'That's it, move for me.' His breath was warm against her neck. She felt the sharp nip of his teeth and knew he would mark her, but she didn't have the strength or the will to stop him. It felt much too good. Desire was getting the better of her. Rational thought seemed to have taken flight the moment her zip had come down. Now all she really wanted was to curl her fingers around his stiff cock, stroke him until he begged her to stop and then feel him thrust inside her so that he filled her to the hilt.

Adie slid her hands down his body from his shoulders to the seat of his trousers, and dug her fingers into the flesh, urging him to fulfil her wish. He altered his motion, teasing a finger around her clit.

'Maybe you're right. My place isn't far, and we won't get arrested there.'

'And Ihsān?'

'Will be easier to contact after dark.'

He surprised her by leading her via the underpass to the south-east of the city, where the electricity cables hung like giant cobwebs between the crypts of the City of the Dead.

'You should see the place on festival days,' he said of the cemetery. 'People come here for picnics.'

Anton unlocked the door to the crypt that was apparently his home and led Adie inside the sepulchre. He lit a candle before sealing the door. To the right stood a small wash-basin and a camping hob. Further in, stone shelves held his clothing, miscellaneous artifacts and a collection of spice jars.

'Have a seat,' he said, pointing to the only real piece of furniture. Adie sat on the mattress.

'Are there any bodies in here?' she asked, her toes already curled inside her boots. She knew that the eerie Northern Cemetery was home to much of Cairo's expanding population, but she hadn't expected Anton to be quite so bohemian.

'They moved out before I arrived. The previous resident sold them to tourists to fund his degree.'

'You are joking?'

Anton shrugged and Adie decided not to pursue it. Instead, she shuffled further on to the bed and watched him calmly light an oil lamp. Yellow-gold light spilled over the walls of the tiny building and turned Anton's skin bronze.

'Where do you keep the tent?' she asked.

'I borrowed it from a friend, just like the horse, although only I ride him. I'm sorry if this isn't quite what you expected.' He tugged his shirt over his head and cast it across the room in the direction of the wicker laundry basket. 'Now, where were we?' He unzipped his trousers and walked towards her, revealing a thick meaty erection.

'Oh ... I,' she murmured, but when it bobbed just before her face and the scent of him wafted towards her, the protest died and her lips willingly closed over the shiny head. He seemed to swell in her mouth. Adie held on to his open waistband as he rocked into her with his hips, filling her with increasing urgency, stopping just short of gagging her.

'Adie,' he panted, tugging her shirt up to expose the clasp of her bra. It opened with a quiet twang, and he lifted her heavy breasts from the underwire then cupped them together.

His cock popped out of her open mouth and hung poised before her glistening lips for a moment, then pressed between her breasts as he urged her into a kneeling position on the bed. Slick and wet, he slid between the pale globes, the mahogany-coloured head of his prick peeping up expectantly at her at the culmination of each thrust. She felt him stiffen and thought he'd come in her face, but instead he pushed her backwards, turned her on to all fours and brought his hand down across her rump.

'Ouch!' she cried in surprise. The impact stung but didn't hurt, just leaving her bottom tingling. She tried to wriggle forwards when he brought his palm down a second time but he held her back.

For the second time that day, he unzipped her fatigues and exposed her. Adie's bottom warmed nicely under his hand and his lips were soon pressed to the freshly reddened skin.

She arched her back to the wet and silky caress, groaned aloud and shuffled her legs wider apart. His tongue teased around her clit. He stroked her with his thumb-tip until she was sweating, trembling, begging for a thicker pole on which to slide.

Adie clutched at the sheets. His silky-soft hair was brushing her back, driving her to distraction. 'Anton,' she begged unintelligibly. She grabbed his hand and pressed it more firmly to her crotch, making his fingers mash against her overeager nub. 'Harder!' She pushed back against him so that his cock and balls slapped against her cheeks.

Anton clawed at the shelf to his left and picked up a fresh thick white candle. 'Use it on your *cush*,' he instructed, pressing it into her palm.

Without hesitation, Adie played the waxy shaft around her sensitive opening. Her sex throbbed. Acting on instinct, she pushed it inside. Her muscles clenched around the stem.

Anton moved to her front, and pressed his cock-tip to her lips again. Adie swallowed him to the root and milked him with long loving gulps. Her climax began to tingle through her. At the same moment, he erupted in her mouth. She screamed in pleasure, while her body jerked back and forth on the improvised dildo.

Adie collapsed on to the sheets, panting and shaking from the aftershock. Sex with Anton was unpredictable and fun, but she realised that she'd have to give him up sooner rather than later if she wanted Killian.

Anton laid a gentle hand on her shoulder, then nestled beside her. She pressed back against the heat of his body, wanting the comfort. A beetle scuttled along a long gash in the low stone ceiling and disappeared into the shadows of the shelves.

'Does Killian know about your hunt?' Anton asked. 'Because frankly it doesn't sound like something he'd approve of.'

Adie turned her head, suddenly curious about the enigmatic, self-assured man beside her. 'You were close, weren't you?' she asked, fixing her gaze on his upturned face.

The mattress rocked as Anton propped himself up. He reached out and touched her thigh. Adie met his brown gaze. 'We were partners, Adie. Of course we were close.' He bit his lower lip then sighed. 'I haven't seen him for years, though. It ended badly.'

Adie rose to lean on one elbow and stroked his hair where it lay across his neck. 'I can't imagine you working together. I mean, what do you have in common?'

Anton shifted into an upright position. The springs chirped as he folded his legs beneath him. 'We've more in common than you think, or we did have. People change.'

She watched the lamplight flicker across the muscles of his back as he leaned over the bedside, lifted a large ceramic vase, and retrieved the tatty shoebox it had been standing on. He sifted through the contents of old luggage labels, receipts and dried-up biros, and finally pulled out a dog-eared photograph of three men.

'Here, if you're interested.'

The glossy print was scuffed in one corner.

Adie stared at the frozen image. She'd seen this before, framed in Joe Levine's house, but had never known the two other faces in the picture. It was of some past graduation day. The central figure was her old supervisor, and his kindly face managed to tease a smile on to her tight lips. He hadn't changed much, just gained a few more lines around the eyes. The same couldn't be said of the other two figures.

To Joe's left stood a younger version of the man before her. His dark hair was cropped very close and his skin was several shades lighter. On the right, Killian was virtually unrecognisable, with an unruly tangle of dark-brown hair and a wide self-indulgent grin. He had the glazed expression of someone who'd been drinking free champagne all day, but it didn't mask his look of hungry enthusiasm.

'My god! He looks so different.'

'So do I,' said Anton. But Adie shook her head.

'No, not in the same way. Your hair's changed and you're older but it's still the same you. Killian's completely different. You do know that his hair's gone white these days, don't you?'

'I didn't, but it's hardly a surprise. His father had white hair, and the stress would have done it if his genes hadn't.'

'He doesn't look terribly stressed in this picture.'

Anton shook his head. 'That came later, when things started to go wrong. Dareth Sadler has a lot to answer for.' He rubbed his lips thoughtfully. 'Explain to me how a maverick like you ended up on Killian's team. You're intuitive and impulsive, two qualities he despises these days.' He stared hard at her for a moment. 'Are you sleeping with him?'

Adie lowered the photograph. She opened her mouth and suddenly realised she didn't know what to say. The truth seemed to stick in her throat. No, she screamed inwardly. It wasn't like that; she'd won her position fairly. It was only since then that things had become more complicated.

Anton began to laugh, a low bitter laugh that seemed to be as much at his expense as hers. 'Well, if things aren't royally screwed up,' he chuckled. 'We used to share everything, but times have changed a little, don't you think?'

Adie nodded. Suddenly all the pieces were coming together into one complicated whole. 'Why did you leave? Surely he needed his friends?'

Anton took the photograph off her and replaced it in the shoebox. 'I didn't walk out on him, if that's what you're thinking. The Sadler thing was eight months in the past, and we weren't even in Egypt any more. We were drifting apart. All Killian cared about was his damn reputation, while I was on a collision course with the establishment over the kind of research I was interested in. We finally parted company when the arguments got way too personal.'

'You must be kicking yourself, considering how well he's done,' she mumbled. She didn't mean the statement to be hurtful, but she immediately regretted it. His wounded expression may have been shame at his apparent poverty, or resentment at his ostracism by his peers.

Anton reached for his trousers. 'You ought to get going.' He tossed over her shirt and Adie reluctantly pulled it over her head.

'I didn't mean it like that,' she said, reaching out to him.

Anton shrugged her off. 'Sure. You seem to be having that problem a lot today. Gather your stuff. I'll walk you to the road so you can get a taxi.'

'What about Ihsān?'

'I said I'd find him. Meet me at the Philosophers' Circle on Monday night and I'll let you know the score. Anything else you want to tell me?'

'Franks,' said Adie. 'Dr David Franks, that's who he was working with, and we're looking for a plaster fragment with a pharaoh's genitals on it.'

'It should be fairly memorable, then.'

As he reached to open the door, it suddenly rattled with someone's knock. 'Get back into the shadows,' Anton hissed, and he pushed Adie towards the rear of the tomb.

She watched him reach up and slide a curved knife off the shelf; holding it with his thumb up and the point down, he inched open the door.

He seemed to relax, opening the door a little wider, although he kept a tight grip on the knife.

Her curiosity roused, Adie slipped forwards silently.

'When?' she heard Anton ask.

'Ten forty-five. It's all set.' There was a pause as if the informant were afraid to continue. 'Anton, do you know what you are doing?'

'Jamāl al-Aziz is going to learn that I take theft seriously.'

'Very well,' said the voice. 'Good luck.'

The door creaked to, and Adie scuttled back into the shadows. 'Are you ready?' Anton asked. He returned the jambiyya to its ornate sheath and put it back on the top shelf, then threw the door wide.

The informant was gone.

'Then let's go.'

'No,' said Adie. 'First tell me what the hell that was about?'

Anton regarded her silently for a moment then rubbed his fingers thoughtfully over his lips. 'I told you. I have business of my own with Jamāl. Now I need you to go, Adie, I have to prepare.'

'For what?'

He shook his head, making the long strands of his hair stir around his shoulders.

'Come on, Anton, don't I have a right to know? He kidnapped me this afternoon and gave me a fucking great bruise. If you're planning revenge, I want in.'

Anton folded his arms across his chest. 'This is serious business, Adie. Go back to your trowels and your books. I'll see you on Monday night.'

Adie shook her head. She had a score of her own to settle with Jamāl and she seriously doubted she'd manage to get an official charge to stick. Teaming up with Anton seemed like a good way of getting some justice. 'I can see it's serious. Nobody else I know answers the door holding a knife. So what's the deal?'

She walked up to him and took the knife from the shelf, remembering the way he'd drawn the cold tip across her skin, and how she'd trembled with fear and excitement. She shivered now. Just visible below the neckline of her top was the faint red mark where he'd scratched her and drawn blood. She shivered. Anton pushed the door closed and fastened the latch.

'It's sharp,' he said and took it from her, returning it to its place.

'I want in,' said Adie.

She watched him sit down on the bed.

'What has he done to you?'

Anton snorted. 'It's a set-up.' He rested his elbows on his knees so that his long dark hair framed his face. 'And it's taken months. You can come, but I can't guarantee your safety or your reputation.' He stared straight at her and his dark eyes seem to burn into her like hot coals.

She met his gaze, and held it. 'I'm a big girl.'

'As you wish. And as for what he's done to me . . .' All the softness in his face vanished. 'He put me through hell, Adie. I owe him for that.'

14

Adie called the Gezira apartment to let Siân know she was going to be late. 'I'm with Anton. He's helping me find Ihsān,' she said. Siân seemed surprised, but didn't press her for details.

'OK. I'm working on the journal, since there's no guarantee that Ihsān will be any use. See you later. Try to stay out of trouble.'

Adie laughed. 'Don't worry. I promise to be a good girl.' She hung up and looked across at Anton. Some promises were made to be broken.

The sky was dark when they finally left the City of the Dead. Anton had dressed in his black bedouin outfit and had insisted upon her wearing a similar disguise, which he shortened with scissors to her height. He'd strapped the jambiyya in its ornate silver scabbard to his waist, where now and then Adie caught a glint of it in the moonlight. They took a taxi south out of the city as far as the village of Abusir. It was a twenty-minute walk from there to the heart of the desert necropolis.

The pockmarked cemetery of North Saqqara was deserted. The tourists and vendors had all retired for the night, and anything that remained knew how to get around without making a sound. Inky darkness filled the broken shells of the early-dynasty tombs, while the dying *khamseen* blew fitfully around them.

'This is the one.' Anton stopped before a first-dynasty mastaba. The entryway was a black slash in the stonework, partially covered by a stone portcullis slab, which was tilted at an angle with wooden splints.

Anton felt around the edge, found a small hurricane lantern and lit it. They'd been navigating by moonlight, and the warming orange flame infused Adie with a primitive feeling of security. 'Careful how you go,' Anton warned her. 'There's only a narrow lip, then a drop.'

Adie squeezed through the entry. The dim lantern-light revealed a small platform, which might once have been the top of a flight of steps. It was now merely a stone column supporting a ladder. Adie looked about nervously. The main chamber below was impossible to make out. The light only revealed flashes of barren stonework. The roof space was more impressive, and stepped, like Djoser's pyramid.

'This place must have been excavated before,' said Adie, following Anton down into the gloom. She was shivering beneath her robes, and she wasn't sure whether it was from excitement, the weird vibe of the place or just fear of meeting Jamāl again. The sudden realisation that Anton wouldn't have a permit to work here only increased her apprehension. She didn't want to think about the consequences if they were caught.

'That doesn't mean there's nothing left to find.' Anton offered her his hand as she stepped off the ladder and held up the lantern. The floor was pitted and cracked, the walls an uneven patchwork of bricks and rubble that reminded her of castle ruins ravaged by time and war. There was no sign of a casket, but two darker archways led into further rooms.

'Storage areas,' said Anton, following her gaze. 'The right one has a small granary. The left side I've been using for storage. It's mostly full of rubble from a cave-in. This is the burial chamber, but the body went long ago.'

'Then what are you looking for?'

'Nothing. I've been trying to catch Jamāl's attention for weeks by coming here, but I guess that Sadler's been keeping him busy. Normally, he'd be too inquisitive not to check out what I was doing.'

'And you're sure he'll come tonight?'

'No. Nothing is ever certain, but I've had a solid tip-off from a reliable source that Jamāl is in Saqqara tonight. And even with Sadler's backing he's not stupid enough to risk robbing your project. He'll come here because he knows the authorities won't be looking this way.'

'What did he actually do to you? You've been pretty vague about it.'

Anton pursed his lips, as if in thought.

'The truth,' she prompted.

'OK. About eighteen months ago, I was working on a mastaba out here, and turning up some promising material. I hadn't worked with Jamāl before, but I'd never had any problems with the al-Aziz clan, so there was no reason to suspect him.' His fist clenched, but he forced it open again. 'It was the usual deal. They got the easily marketable stuff, and I got anything of archaeological significance, to study and eventually pass on to a museum. Everything was fine, until I uncovered a series of reed mats rendered in blue faience tiles, and a casket of jewellery. Then Jamāl got greedy.'

Anton's jaw tightened. 'He spiked my water with a sleeping draught and stripped the place bare. By the time I came around there was literally nothing left. What might have been an important site was now just another hole in the ground. To make it worse, he tipped off the authorities, and I was arrested.'

He paused. For the first time, Adie noticed the shadows around his eyes. Each time they'd met she'd been preoccupied with her own thoughts about Killian, Sadler, or the missing fragment. She'd never given his emotional well-being all that much thought. Even when she'd found out he was Killian's former partner, her thoughts had been on her boss.

She traced her fingers along his jaw line in a gentle caress. Anton took her hand and pressed it against his cheek.

'The charges were eventually dropped because they couldn't prove there'd ever been anything down there.' He released her hand. 'But they took my passport and all my papers while they thought about it.'

'What happened then?'

He lowered his eyes. 'Do you know the Mogamma building on Midan Tahrir?'

Adie nodded. She had heard of the dreaded fourteen-storey monument to the gods of bureaucracy.

'I spent fifty days in there trying to recover my passport, my work permit and my identity. Trying to find one person then the next to sign, countersign and approve all my documents, waiting outside locked offices where "back soon" could mean anything from five minutes to five days.'

'So you want to do the same to him?'

'Something like that. At the very least, I'd like to see him stew for a few hours.' He took her hand, shaking off his anger. 'Let's finish up and get out of here.'

He led her into the right-hand chamber, where he produced a small bag and emptied the contents over the floor.

'What are you doing?' Adie watched him shake the bag out.

'Baiting the trap. Just planting a few trinkets: earrings, a comb. I didn't want to leave this stuff down here in case some other enterprising thief was about.' From another sack, he took a small *ushabtis* statue and a piece of inscribed alabaster, perhaps a fragment from a canopic jar.

'You're going to let him take those?'

'Good fakes, eh?' said Anton grinning. 'A friend of mine did them, although he usually specialises in mummified pets.' He balanced the two items on a shelf just inside the door. Adie lifted the figurine and turned it in her hands. The tiny guardian was about the length of her forearm, and carved as if to appear bandaged. Its face and folded arms were detailed in a dull brown, which gave the impression of age. It was quite convincing, for a fake.

'What's that noise?' Anton suddenly pulled her into the shadows. 'Hell!' he hissed. 'He's early.'

Adie felt all the blood drain from her face. She'd figured out enough of the plan to realise that they were supposed to be outside while Jamāl was down here, not trapped inside with him blocking their escape.

'Stay here,' he urged. 'And not a sound.'

The side chamber fell into shadow as Anton moved into the burial vault with the lantern. Jamāl's raspy vocals sounded loud and close.

'Good evening, Mr Kelly. You're out late. Are the authorities aware of this excavation?'

'What do you want?'

'My property, which you stole when you left your calling card. I need that book. Now!'

'I have no idea what you're talking about.'

Adie missed Jamāl's reply. Then as suddenly as the argument had started, it was over.

Adie heard a muffled curse, followed by a scraping noise.

It was no good. She had to know what was going on.

She inched along the wall and strained forwards to peer around the archway. Two lamps now lit the central chamber. The men were only a few paces apart, Jamāl at the bottom of the ladder, blocking the exit, with Anton opposite him. There was fire in Jamāl's eyes and a cruel smirk on his scarred face. He was holding a knife, not an ornate and traditional jambiyya, but a long straight-handled weapon that he clasped in a backhanded grip with the blade protruding from the bottom of his fist.

Anton had not drawn his own knife. Instead, he had pulled the sash from around his waist, and was holding it loosely in both hands.

Jamāl hissed as he lunged forwards. The blade streaked twice through the air in front of Anton's face, forcing him backwards. Then it swept upwards towards his throat.

Adie's mouth opened in horror, but the scream never came. At the last moment Anton dodged, and caught Jamāl's arm in the loop of the sash. He twisted it and jerked Jamāl forwards, sending them both careening into the back wall where the blade skittered off the stonework.

Adie held her breath as she watched Anton scramble away with Jamāl in pursuit. This time the Egyptian stabbed down towards the top of Anton's head. Again, Anton parried, with the scarf pulled taut between both hands. It stopped the attack, but Jamāl drew back the knife, slicing the cloth in two.

Anton was cornered.

Jamāl's vicious grin widened, and he hissed what sounded like an insult. He began to weave the knife back and forth. She watched the lamplight play across the surface of the metal. The dancing waves of orange and gold were hypnotic, lulling.

Suddenly, Jamāl swooped in low. There was a sound of ripping cloth. Realising that she still had the statue, Adie launched herself out of the granary and brought it down as hard as she could on the back of Jamāl's head. He dropped to his knees in a daze.

'Run!' shouted Anton. Adie dropped the statue and leaped on to the ladder, which wobbled alarmingly. She scrambled up the rungs, and out into the cool night air.

There was a clatter behind her; Anton had kicked the ladder free of its mooring. He squeezed through the entry-way behind her. 'Help me with these splints,' he yelled, kicking at the wedges supporting the portcullis slab. Adie grabbed the largest and pulled as he kicked at it. She fell back as it shot loose. The stone shuddered. She tore at another with her fingers while Anton put his weight to the stone. It rocked unsteadily, snapping several of the smaller wedges, before crashing into place, sealing Jamāl inside.

On her knees, Adie stared at the stone slab. They were safe. She was safe. Why the hell had she come along?

Anton pressed a reassuring hand to her shoulder. 'It's OK,' he said, and she realised that the low keen on the wind was coming from her own throat. She shook herself.

'Are you hurt?' she asked. There was a long tear in the left side of his *galabeyya*.

Anton felt beneath the cloth, and his hand came back bloody. 'It's just a scrape. Not deep. He caught me just before you struck.'

Adie pushed herself to her feet. She wanted to go home to bed, where it was safe and warm and crazy Egyptians didn't leap at you with a knife.

'Why didn't you use that?' she said, staring at his jambiyya.

'Because I don't want to face a murder charge.'

He walked back over to the door. The slab wasn't a perfect fit, so Jamāl wasn't about to suffocate, but releasing him would take time. 'What next?' she asked. 'We're not going to leave him down there?'

Anton snorted. 'Aren't we?'

Adie peered at him nervously. She couldn't tell if he was joking.

'Stop fretting, Adie,' he said. He began to walk back the way they'd come across the desert from Abusir. 'I'm not actually going to leave him there to rot. I'll send the authorities for him in the morning.'

He pressed his hand to his leg, and grimaced when it came away red again. 'Damn it. Let's move. I need to get this treated.'

Adie caught up with him. 'Let me look.' She lifted the

hem of his robe and found the knife wound. There were smears of blood across his thigh and rivulets down his leg. 'It's not deep but it's clean; that's why it won't stop. Have you got another scarf you can wrap around it?'

He loosened a long black streamer of silk from around his neck and handed it to her. Adie tied it around his thigh as a temporary dressing. She remembered Killian doing the same for her, and a wry smile tweaked her lips. Best if he never found out about tonight's adventure.

'I assume the journal he wants is the one your enterprising friend stole. I must thank her sometime for adding that detail to the plan,' said Anton.

'So what now?'

He shrugged. 'Once I've finished with Jamãl, I'm heading into the desert towards Bahariya. There's more scope for my line of work there. I assume you've heard of the Valley of the Golden Mummies. Anyway, it's a huge necropolis of common and middle-class burials from the Greco-Roman period, which they've hardly begun excavating.'

Adie nodded. 'I can see why you'd be interested.'

'You're welcome to come along.'

She shook her head. 'I don't think so.'

Anton caressed her cheek with his thumb. 'Neither did I. But I thought I'd be polite and ask.'

They shared a smile. Adie curled her fingers around his hand. She wondered if they'd still be friends after Monday night.

'You're still going to talk to Ihsãn for me, aren't you?'

He nodded. 'I said I would, didn't I? I'll be at the Philosophers' Circle, as we arranged.'

It was almost one when Adie reached the apartment. Jason let her in. 'We were starting to worry about you.' He yawned. 'We thought we might have to send out a search party. Siân seemed to think you were fine, though.'

Adie gave him an apologetic smile. 'Any chance of a coffee?'

'Sure. Siân's in the lounge. She's been in there most of the day.' He turned, and headed off towards the kitchen.

Siân was sitting cross-legged on the floor, engrossed in Jacob's journal. There was a pint-sized mug of coffee next to her elbow, and an array of papers arranged in a semicircle around her. She looked up when Adie came in.

'What the hell happened to your head?'

Adie dropped on to the sofa to Sian's left. She ran her fingers over the bump, which had provoked Siân's remark. It felt like days had passed since Jamāl had given her that memento, but hopefully he had a lump of his own where she'd clobbered him with the statue.

'One of Sadler's goons caught me in the bazaar and forced me to a meeting with his boss. The creepy bastard had learned about us gatecrashing his party and tried to blackmail me into helping him.'

'You didn't tell him anything?'

'Of course not.'

Jason came in and handed Adie her coffee. 'Want a top-up?' he asked Siân. She shook her head. 'All right. I'm turning in. Happy hunting and remember to get some sleep.'

'Goodnight,' they both said.

Siân waited until he'd closed the door. 'Now, what have you been up to this time?'

Adie stared down into her mug and let the rising steam warm her face.

'I'm guessing that you haven't seen Ihsān or you would have said so already, and I doubt you've been doing anything as useful as talking. You're gonna have to decide which one of them is for keeps, you know, because Killian won't tolerate another lover, regardless of anything else.'

Adie blew on her coffee, making ripples on the surface. She took a sip, and said nothing.

Siân shook her head, disapprovingly. She raised her own mug to her lips and held it there a moment before asking, 'What is happening about Ihsān?'

'Anton's going to talk to him, then meet me on Monday night at the Philosophers' Circle with any news.'

'Is that it? Took a bloody long time to decide that.'

Adie let the remark go. She didn't want to explain the risks she'd taken that night.

'Aren't you even going to make any excuses?'

Adie shook her head. 'We were tying up loose ends. It's over between us now, or it will be after Monday night.'

'I still think you're crazy.' Siân flipped over another page of the journal. 'But I guess you think it's going somewhere with Killian?'

'Maybe.'

'You might want to check your email, then. You've had something from Professor Levine.'

'How do you know? Have you been snooping on my account?'

'You left yourself signed in last night.'

Adie got up and turned on the computer. 'Have you found anything useful?' she asked as she waited for it to boot up.

'Not exactly, but it's interesting reading. Jacobs spent some time at Giza with Flinders Petrie. As for the fragment, there's just what we already knew about him chipping it out. It does tell us where he went next, though, so my guess is that Sadler is working through the list looking for clues. I've made us some notes.' She picked up one of the sheets from the semicircle. 'But it's one hell of a paper-chase to follow all these leads. I can see why Sadler tried to pump you for information.'

Adie frowned at the innuendo. 'You're telling me that if Ihsān doesn't come through, we're screwed, right?'

'Pretty much.' Siân linked her fingers and stretched.

'What's it say?' she asked, nodding towards the computer screen.

Adie swivelled around on the chair. She clicked on Joe's message and braced herself for a lecture, but all she got was a single sentence. No greeting, just 'Ask him about Petra.' And that was it.

'I don't suppose you know who Petra is?' she asked Siân.

Her friend rose and joined her by the computer. 'Nope.'

Adie stared at Siân and bit her lip.

'Really, I don't know. You're just going to have to take a chance and ask him. Personally, I can live without knowing all the sordid details of Killian's past.'

'What exactly happened between you two?'

For once Siân looked uncomfortable. 'What do you mean?' She turned her back, picked up the journal and crossed to the farthest armchair, where she sat down and curled up.

'There's this weird, protective, touchy vibe you give off whenever we talk about him like this. It's as if I'm asking you about your brother or an old flame or something.'

'He blew me off, OK.' Siân forced a smile. 'In the nicest possible way. I offered him a blow job and he told me to back off before he moved in with his emotional baggage.'

'Oh!' said Adie. 'So then what?'

'We sat down and got drunk together, OK. He hired Bill two weeks later so I fucked him instead, but he came on a bit strong, so when Matthew came along I moved on to him. Satisfied now?'

Adie nodded. 'Doesn't tell me who Petra is, though. I guess I'll just have to think of a way of asking him.'

Siân hit her own forehead with the book. 'You know, Adie, sometimes it's better to let things go.'

After all her adventures, Adie slept late the following day. Samih eventually woke her around midday. Siân had spent the night on the sofa, and was still there, yawning into the last few pages of the journal. The lump on Adie's head had gone down overnight, although the bruise had turned a venomous shade of yellow. After a long shower, she did her best to hide it with her hair and make-up.

It was nearly four when they finally arrived back at the *dahabiyya*. Matthew and Lucas were translating plaster seals. Killian was in the kitchen. Adie watched him a moment from the door as he got out the pans and chopping board. 'You cook!' she said when he finally noticed her.

'Badly,' he confessed, adding two large onions to the pile of vegetables. 'I do three dishes: chilli, prawns with piri piri, and tapioca pudding. Which is why I only cook once a month.' He opened a cupboard and placed a tin of kidney beans on to the central table, followed by a selection of peppers.

'I'm guessing it's not tapioca for tea.'

'Less of the wisecracks in my kitchen.' He rolled the onions in her direction. 'Grab a knife and you can help chop.'

Adie rolled up her sleeves and joined him by the table. She picked up an onion and started peeling it, while he opened the tin. 'Why tapioca?' she asked.

'My grandmother used to make it. I helped her. Shame I never mastered her chicken soup or Yorkshire puddings. I miss those.'

'Do you ever visit?'

Killian tipped the beans into a pan. 'Sometimes. She's in her nineties now and a bit frail. She likes to hear what I've been up to.'

Adie gazed wistfully at him. He'd never mentioned any family before; she'd always assumed that he was alone, like her. She finished the onions and watched him throw them into a frying pan to brown.

'Any luck with your treasure hunt?' he asked.

'Er, no,' she lied. Maybe in a couple of days, when she had the fragment, she'd enjoy this conversation, but right now it was the last thing she wanted to talk about. She didn't want to let slip about Anton, or Matthew's photo session, or her run-ins with Sadler.

'Masud has you on a wild goose chase, you know. If you want a side project I can find you something.'

'Are you frightened I'll actually find it?'

'What's your point?'

'I just thought you'd like to see the mural complete.'

He didn't reply, so she left it at that.

They worked in silence for a while, chopping vegetables and tossing them into the pan. Eventually they finished. Killian put on the lid and left it to simmer. 'You've gone serious on me,' he said. He opened a bottle of red wine and poured two glasses.

Adie accepted one and sat down at the chair he pulled out for her.

'What's on your mind?' Killian reached out and rubbed his thumb across the back of her hand.

Adie stared at the point of contact, watching him press a fleeting touch to the wedding band he'd given her. Maybe this was the right time.

Killian slid his hand into hers and began to brush her wrist with his middle finger. 'You still want to know about Sadler, right? Why is it so important?'

Adie shrugged. She wanted to know what all the fuss was about, what the great secret was, but mostly she just wanted to know about him. 'Who's Petra?' she asked.

Killian pulled his hand away. The softness in his grey eyes turned to ice. Adie recoiled into her chair and nervously licked her lips. Joe had dropped her in it again.

Killian took a sip from his glass. He looked at her, and Adie looked back. 'Josef?' he asked.

'I emailed him about Sadler. He didn't tell me anything. He just said I should ask you that.'

Killian sat in silence, his thoughts turned inwards. Adie bit her thumbnail.

'Who was she?' she asked. 'Was she important to you?'

'Petra,' replied Killian, and his voice was low and husky. 'Not who, but where.' He raised his hands to his face and massaged his temples. 'After Sadler published his damn book my career in Egypt collapsed. I had no choice but to leave. I went to work at Petra, in Jordan, as an extra hand for Professor Wojcek of Harvard, while all the fuss died down.'

He pushed his chair back, rose and paced over to the hob. 'How much do you actually know?'

Adie shrugged.

'Very well; I'll start at the beginning. In the early days, I believed in a hands-on approach. If I found a sculpture or a pot, I wanted to try my hand at making it. If there was a ritual, I'd recreate it. I thought it gave me a valuable perspective on the past, but really, I was just young, ambitious and full of shit. Sadler turned up during my first big project. I was working with a guy called Anton Kelly, a friend from university. Courtesy of Joe Levine's connections, we were working on the western massifs of Djoser's pyramid complex.

'Sadler said he was writing a book, so we talked. He was interested in our reconstructions, especially those involving spells. It wasn't until his book came out that I realised he was targeting the sensationalist market, and that I'd been used.'

He sighed, and shook his head. 'He made me a laughing-stock, Adie, and despite Joe's reassurances, the backers pulled out one after another until the project collapsed.'

'That's when you went to Petra, right?'

Killian nodded. 'Anton and I were working in the ancient burial chambers, which are part of the stone city out there. I guess I wasn't very good company, and things

did this come from?' He swept her hair back
ace, and gently ran his thumb over the bruise.
brow crinkled. It was too vibrant to claim she'd
the dig.

dusted her cheek.

a spot of bother in the market.'

d came up.

g like that.' She grasped his upper arm and
m back into an embrace. 'It was just a mis-
nding, and there's no problem, it's all sorted

eyed her warily. 'Is that right?'

n't seem entirely convinced, though he took her
rd and let it ride.
.'

will happen if Sadler publishes something based
rrent project?'

left the bed and crossed the room. Adie pushed
on to her elbows. She noticed him briefly clasp
quare of cloth, then push it into the top drawer
t-stand. It didn't look as if she was about to get

ed towards her. 'What knickers are you wear-
ked purposefully.

t up straight. 'What's that got to do with
g.'

tton,' she answered.

ought a smile. 'How very Enid Blyton of you.
off.'

m off.'

off the bed and undid the button at her waist.
d before lowering the zip. 'Why?'

came to a head. We argued. He left, and that was it. My
last ally was gone and I had nothing.'

Killian took the lid off the pan and stirred it furiously.
'I haven't seen him since, but I think he took something
from me the day he walked away.'

Adie saw the look of bitter regret in Killian's eyes, and
realised for the first time just what it had cost him to
rebuild his career. She felt she should say something, but
couldn't find the right words. Instead, she left her chair
and went to him. Cautiously, she reached out, hesitated,
and then curled her fingers around his shoulder.

'What happened then?'

'I didn't leave that tomb until I had a plan. I kept my
head down for the rest of the season, then came back to
Egypt and started working hard, any archaeological dog-
work I could get. I got lucky the day I met Masud. He was
prepared to take a chance on me, but it still took me five
years to claw my way back.'

Killian reclaimed his glass and topped it up.

'How did you meet?'

He took a sip of wine. 'In a hotel bar in Luxor. He was
trying to make a long-distance phone call, and kept getting cut off. We exchanged a few sympathies, had a drink
and it went from there. He's been my main sponsor ever
since.'

He squeezed her hand. 'Am I boring you yet?'

Adie shook her head. He'd given her a lot to think
about. After he'd shared so much, it seemed only fair to
tell him about the photographs, Sadler, Ihsān and Anton.
But she had no idea how he'd react.

She picked up her own glass, using the action as a
means of breaking eye contact with him, and took a deep
breath.

'Smells nice,' said Siân from the galley door. 'Lucas
mentioned you were cooking, so I thought I'd better check
up on you.'

She came over, dipped a spoon in the pot and had a taste. 'Mmm, not bad. It needs something, though.' Adie watched her open a cupboard and take out a bottle of chilli sauce.

'Siân,' Killian warned.

'It's only a little juju.' She added a generous splash before Killian could stop her. 'You know Lucas likes it hot,' she said, grinning evilly.

'I told him I'd make it mild.' Killian took the bottle from her and placed it on the highest shelf he could find, then turned to Adie. 'Any complaints about dinner, and you can direct them at Siân. I don't know if you've noticed yet but she gets a kick out of winding people up.'

The juju had worked its magic. The chilli was hot. They ate on deck, shielded from the sun by a large striped canopy. Lucas ate without complaint, one mouthful to two of water, while Adie tried hard not to laugh. She was finding it tough going herself, but Siân apparently had lips made of asbestos, because she finished first and helped herself to another plateful.

'What's the plan for tomorrow?' Adie asked.

'Carry on with the translations, and take some photos of the burial chamber,' said Killian. 'I want an accurate record of everything before we start tampering.' He left his seat and wandered over to the railing. 'I want this done properly.'

Siân helped herself to a glass of wine. 'Is Adie allowed to help?' Adie kicked her under the table, but the words were already out. 'Or do you still not trust her?'

'She can work with you on the tracings.' He turned to Lucas, who was the only one not drinking wine. 'What have you got so far?'

'We're getting the same name again and again. I'd say there's a high probability that the tomb was intended for Huni. We'll have to see what we find tomorrow, but we

might finally be able to substa
mentary evidence for the early
sketchy, as you know.'

Killian nodded. 'The level
unusual, though. Detail like th
fifth dynasty. No speculations.
Let's go into it fresh in the morn

The conversation soon lapsed
wandered off towards his cabin.
of Siân and Lucas uncovering a
mified cats, then slipped away
room. He hadn't really answer
Sadler, but she realised there wa
Sadler had robbed him of his d
apart. What he'd rebuilt was very
have been.

She knocked, and answered his
lying on the bed.

'Tired?'

'Thinking,' he said, stretching
too much. Care to take my mind o

Adie took off her boots and st
She wondered if he'd be so eager
if he found out about Anton, or t
gut-level feeling of guilt made h
course, they hadn't agreed to
hadn't really agreed to be anythi
there seemed to be an awful lot o
on every other level.

Killian wrapped an arm arou
do anything else. He also seeme
caused the knots in her stomac
full of questions,' he said.

She rolled on to her back. For
looked at her, while Adie praye
in her expression that would be

Killian lifted a Gillette razor and rolled it between his forefinger and thumb. 'I wondered if you'd like a trim.'

Well now Anton had stolen a curl, did Killian intend to shave her completely? How would it feel to be completely smooth down there? She'd always loved the silky feeling of her skin after she'd waxed her legs. And what would this do in terms of sensitivity?

Adie slowly unfastened her zip, then turned her back to him as she pushed her trousers down, bending to give him a good view of her behind. She gave a wiggle, and tentatively lowered her pants, then turned to face him again, coyly covering herself behind her crossed hands.

Killian filled a bowl with warm soapy water from his basin and brought it over, along with a stool and a towel. 'Sit,' he said, throwing the towel over the polished wood. Adie did as instructed and sat on the fluffy Egyptian cotton with her legs spread. She watched in fascination as he lathered her curls, working his fingers over her mound, until her hairs clung together in soapy locks.

She'd shared baths with one or two of her lovers but none of them had ever washed her this intimately before. It was strangely luxurious letting someone else take care of such a basic need, but at the same time seemed rather subversive.

Adie wriggled at his touch. The warm water, coupled with the delicate massage of his fingertips, was causing her sex to plump. Desire tightened in her womb, making it hard to maintain her pose. She wanted to capture his hand between her thighs and squeeze while he rubbed her clit with the knuckle of his thumb. Her orgasm would be sharp and hard. Adie gripped the edge of the stool with both hands and leaned back, ready for just such a touch.

'Watch,' said Killian, dragging her vision back from the ceiling to her exposed crotch.

His fingers ceased their dance, and closed around the haft of the razor. Heat seemed to seep from her every pore as the twin blades slid over her delicate parts. He followed each crease, each curve, gently and carefully removing the silky down, leaving her feeling naked and exposed.

Adie's breathing grew shallow, until she couldn't prevent a gasp.

She was bare.

Killian dabbed away the last of the foam with a moist flannel, then patted her dry with a corner of the towel.

'Now what?' she murmured.

Killian stood. He grasped her hand and Adie allowed him to pull her to her feet, expecting him to lead her to the bed and finish undressing her. Instead, he held her knickers for her to step into.

'Aren't we going to . . .'

The soft cotton covered her freshly shaved mound, brushing the pink and sensitive skin, causing her to wriggle in delight and frustration.

'We've work to do.' He patted her bum. 'There are thousands of fragments to piece together. Can you think of a better way to spend Sunday night?'

'I . . . I thought . . . You bastard,' she swore, realising that he was grinning. She swatted at his chest.

Killian laughed and dropped to his knees. He snagged his index fingers under the leg elastic of her pants and pulled her forwards on to his mouth.

'Oh!' Adie groaned, as his tongue probed her slit through the cotton. The addition of the soft barrier gave his touch a feathery quality, tantalising and subtle, but oh so sweet. She felt unsteady, dizzy, as he sucked on her clit, loving the tiny nub so hard it trembled, making her shake.

'Slow down,' she begged. 'I want to come with you inside me. Please.'

Killian looked up at her, his nose still pressed to her pussy.

'Please.'

'All right,' he agreed, taking her by the hand and leading her to the bed. 'But the knickers stay on.'

15

Dareth Sadler stepped on to the red carpet of the old film house. The bribes and bullying had paid off and he was about to meet with a promising contact. He checked his watch. Where the hell was Jamāl? Probably hiding until he'd managed to locate the journal.

Dareth slipped into a faded-red plush seat and nodded to the figure to his left. On the big screen, Sean Connery was about to take a beating from Bambi and Thumper in *Diamonds are Forever*. He watched their gymnastics for a moment with mild interest, while the young men around him shouted crude encouragement. Once, he'd fantasised over the powerful embrace of those thighs, but these days he preferred to be on top.

'You are late, Mr Sadler,' said the white-robed figure beside him. 'My brother-in-law is an important man. He will not wait. He is not as generous as I am.'

Dareth turned away from the screen and put on his best convention smile. 'My sincere apologies. I understand he's something of an expert on erotic art.'

The man clasped Dareth's hand over the armrest. 'Come, let us reason together. We know what you are looking for. Other parties are also interested in this item. What incentive do you offer?' The man gave a rather toothy grin. Dareth pulled his arm away.

'First let's be clear on what exactly I'm getting. I don't suppose you happen to have the piece in your possession?'

'My brother-in-law is the one with the details,' said the man, evading the question. 'You must discuss with him whether you are buying goods or information. Obviously, an artifact will cost more.'

'And when is your brother-in-law going to arrive?' Dareth searched the rows of the darkened movie house, wondering if the elusive Ihsān Fuād was here. The cinema had seemed an eccentric choice of venue, but it had advantages, as the constant chatter of the viewers over the English soundtrack made eavesdropping impossible. There could also be any number of Fuād's people seated nearby. 'Jamāl led me to believe that he'd meet me himself.'

'Unfortunately, he is unavailable. The earliest he can possibly see you is midday Tuesday.'

Dareth turned his attention back to the screen, with its oversized Arabic subtitles. Time was running out. Carmichael's women were working just as hard as he was to locate the piece. But this was the only concrete lead he had, and he'd have to take that risk. 'Tuesday midday – where?'

'The Gamal Cafeteria off Al-Muizz Il Allah. But I must know that you are not wasting our time, Mr Sadler. What can you offer?'

'Cash or kind,' said Dareth. Jamāl had taught him one thing: how to cut a deal with rogues.

'Ah, a man who knows how to bargain! Tuesday, Mr Sadler, and bring your assistant.' The little man stood and shuffled off along the aisle, his bright-white clothing making him appear ghostlike in the dark.

Dareth settled back into his seat to enjoy the film. He had a feeling that Tuesday would only provide him with a map, but hopefully one with a large X marked on it. Then it would just be a matter of collecting the item. He was looking forward to the reactions of Carmichael's team when he produced the fragment at his book launch. Meanwhile he'd take a trip around the bazaars tomorrow and hone his haggling skills. He fancied a new carpet to roll Lana in.

* * *

Adie peered along the eerie rock-cut corridors of the Serapeum. She and Siân were killing time in the vast burial vault of the sacred Apis bulls, while they waited for Anton. Once she'd contacted Ihsān Fuād and found the fragment, Adie was convinced that the threat of Dareth Sadler would vanish. The fact that Fuād might not have the information she needed was not something she was prepared to consider.

Adie glanced at Siân, who was squinting at her wristwatch. She'd insisted on coming along.

'Five minutes,' said Siân. 'Let's head over.'

Below the sand in Huni's empty tomb, Matthew winced as the hard white flash of Killian's camera lit the gloomy burial vault. He'd been ordered to work late, and was having to hide his resentment. Even worse, the narrow tunnels had prevented them from setting up proper lighting, and now every shot was a stark reminder of the photographs Lana had taken. And it wasn't just Killian's reaction that worried him. He was afraid that his arse would become world-famous as the subject of some hilarious email attachment.

While his boss repositioned the tripod, Matthew wiped the sweat from his face and slumped against the mausoleum wall. It was such a pity. He'd finally found a woman who was prepared to treat him badly; who'd whipped him and fucked him, driven him crazy with lust, and then she'd screwed him.

'Place the ruler about four feet up,' said Killian. He paused, and gave Matthew a hard stare. 'OK, what are they up to?'

'What? Nothing.' Matthew pushed himself off the wall as if it was electrified. He didn't actually know what Siân and Adie were doing, only that they were meeting someone. 'Why are you so suspicious?'

Killian snorted in response. He tilted his head and

looked at Matthew along the length of the zoom lens. 'Because you look so guilty. Besides, the Apis bulls aren't that exciting. Line it up so that Hathor is central.'

Matthew fumbled with the metal ruler, laying it alongside the goddess. He realised it was all about to come out. He had the same feeling he got when he knew he was about to vomit.

'Let me guess: they're out wasting their time on that damn fragment. I'll assume they haven't found anything, since they haven't even had the courtesy to keep me informed.'

Matthew licked his lips. He reached for his water bottle but it wasn't there – he must have left it in the other chamber.

'Matthew,' said Killian. 'I'm expecting an answer.'

'I'm not sure. Meeting someone, I think.'

'And you don't know who?'

'No.' Matthew wetted his lips again. 'Look, Killian, there's something I've got to tell you. Something I should have told you last week.'

Killian straightened to his full height and stepped around the tripod. 'Go on.'

'I let somebody on to the site on Thursday. It was an accident,' he blurted. 'They took some photos of the mural. I think they were working for Dareth Sadler.'

'You stupid bastard.' Killian raised his hand with his fingers flexed. 'Why are you telling me this now?'

Matthew stared at the wall. 'Adie thought she could get them back.'

'You mean you told Siân and Adie instead of me. And now they think they're helping me by bargaining with Sadler over at the Serapeum.' He kicked a stone, which ricocheted off the side of the sarcophagus casing, chipping the relief. 'Idiots!' he growled. He turned on his heel and stormed out of the chamber.

Matthew waited a moment, then cautiously followed

Killian as far as the robbers' tunnel. He hadn't meant to drop the two women in it. Killian had drawn his own conclusions, and now there'd be hell to pay.

Killian's temper flared inside the confines of his skull, until it had pushed out any room for rational thought. By the time he'd trekked as far as the rest-house, he felt sure that he'd find them striking some crackpot deal with Sadler, who would find out everything they knew and then betray them regardless.

Bloody fools. He'd thought better of Siân, and hoped better of Adie. Hell, he'd even begun to trust her.

He struck off across the pockmarked landscape, directly towards the Serapeum. Further down, beneath their protective roof, the statues of the Greek philosophers and poets – known as the Philosophers' Circle – stared solemnly across the horizon. He could just make out three figures, one of whom was seated by the feet of Homer. He recognised Siân's blonde plait a moment later.

So they weren't even at the Serapeum. He gritted his teeth. More lies and deceit. He pumped his legs harder, gaining momentum as he strode towards them. Feelings of anger and betrayal pulsed in his temples. He burst into the circle. The two women stared at him in shock. 'Fools,' he said, and turned his back on them to face his enemy.

But it wasn't Sadler.

Anton.

They stared at each other for several seconds. His former friend had changed in the years since they'd parted ways; once short-cropped hair had grown long and wild, and fine webs of laughter lines were etched around his eyes, but Killian would have known him anywhere. He took an involuntary step forwards, then stopped himself. He remembered how big their dreams had been, how the whole of human history had been theirs to discover. Then he remembered the article ridiculing him, how they had fled and hid themselves in an ancient rock fortress, and finally how even his closest friend and ally had betrayed him. Now, just like that other bad penny, Sadler, he'd come back into his life when the stakes were too high.

Killian didn't believe in coincidence. It couldn't be chance that both men had turned up again after all this time. 'What the bloody hell are you up to?' he demanded.

Before Anton could respond, Adie darted forwards and positioned herself between them. She grasped Killian's hand. 'He's helping us. He's arranged a meeting with Ihsān Fuād, for tomorrow morning. The partner of the man Masud told us about.'

'Adie. Shut up.' He stepped around her to face Anton. His rage had suddenly cooled to bitterness. 'What are you doing here?'

Anton stared at him for a long time, long enough for Killian to realise that this was probably difficult for him too. 'Helping a friend,' he eventually replied.

'I'd rather you didn't. This is a reputable team and we don't consort with grave robbers.'

Anton stiffened. 'I'm not a grave robber.'

'Aren't you?' Killian flung back. 'You've built quite a reputation for yourself, and it's not a good one. I know the museum takes finds from you, because no one can prove you're breaking the law. But your stupid *Boy's Own* adventures will jeopardise my career all over again.' Killian stopped talking, as he realised where his point had taken him. 'I . . . I can't talk to you,' he finished softly.

'Yeah, missed you too,' replied Anton.

Killian took in the sight of what Anton had become and mentally compared the image with himself. Looking back, he'd been so uptight at Petra that he'd have walked out on himself if it had been possible. But in this place, at this time, they couldn't be friends. Not now, perhaps not ever.

He offered his hand to Anton, who cautiously took it. 'It's good to see you,' Killian said.

Anton briefly smiled. 'I'd better go.'

His robe swirled around him as he turned, and then he was gone, into the twilight.

Killian turned back to Adie. 'You're not meeting Ihsān Fuād. He's a criminal.'

'You know him,' she said, incredulously.

'No, I don't know him, but I know of him. I don't lock the dig site just to keep Sadler out. Although from what Matthew's just told me, I needn't have bothered.'

Neither Siân nor Adie spoke. They obviously hadn't expected Matthew to crack.

'I thought you had more sense,' he said, looking at Siân.

She shrugged, but made no apology. 'If Ihsān can lead us to the fragment, the pictures won't matter.'

'You shouldn't have kept this to yourselves.'

'Maybe not, but that's the way it panned out.' Siân reached out and leaned against the statue of Heraclitus.

'You should have told me about Sadler and those photographs on Thursday night, when I could have done something about them.'

Adie replied this time. 'But the photos will be useless if we complete the mural. Sadler's book's based purely on conjecture. We'll know the truth.'

Killian shook his head in exasperation. They were out of time, and he needed to resolve this quickly. 'Listen, both of you. I want everyone back on the boat so we can sort out this mess and call an immediate press conference. I hate to do it, but Sadler's forced our hand. We need to announce our findings before he releases the pictures and grabs an exclusive. We can take the emphasis off the mural and shift it on to what we've discovered in the burial chamber.'

'Which is fuck-all,' said Siân bluntly.

'Maybe, but you two seem remarkably good at making up stories, so I'm sure you can manage to find something to hype.'

'What about the fragment?' said Adie.

'I meant what I said, we don't consort with criminals. You can search the museum records later.'

Fifteen minutes later, Adie rode in the passenger seat of Siân's Land Rover as they headed towards the river. 'I can't go back to the boat,' she muttered to herself. 'If I do, we'll never find that fragment. Ihsān will sell the information to Sadler instead. He said as much to Anton.' She stared sullenly out of the windscreen at the powder-puff clouds on the horizon. 'You're not saying much.'

'What's there to say? Killian calls the shots, and he doesn't take risks. We've got to say something interesting about an empty room, or Sadler will shaft us.'

Adie set her jaw. She wasn't prepared to give up yet. If Sadler found the piece first, the backlash would mean she'd be out of a job, anyway.

'Where's the nearest railway station?' she asked.

'Don't be stupid, Adie.'

Adie dug out the local map from beneath her seat. 'Al-Badrashein.' She jabbed a finger at the village that lay just north of where the houseboat was moored. 'Please, Siân, don't make me waste our only chance. All you have to do is drop me off.'

From Al-Badrashein, Adie caught an incredibly slow train to Cairo. The two-hour journey and the subsequent sleepless night in the empty Gezira apartment – Jason and Samih had been summoned to the houseboat – was the loneliest time she'd ever spent. At least there wasn't a phone on the boat. She just hoped that Killian didn't take it out on Siân.

Late the next morning, Adie headed south past the

black-and-white-striped buildings of the Al-Ghoriyya complex in the heart of town, as Anton had instructed. The distant hum of lunchtime traffic throbbed in the dry air of the city. The cafeteria where she was to meet Ihsān was nestled between one of Cairo's last remaining *tarboosh*-makers and a bizarre curio shop, with dried hedgehogs hung in the window. Adie eyed the saloon-style doors apprehensively. Even out here on the street she caught the reek of tobacco smoke and sweat. Siân had repeatedly warned her to stay clear of the *baladi* bars, where the only women were prostitutes. But she had no choice. If she turned away now, the tide of publicity generated by Sadler's book would most likely sink the project and Killian's career, along with every member on the team. With virtually no experience, she was unlikely to find anything else. 'Be brave,' she told herself. 'Your future depends on it.'

Her eyes adjusted slowly to the dimly lit interior. Six stone steps led down into a small square room, cluttered with tables, where coiling tobacco smoke hung like a cloud at shoulder level, obscuring both the customers and the bar. There were few patrons: a group of three old men positioned around a backgammon board, and two loners, one at the bar, the other drawing heavily on an apple-scented *sheesha*.

The clack of gaming pieces and the low burbling of the water pipe ceased as she crossed the bare floor. She could feel the eyes of the patrons on her body, appraising and undressing her. She kept her head pointed forwards and her gaze lowered. The last thing she wanted was to make eye contact and for one of them to actually proposition her.

Adie clenched her fists tight and tried to take comfort in the bite of her fake wedding band. Anton had told her to ask at the bar. He'd given her a note in Arabic just in case, which he seemed to think would ensure her safety. She didn't have much confidence in it.

'I'm here to meet Ihsān Fuād. Is he here?' she asked the gaudily dressed bartender, whose washed-out *galabeyya* seemed to be made of tie-dyed polyester. He nodded, and to her dismay pointed towards a beaded curtain at the rear, leading into a darkened back room, away from even the doubtful safety of the public bar.

Adie scurried between the tables, then paused before the tacky curtain. This was crazy. She glanced back at the male patrons, then parted the curtain warily, before she lost her nerve and ran for it.

In the centre of the small room beyond was a pitted table, surrounded by wooden chairs. Thick tapestries covered the stone walls, and rosy light spilled from an ornate glass lantern overhead. It looked like someone had looted a seraglio for soft furnishings to decorate a prison cell, but it was still a far more appealing room than the main bar. However, there was no occupant. Fearing a trap, Adie took a hurried step back, only to feel the terrifying sensation of warm breath stirring the hairs on the back of her neck. She froze. She shouldn't have come here, not alone. Too late, she realised that the back room didn't have another exit.

'Dr Hamilton,' said a voice. The third member of the backgammon trio stood beside her in the doorway and gestured into the room. 'I am Ihsān Fuād. Will you join me?'

Adie glanced suspiciously at the wizened man; she'd expected a swarthy low-life.

'I see you are cautious,' he said in response to her hesitation. His speech was curiously polite, school-book English. 'You are wise, but I assure you I am who I claim to be. Dr Kelly gave you a note, did he not?'

'Yes,' she said. 'Did you want it?'

'No, I am confident that you are who you say you are. Please come inside, where we may speak freely. Some refreshment?'

'I'm fine.' Adie crossed to the table and perched on a chair, facing the beaded curtain. Ihsān sat opposite, taking a moment to observe her. Adie nervously toyed with her hair. His aura of absolute calm only heightened her sense of trepidation. 'I'm looking for a missing fragment of mural, from one of the tombs out at Saqqara. Dr Franks said you might know where to find it,' she blurted.

Ihsān raised his hand. 'Dr Kelly explained. I know where you can find something of that nature. Whether it truly is the piece you seek is uncertain. However, let us not be hasty, Dr Hamilton. Tell me about yourself before we barter. I like to know whom I'm dealing with.'

'OK.' Adie clasped her hands in her lap. 'But I am in a hurry. This fragment would be beneficial to my project. I'm an archaeologist, like you were once.'

'And still am. One's vocation remains, always.' He rubbed his fingers across his lips and smiled. 'Tell me more.'

Adie hesitated. She was sure he didn't want to hear about her favourite books and restaurants. 'There isn't much to say. I've always been into archaeology, ever since I was a child. Coming to Egypt was my biggest ambition,' she finished simply.

'That Egypt ceased to exist over two thousand years ago. Like all your kind, you only love the past.'

Adie stared at him. Was there any reproach, or was he making fun of her? She thought of everything that Anton had shown her, the boy in the market, even the traffic in Cairo.

'Since I came here, I've learned that Egypt is full of the living, as well as the dead. Also that the lives of commoners are just as precious as kings. I've been given a lot to think about.'

Ihsān regarded her. He seemed satisfied.

'Before we continue, Dr Hamilton. I want you to understand that I agreed to meet you first – for there are other interested parties – because Dr Kelly has helped my associates in the past. However, if we cannot reach a suitable agreement today, I will begin other negotiations, and I cannot promise to agree to a second meeting, even for a friend of Anton Kelly.'

'I understand, but what guarantees do I have?'

'None. You will have to trust me. I am, however, confident that the piece will still be where I left it. It was well hidden.'

'Hidden? Why?'

'Because I had planned to steal it, before I was dismissed.'

'Were you fired for stealing?' she asked.

'There was no evidence, only suspicion.'

'So how do I find it?'

Ihsān steepled his fingers and tapped them on his lips. 'You are very impatient for an archaeologist, Dr Hamilton, even more impatient than Mr Sadler. I will explain, but first I think we must discuss payment.'

So, he was already negotiating with Sadler. Adie clenched the edge of the table. There was an avaricious twinkle in Ihsān's dark eyes, made more apparent by the web of lines around them. It made her wonder if the wad of old notes stuffed into her pocket would be enough to satisfy him. In a bidding war, Sadler would win easily. 'How much?' she asked.

Ihsān rose from his seat and circled the table until he stood beside her, his emaciated hands resting on the back of the adjacent chair. Adie immediately stiffened. He leaned forwards a little, and looked deep into her eyes. 'I don't want your money, Dr Hamilton.'

Adie's chair scraped noisily against the floor as she jerked up off the seat. She stumbled, then steadied herself against the table.

'Please sit down, my dear.' Ihsān gestured towards her seat, but Adie stubbornly ignored him. She preferred to be on her feet in case she had to run. Ihsān shook his head and sighed. 'Very well. I wish to show you something.'

He drew a package, roughly twelve inches long, from the pocket of his jacket. Adie stared at the battered Jiffy bag in trepidation. Inside the bag was a roll of bubble wrap, which Ihsān unrolled across the table to reveal a smooth marble cock, the severed pride of some ancient sculpture. Adie frowned. What did he want her to do – identify it?

'Greek, I believe,' he said, dispelling that possibility. 'Probably fifth century BC. I had it shipped from Alexandria last week. I have a buyer ready, but he has rather specialised tastes. Which is where I require your assistance.'

Adie's frown deepened. Her gaze shifted uneasily between the white marble cock and Ihsān's leary expression. 'What exactly are you asking of me?'

'Think of it as an exchange of favours. I provide you with all the information you need to find your precious missing fragment, and in return you apply some polish to this artifact.' He locked eyes with her again.

Adie sat down uncomfortably. He clearly didn't mean with a duster. Her mouth opened but no sound could express her outrage. She prepared to refuse, but the words never left her lips. Without Ihsān's help she would never find the fragment.

'You want me to masturbate with it?' she squeaked. It was almost unthinkable. There was only a beaded curtain between this room and the bar. Anyone could walk in.

Ihsān grinned, revealing a row of discoloured teeth. 'To put it bluntly, yes. Do you agree to my terms? I'll need a photograph as proof.' He rose and fetched a Polaroid camera from a shelf.

Adie swallowed the lump in her throat. If she didn't

agree, Dareth Sadler was sure to find someone willing to perform with a stone cock on his behalf, Lana most likely. 'I don't know,' she said cagily. 'Anyone could walk in.'

'Nobody will enter. You have my word.'

Adie shook her head. It was too risky, and too sordid. Was it worth prostituting herself for Killian and the project? But this was the only lead she had, and time was running out. Five, ten minutes of performance art would be over quickly and nobody needed ever know.

'Any pictures you take, you leave my face off.' He shrugged, then nodded. 'You'd better not be bullshitting me,' she continued.

Ihsān lifted the stone cock and handed it to her by the base. 'I promise that you will be given an exact location of a box, and to the best of my knowledge that box contains the item you are looking for.'

Adie dazedly accepted the object.

The marble was cold in her hand, much heavier than she'd expected, and strangely tactile. She curled her fingers around the shaft while focusing on the bulbous tip. It was more detailed than any of the vibrators she'd ever owned. You couldn't get these from an Ann Summers party.

Ihsān hoisted a chair in one hand and set it down just to the left of the beaded doorway. She watched him glance out into the smoky main room, before settling himself comfortably. 'Whenever you are ready.'

Adie hesitated, aware of a sudden heat in her cheeks. She felt awkward – deeply embarrassed. She'd have to pretend he wasn't there. She stared at the elaborate wall-hangings. They reminded her of Anton's silk palace. Self-consciously she stroked the cool tip of the dildo across her collarbone and down over one breast, where she circled the nipple. There was no spark of excitement, just a dull sense of unreality and a desire to flee.

'Relax,' Ihsān encouraged. 'Pretend that you are performing for a lover. I am sure you have one. Perhaps it is Dr Kelly.' He smirked knowingly. 'Think of him.'

That's what I was trying to do, she thought. 'I think it best if you don't talk.' She shut her eyes and forced her hunched shoulders down, despite the knots of tension, and concentrated on her memories of the silk pavilion. Gradually, the busy thoughts in her head stilled into a vision of Anton, his dark hair fanned out across her body, how they'd lain after they'd last made love. That was before he'd come face to face with Killian again.

Suddenly her mind was full of Killian. She saw him as he'd appeared last night, furious and thin-lipped, but the dark image fractured under her caress into one of him standing by the tomb's entrance, with the Saqqara dawn gilding the snowy strands of his hair. The light added a touch of lavender to his irises, which made them look the way they did when he'd just come.

Finally, the tension drained out of her limbs. She unbuttoned her shirt and, still seeing Killian, brushed the stone phallus against her exposed skin. The marble was cold, pleasantly so, as she rubbed it luxuriously around her peaking nipples and down towards her waist.

This was all about Killian. It always had been: everything she'd done since that fateful night outside Joe's office. It was only right that he should share this part of the journey too, and so it was his hand she envisioned manipulating the stone cock, and lowering the zip of her jeans.

The smooth tip prodded against the front of her panties, giving rise to an unexpected shiver of pleasure. Gravity slowly tugged her jeans downwards and off her hips. They briefly clung around her thighs then slithered to her ankles. Adie kicked them off and returned to her seat, where she sat with her ankles hooked neatly behind the front legs as if restrained, just how she imagined Killian would tie her.

She risked a look at Ihsān. The slight, one-time scholar was slouched in his chair, his hands pushed inside the crotch of his baggy white trousers. She caught his gaze, seeing not him but Killian, and with his full attention she put her tongue to the cock-tip before closing her lips around it. Ihsān's salt-and-pepper hair clung to his forehead, stuck with beads of perspiration. He let out a long breath, while working his hand faster. Adie shuffled forwards to the edge of her seat. With one hand she tugged aside the cloth, and tapped a finger against her clit. She was wet from her thoughts of Killian, and a zing of urgent desire sparked beneath her touch. She wriggled, trying to find just the right spot, and replaced her finger with the heavy cock. Lubricated with her saliva, it glided easily against her, polishing her nub until her lower body twitched of its own volition. 'Killian, Killian...' she mouthed, imagining his lips on her throat and his penis between her legs, poised to take her. She lifted her hips and her flesh closed around the shaft, its coolness striking her core like a lance until her orgasm broke around her.

Killian smiled at her, then the conjured image faded, and to her horror she found herself staring at Ihsān. He returned her stare, while he wiped himself with what looked like a free take-away serviette. Appalled, Adie looked down at her semi-naked body and the stone cock jutting obscenely from between her thighs, and felt herself flush in embarrassment. She tugged her shirt across her chest and hurriedly buttoned up. The dildo she dropped on to the table, creating a new dent.

She shuffled back into her jeans. It was over. She just needed the information now and she'd be gone.

Ihsān retrieved the phallus, carefully rolled it in its original bubble wrap and stowed it safely in his pocket, along with the headless Polaroid snap. God knows when he'd taken it. It looked like an anonymous happy snap, the kind you saw on Internet revenge sites.

'Now keep your promise,' she demanded.

He patted his pocket, and smiled. 'Of course.'

Adie moved cautiously through the storage area of the Cairo Museum. Harsh light from the fluorescent tubes overhead illuminated rows of crates and torn packages, which rested on utilitarian metal shelves.

The dash through Cairo had removed the scent of sex from her clothes, but she still felt grimy and soiled from her encounter in the bar. She didn't know if she could trust Ihsān Fuād, or if her search would end in frustration, but this was it – she was about to find out.

She checked off the numbered boxes as she passed them, while listening for the sound of footsteps. Ihsān had directed her to the storage areas, where she'd slipped under the rope barrier while no one was paying attention.

Suddenly a shape loomed at her from between a gap in the shelves. A life-sized statue of Anubis with a missing ear glared at her from the shadows. Ihsān had told her to watch for this. So far so good. If her luck held, she wouldn't meet any other custodians.

Adie moved on from the landmark to a new shelf. What if it wasn't here? Even if Fuād wasn't lying, would the fragment still be here after twenty years? Could she trust the old man's memory? Think positively, she told herself. Her heart was racing. Adie walked faster, scanning the crates. Faded Arabic writing gave little indication of what the boxes contained, but broken statues peered mournfully at her from antiquity.

There.

The Grecian urn Ihsān had told her to seek. She reached out, and saw that her hands were trembling. Taking a breath to steady herself, she lifted the lid. The pungent smell of decaying mouse wafted upwards. Adie wiped her sticky palms on her denim-covered thighs then nervously pushed her hand into the darkness that the urn contained. Her fingers grazed cardboard, and she grasped a box. It was slightly nibbled, and some of the protective cotton packaging had been tugged out and shredded, but the weight of it was encouraging.

Ancient tape secured the box from both sides, crossing over on the lid. X marks the spot, she thought. Her heart pounded with redoubled effort. Excitement tingled in her fingertips, making her so clumsy as she picked at the tape that she nearly dropped it. The lid came off with a prophetic sigh, and she stared down at the chipped fragment within, at the familiar palette of faded but once vibrant colours.

She squinted at it, unable to put the image into context. There was no time. She had to get back to Saqqara. She carefully wrapped the fragile piece in a scarf, clutched it to her body, and headed back towards the public areas.

Back at the entrance, she was just working out how to slip past the security checkpoint at the entrance, when a commotion broke out on the steps. Sadler appeared, flanked by journalists, with Lana in close attendance.

He could only be here for one reason. Ihsān Fuād had sold the same information twice, and now they were here for the fragment. He wouldn't be pleased to find he'd been beaten to the prize.

Adie bowed her head and brushed past the distracted guard, with the hope of losing herself in the crowd of tourists outside. Just as she was about flee down the steps, she saw Lana grab Sadler's arm and point in her direction.

'Miss Hamilton! Stop!'

She turned her back on the voice and ran out into the sunlight, then dodged across the forecourt and recklessly sprinted on to the Corniche el-Nil.

The main thoroughfare along the Nile bank was choked with traffic. Heedless of any danger, Adie squeezed between a donkey-cart and a microbus and darted across the lanes. Lana and Sadler wouldn't be far behind her, and might even have alerted the museum staff. Confused and unsure where to turn, Adie ran along the river-bank. Further on, she braved the traffic again and darted into a small telephone kiosk. She bashed out Anton's number on the keypad from the note he'd written her, and willed him to answer, and not some stranger picked at random by the phone exchange.

'Hello.'

The connection was good. 'Anton, I'm being chased,' she blurted. 'I don't know what to do, they're just behind me.'

'Where are you?'

'Just along from the Tahrir Bridge,' said Adie, relieved at his calm acceptance of the situation.

'Listen, there's a felucca landing, just south of there. Get on the river-bus and I'll meet you upstream at the Giza stop. Can you do that?'

'I think so.'

'Go, then.'

The line went dead. Adie dropped the receiver. She'd already seen the river-boat as she'd sprinted along the bank; it was only a short distance to the landing. Adie stuck her head around the kiosk doorway. She could just make out Sadler on the bridge. She weighed the odds, and ran for it.

16

'Anton. Thank god.'

Adie rushed towards him along the quay, clutching the fragile mural fragment in her arms. 'I've got it,' she gasped. 'It was in the museum.'

'Adie,' he said sternly.

His tone didn't register. 'I was so scared. Sadler's after me. He saw me get on the boat. But if he's come the same way, he'll be at least half an hour. I read the timetable; only every other boat comes this far downriver.' She held the fragment tightly to her chest. 'I need to get this to Saqqara, fast.'

'Adie!'

She finally paused for breath.

'Tell me you didn't just walk out of the Cairo Museum with an artifact.'

A wash of scarlet seeped into her cheeks.

'Damn it, Adie! You're not bloody Lara Croft. You can't just take whatever you want. You're supposed to fill in the paperwork. I thought you were a pro.'

'We don't have time for this,' she snapped. 'It's an emergency. If I don't get this back, the project might go belly-up. Sadler's going to shaft us.'

'Sadler's got nothing on you. If anything's going to sink the project it's one of the team being arrested for stealing antiquities.'

Adie frowned. She pursed her lips, while the threat of tears stung her eyes. 'I had no choice. If I'd tried to get it legitimately, Sadler would have pulled strings. He knows people.' She'd never even considered obtaining it legitimately, but Anton didn't need to know that. 'He'd have ruined Killian with it,' she continued, defensively.

'Speaking of whom, you realise he's going to go ballistic when he hears about this? Or didn't you hear last night's lecture?'

'Of course I did.' Adie chewed her lip. And she'd deliberately ignored it. Now she realised that Killian probably wouldn't accept the fragment unless she could prove she'd obtained it legitimately. If she'd filled in the requisite paperwork, he'd have got over it eventually. Now who knew what he'd do? Order her to take it back? At least they'd know where it was, and so would the Egyptian Antiquities Organisation. Sadler wouldn't be able to claim it as his discovery.

'Do you think I should take it back?'

'It's too late for that. The damage is done.' Anton rubbed a hand across his brow, brushing his long hair out of his eyes. 'Sadler's probably already notified the EAO. Let's get you out to Saqqara and see what happens.'

Adie nodded. She may as well go all the way. 'You'll come with me?'

Anton sighed. 'All right, but I don't want to meet Killian again. And we'd better stay off the road. You don't want to meet Sadler, or anyone else he's brought with him. At least Jamāl is out of the frame; the police picked him up on Sunday morning.'

They hired horses from a tout on the Pyramids' Road. Adie had a little riding experience, but she was too busy worrying to enjoy the wild gallop across the desert. It was nearly three when they reached the excavation site, which had become the centre of frenzied activity. There was a van with a satellite dish mounted on the roof, bearing the BBC logo on the side, and several strangers hanging around the site entrance. Adie spotted Siân sitting on the back step of her Land Rover some distance away.

'Somebody called the cavalry,' said Siân humourlessly, as they drew close. 'Killian's instructions were to tell you that you're fired.' She turned her head from Adie and stared at Anton, clearly surprised to see him again.

Adie slid gracelessly off the horse. This might be her last desperate gamble, but she was convinced she held an ace. 'I've got it,' she said.

Siân was suddenly paying attention. 'Well, what are you waiting for? It's not a live broadcast, but the cameras are rolling. Lucas has drafted a press release and the find will be online within a couple of hours. Oh, and there's a representative from the EAO down there.'

Anton pointed across the sand towards the direction of the ticket office. 'There's about to be a few more.'

Adie followed the line of his gaze. Sadler had arrived with two dark-suited Egyptian gentlemen, and a couple of members of the tourist police. They were having a heated discussion, which stopped abruptly as they began to move towards her.

Anton tapped her shoulder. 'Time to make your move.' They were getting closer.

Adie clasped the fragment tightly to her chest, and sprinted towards the tomb. Ignoring the gathered figures, she ducked into the low doorway.

Voices drifted up from below. She said a brief prayer to any gods who were listening, then carried on down the stairs.

Nobody paid her any attention as she slipped into the mural chamber. Killian was standing before the mural with a reporter and another Egyptian, while a cameraman and sound technician did their jobs with calm efficiency.

'Yes, it's a shame that this otherwise splendid mural has been defaced so casually,' said the Egyptian in an erudite tone. 'Do we have any hope of recovering the lost fragment?'

Now.

'Right here.' Adie stepped forwards into the camera eye.

Killian froze.

The boom hesitated for a moment, then hovered over her head.

Adie unwrapped the fragment and thought for a moment, before handing it to Killian. He stared at her, his grey eyes like flint, then wordlessly moved to set it in place.

The fit wasn't perfect. A century of erosion had enlarged the cracks made by Jacobs' chisel, and several splinters had been lost, but the picture was complete, with enough detail to see exactly what was going on.

'Goodness,' said the man from the EAO.

'Blimey. That's gotta hurt,' muttered the sound technician.

Adie stared at the completed picture. Weeks of working in close proximity had deadened its impact, but she remembered now how she'd been struck by its beauty and artistry the first time she'd seen it, and the feeling returned, tugging her mouth into a wide smile.

A moment later, her smile faded as Sadler entered the chamber, his retinue crowding in behind him.

'Very interesting,' said the EAO representative. The camera was still rolling. 'And now we see it in its entirety. You are lucky to have an assistant with such initiative, Dr Carmichael. Can you explain the significance of your magnificent discovery?'

Killian glared at Adie. Then his instinctive profession-alism took over. He swept his hand through his hair, and half-turned to the mural. 'This is perhaps a unique discov-ery. The images suggest that the pharaoh Huni is under-going ritual castration, as part of a re-enactment of the

Osiris myth. Osiris, as I'm sure you are aware, was restored to life without his phallus, before his consort Isis fashioned a replacement, rendering him potent again.'

'And why would this be considered important to the pharaoh?' asked the reporter.

'Osiris is associated with divinity. Presumably by emulating his fate, the pharaoh hoped to attain divine status.'

While Killian was speaking, Adie noticed Sadler's face whiten. He took two paces backwards into the shadows, and slunk off up the stairs. Good riddance, she thought. She'd have loved to see him base a ritual on this.

Killian's impromptu explanation ended. The reporter thanked him, and then, surprisingly, the EAO representative began to applaud. His colleagues, lost for purpose, joined him, as did the tourist police. Adie began to clap herself. It finally seemed that everything would be fine.

After Adie retreated into the tomb, Siân watched Sadler follow her. 'So much for that,' she muttered. Ever since the press had arrived, she'd been surplus to requirements. Now the find belonged to Egypt and the world. Killian would start doing the rounds of interviews and lectures, and they'd lose the student camaraderie of the last few weeks.

'You seem disappointed.' Anton cut in on her thoughts.

'No. Yes.' Siân looked up at Killian's one-time partner. 'If Adie pulls this off, and I think she will, life is going to get pretty boring around here.'

'Don't you like being an archaeologist?' There was laughter in his eyes.

'You're mocking me. I like the fieldwork. And I like getting there first.'

'That's very honest. You'd make a good grave robber.'

Siân kicked the back tyre of the Land Rover with the toe of her boot. 'I thought you said stealing was wrong.'

'It's not stealing if you give it back.'

'Right.' Siân rolled her eyes heavenwards. The *kham-seen* had died off overnight and now there was only a slight breeze. She shifted her gaze back to Anton, and watched his long hair whisper around his shoulders. 'Have you ever found any gold?'

'Not yet.' Anton examined Siân's face. 'Although I'm heading west to the Valley of the Golden Mummies tomorrow. Do you want to come with me?'

Siân looked up at him, and laughed. 'For a life of crime?'

'For a life of adventure.'

Siân stopped laughing. 'I hardly know you. And what about Adie?'

'It would never have worked out. She's too much like him to work from the shadows, following stories and mysteries to places that aren't on any map. She wants recognition.'

Siân drummed her fingers against the scorching metal of the car, considering his words. It was true. Adie would never be satisfied with just making discoveries. She wanted the world to know about them.

Anton leaned forwards and caught up the reigns of Adie's mount. 'I'll be waiting by the river-bank at dawn tomorrow. Maybe I'll see you there.' He sat up in the saddle, kicked his heels and rode away like a prince.

Siân watched him go, and slowly licked her lips.

Eventually everyone else departed, leaving Adie and Killian alone below ground. She watched him pace the chamber perimeter, turning off the lights, until a single spotlight lit the restored pharaoh.

'I suppose you're expecting me to congratulate you,' Killian said, his tone strangely neutral. He gazed up at the mural. 'It certainly looks better now it's complete. Masud will be pleased. Where did you find it?'

Adie apprehensively sucked her lower lip.

It was inevitable that he would ask. She'd even rehearsed her explanation on the ride to Saqqara. But when he'd slotted the piece into place, she'd thought it was all over and she wouldn't have to explain any more. 'I got it from the museum,' she eventually replied.

Killian inclined his head, as if that was the reply he'd expected. 'And you probably dealt with Fuād to get there. I guess, judging by the fact the police followed you in, that you stole it.'

Adie took a breath. 'Sorry.'

Killian turned towards her. His eyes were cold. 'I'm glad you're sorry. I think you need to say that to the rest of the team as well. Matthew and Sadler nearly sank us, but so did you.'

'I know,' she said very quietly.

'I'm not going to sack you, Adie.' He turned back to the mural. 'But if you want to be in my team you have to learn to trust me, and you have to play by the rules. From now on, no more secrets, and no more dealing with criminals. Is that clear?'

Adie nodded, then, realising that he wasn't looking at her, said, 'Yes.'

'Good. Then the job's still yours. And you can prove yourself willing by finding Lucas and helping him redraft the press release. I know it's explicit, but keep it clean. I don't want to encourage the editorial teams to chop it up and misquote us.'

Adie hesitated. There were still unresolved issues between them. She needed to know if they still had a relationship or not.

'You're still here,' he said.

'Killian,' Adie said quietly. 'What about us? I know I've betrayed your trust, but . . .' Her words trailed off and she unconsciously tapped the gold wedding band against her teeth.

Killian turned. He seemed faintly surprised, as if he

hadn't really thought about it. 'But what?' He arched an eyebrow. 'Do you expect me to punish you?'

Adie shuffled uncomfortably on the spot. Yes, that was exactly it. She'd wronged him, and he didn't know the half of it. But if he laid her over his lap and spanked her for her insolence and misbehaviour, then they definitely had a relationship, right? Her heart gave an excited jump at the thought of his cock pressing against her midriff as he warmed her bared cheeks with his hand. She suspected a proper spanking would be rather sensual.

She tilted her chin upwards. 'Don't I deserve it?'

'Deserve it?' Killian shrugged. He crossed the gloomy chamber to one of the work trunks and took out a roll of masking tape. 'Need it, more like.'

Adie watched him warily. If he was going to spank her, what the hell was the tape for?

'What are you waiting for? Strip,' Killian said. 'You want punishing, don't you?'

Adie partially unbuttoned her shirt. 'Aren't you going to do it?'

'No. That would make it a reward.'

Adie frowned, but finished loosening her shirt, and pulled her vest over her head. She lowered her jeans and knickers, and with a bit of tugging managed to pull them off over her boots.

'Over here. Where you can better contemplate the error of your ways.' He'd improvised a post with a crossbar out of the equipment, in front of the restored pharaoh. Adie shuffled over, and he secured her wrists to the crossbar with tape. 'Now head up, bottom out and curve your spine.'

Adie did as instructed and wiggled her bottom for good measure, anticipating the sting of his palm, and the delicious slow heat spreading throughout her lower body. When the slap didn't come, she wriggled again, trying to incite him.

'Stand still.'

He placed fabric over her eyes and tied it behind her head, effectively blinding her.

'More bandages?' she asked.

'Keep still, and speak only when spoken to.'

'Yes, master,' she said impertinently.

Killian still didn't react. Adie frowned beneath the blindfold. Deprived of her sight, she wondered if he was just going to let her stand there and sweat. Was this her punishment? She strained her ears trying to figure out where he was. Fear and helplessness heightened her awareness, until she could sense every whisper of motion in the silent chamber. Her own breathing sounded loud in her ears and Killian's slow footfalls seemed both close and strangely distant. Any minute, she thought, the first strike would come. She felt herself tense.

Nothing.

Then she felt a splash. Something viscous tickled a spot between her shoulder-blades. It hung there heavy with its own weight, then began to trickle very slowly down her spine, teasing each individual hair and nerve-ending. Adie gave an involuntary shiver, but the droplet continued at its torturous pace.

There was a second splash as another droplet began its gradual descent, followed by yet another, each following the same slow, sensuous course. They pooled in the small of her back, lapping at her tailbone. Eventually, a single bead of oil trickled between her cheeks, making her want to clench and shake her buttocks. The path of the oil became the sum of her senses. There was nothing else.

A second puddle formed over her anus, making her tremble in anticipation of the sweet invasion of his finger or maybe even his cock, but he didn't touch her.

Adie could hear his controlled inhalations while her own breaths grew shallower and more ragged, as the oil slid closer to her cunt. She desperately wanted to rub her thighs together.

The first drop reached her clit, where it hung until it grew heavy, swollen by a second droplet. Heat bloomed across her face and neck. Her legs trembled. After the oil, would he spank her or fuck her?

The bead fell; it splashed against her foot.

'Oh!' she gasped. Something stirred inside her, and her body responded with a gush of cream. Adie clasped the crossbar tight to steady herself.

Killian laid a gentle hand on her out-thrust bottom. 'The line's been drawn,' he said, and she realised that whatever came next would determine their future. Obey and trust him, and they would be partners, equals. Try to top him, and he'd never be anything more than her boss.

She felt his breath against her back, so recently sensitised by the oil. His thumb stroked between her cheeks, circling around the whorl of her anus. He ran his open palm down her inner thighs, his touch feather-light but purposeful. The air stirred against her skin as he stepped around her.

'You need to learn patience.' His tongue flicked out and circled around one nipple. 'You're always in too much of a rush.'

He did the same to her other nipple, then his attention moved to her navel, massaging the delicate button with his tongue until she was shaking with need.

Her nerves were virtually buzzing; a connective line seemed to have been drawn between her belly-button and her cunt. Adie whimpered. Slowly was bringing her on fast.

'Killian, please, no more. I can't take it.'

'Are you begging?' He sounded amused.

Adie realised it was time to give in. 'Yes,' she said. 'Yes.'

'Very well.' He stepped away, and a moment later he took a firm hold of her hips and pulled her back against his erection. The heat of his loins warmed her bottom while his cock slid into her sex, aided by the pooled oil. God, she wanted this, wanted it so badly. She wanted to lean back into his arms, while his hands explored her body; wanted to feel him coax her gently to orgasm, as he lay hard inside her. But she obediently held her position.

'Slowly,' she whispered, and he began to rock against her. Adie gripped the crossbar and lifted herself on to her toes to allow him deeper penetration. All her senses seemed to congregate at the point of contact. She clasped him with her muscles, loving the thrill of his cock inside her. The position was precarious, but it was also exquisite.

Killian nuzzled against her back. His breath was hot as his lips moved across her shoulder, while his hands roved across her breasts, over her stomach and down to her thighs.

Adie groaned, the noise welling up from the depths of her soul. She was lost in him and the moment, living, breathing and loving with every pore.

His cock bucked inside her and his fingers slipped over her bare mound to pet her naked clit. It was too much. Her muscles clenched and she was lost, spiralling into orgasm.

She fell forwards in her bonds. Killian's hard shaft dipped again into her eager core, and he rode her until his own climax tossed them both like windborne leaves, Adie hitting another peak as he pulsed inside her.

He supported her in the afterglow, while the echoes of her orgasm died away. Then he lifted the blindfold and tore away the masking tape to free her.

They stared at each other.

Adie swayed, giddy and disoriented by the sudden return of her sight. Killian steadied her, and then kissed her lightly on the forehead. She touched his cheek, pleading with her eyes for more. He relented and kissed her firmly on the lips.

'Consider yourself punished.'

'That was hardly a deterrent.'

He shrugged.

Adie rubbed at her wrists, restoring the circulation. 'What about Matthew?'

'He's already punishing himself with fear. I think I'll enjoy that for a while.'

Killian began to dress and Adie followed suit, only for him to stop her as she pulled on her jeans. He pulled down her pants and taped an X on her bum.

'What's that for?'

'That's where I'm going to spank you if you don't write a damn good press release. Now quit smirking and let's get going.'

Taking him at his word, Adie scampered towards the stairs. The X felt deliciously foreboding, but the press release was important and she wouldn't muck it up just to give him an excuse. She'd find another way of doing that: she still thought a spanking might be fun.

'And Adie?' he called when she was halfway up. She glanced back over her shoulder. The dim torchlight caught in his silver-grey eyes, filling them with warmth.

He smiled.

'Well done.'

LOOK OUT FOR THE ALL-NEW BLACK LACE BOOKS – AVAILABLE NOW!

All books priced £7.99 in the UK. Please note publication dates apply to the UK only. For other territories, please contact your retailer.

PAGAN HEAT
Monica Belle
ISBN O 352 33974 8

For Sophie Page, the job of warden at Elmcote Hall is a dream come true. The beauty of the ruined house and the overgrown grounds speaks to her love of nature. As a venue for weddings, films and exotic parties the Hall draws curious and interesting people, including the handsome Richard Fox and his friends – who are equally alluring and more puzzling still. Her aim is to be with Richard, but it quickly becomes plain that he wants rather more than she had expected to give. She suspects he may have something to do with the sexually charged and sinister events taking place by night in the woods around the Hall. Sophie wants to give in to her desires, but the consequences of doing that threaten to take her down a road she hardly dare consider.

LORD WRAXALL'S FANCY
Anna Lieff Saxby
ISBN 0 352 33080 5

The year is 1720 and Lady Celine Fortescue is summoned by her father, Sir James, to join him on St Cecilia, the turbulent tropical island which he governs. But the girl who steps off the boat into the languid and intoxicating heat isn't the same girl who was content to stay at needlework in a dull Surrey mansion. On a moonlit night, perfumed with the scent of night-blooming flowers, Celine liaises with Liam O'Brian, one of the ship's officers to whom she became secretly betrothed on the long sea voyage. When Liam falls victim to a plot that threatens his life, the debauched Lord Wraxall promises to intervene, in return for Celine's hand in marriage. Celine, however, has other ideas. Exotic and opulent, this story of indulgent luxury is stimulation for the senses.

CONFESSIONAL
Judith Roycroft
ISBN 0 352 33421 5

Faren Lonsdale is an ambitious young reporter, always searching for the scoop that will rocket her to journalistic fame. In search of a story she infiltrates St Peter's, a seminary for young men who are about to sacrifice earthly pleasures for a life of devotion and abstinence. What she unveils are nocturnal shenanigans in a cloistered world that is anything but chaste. But will she reveal the secrets of St Peter's to the outside world, or will she be complicit in keeping quiet about the activities of the gentlemen priests?

Coming in October

THE PRIDE
Edie Bingham
ISBN O 352 33997 7

Those in the little Turkish village see beautiful tour guide Kami Osbank as a seductive, formidable woman. But she is so much more than that: she is a renegade member of a hidden race of supernatural beings known as the Pride. Incredibly fit, strong and sensual, she treats unsuspecting men as fleeting diversions to slake her lust, never leaving herself vulnerable. All that changes with the arrival of English tourist Mark Healey, who is there with his mates for a lads' holiday in the sun. The energy between Mark and Kami is intense, and their mutual attraction leads them to open up to each other in ways that shock and stun both of them. But their new-found bliss is cut short when Kami is abducted and returned to her strife-ridden people to serve as mate to their leader. This leads Mark, along with Kami's friend Janeane, to risk all in an attempt to free her before tensions within the Pride erupt and perhaps tear it apart.

GONE WILD
Maria Eppie
ISBN 0 352 33670 6

Zita seems to have it all – a great job in TV, a cool flat and a fit cameraman boyfriend. But when the boyfriend heads off on a 10-week shoot in Cuba, telling Zita not to get up to any mischief, that's exactly what she does. Soon she is discovering her bisexual side with her girl pal Nadine, and partying for all she's worth. But it's when she agrees to shoot a promo for Nadine's DJ set that things get really wild; dozens of loved-up clubbers are about to descend on Nadine's country house retreat for a weekend of orgiastic hedonism that's bound to get out of hand. On top of this, Zita is growing increasingly attracted to Cy – an enigmatic buff young painter and t'ai chi naturist. When things get too hot to handle, Zita's option is to fly out to Cuba to see how her boyfriend is getting on. What she's about to discover throws their relationship – and Zita's libido – into overdrive.

Black Lace Booklist

Information is correct at time of printing. To avoid disappointment check availability before ordering. Go to www.blacklace-books.co.uk. All books are priced £6.99 unless another price is given.

BLACK LACE BOOKS WITH A CONTEMPORARY SETTING

☐ SHAMELESS Stella Black	ISBN O 352 33485 1	£5.99
☐ INTENSE BLUE Lyn Wood	ISBN O 352 33496 7	£5.99
☐ ON THE EDGE Laura Hamilton	ISBN O 352 33534 3	£5.99
☐ LURED BY LUST Tania Picarda	ISBN O 352 33533 5	£5.99
☐ THE NINETY DAYS OF GENEVIEVE Lucinda Carrington	ISBN O 352 33070 8	£5.99
☐ DREAMING SPIRES Juliet Hastings	ISBN O 352 33584 X	
☐ THE TRANSFORMATION Natasha Rostova	ISBN O 352 33311 1	
☐ SIN.NET Helena Ravenscroft	ISBN O 352 33598 X	
☐ TWO WEEKS IN TANGIER Annabel Lee	ISBN O 352 33599 8	
☐ PLAYING HARD Tina Troy	ISBN O 352 33617 X	
☐ SYMPHONY X Jasmine Stone	ISBN O 352 33629 3	
☐ SUMMER FEVER Anna Ricci	ISBN O 352 33625 0	
☐ A SECRET PLACE Ella Broussard	ISBN O 352 33307 3	
☐ THE GIFT OF SHAME Sara Hope-Walker	ISBN O 352 29935 1	
☐ GOING TOO FAR Laura Hamilton	ISBN O 352 33657 9	
☐ THE STALLION Georgina Brown	ISBN O 352 33005 8	
☐ SWEET THING Alison Tyler	ISBN O 352 33682 X	
☐ TIGER LILY Kimberly Dean	ISBN O 352 33685 4	
☐ RELEASE ME Suki Cunningham	ISBN O 352 33671 4	
☐ KING'S PAWN Ruth Fox	ISBN O 352 33684 6	
☐ SLAVE TO SUCCESS Kimberley Raines	ISBN O 352 33687 0	
☐ SHADOWPLAY Portia Da Costa	ISBN O 352 33313 8	
☐ I KNOW YOU, JOANNA Ruth Fox	ISBN O 352 33727 3	
☐ THE HOUSE IN NEW ORLEANS Fleur Reynolds	ISBN O 352 29951 3	
☐ DRAWN TOGETHER Robyn Russell	ISBN O 352 33269 7	
☐ VIRTUOSO Katrina Vincenzi-Thyre	ISBN O 352 32907 6	
☐ FIGHTING OVER YOU Laura Hamilton	ISBN O 352 33795 8	

BLACK LACE BOOKS WITH AN HISTORICAL SETTING

☐ THE LION LOVER Mercedes Kelly   ISBN 0 352 33162 3
☐ THE AMULET Lisette Allen   ISBN 0 352 33019 8
☐ WHITE ROSE ENSNARED Juliet Hastings   ISBN 0 352 33052 X
☐ UNHALLOWED RITES Martine Marquand   ISBN 0 352 33222 0
☐ LA BASQUAISE Angel Strand   ISBN 0 352 32988 2
☐ THE HAND OF AMUN Juliet Hastings   ISBN 0 352 33144 5
☐ THE SENSES BEJEWELLED Cleo Cordell   ISBN 0 352 32904 1
☐ UNDRESSING THE DEVIL Angel Strand   ISBN 0 352 33938 1 £7.99
☐ THE BARBARIAN GEISHA Charlotte Royal   ISBN 0 352 33267 0 £7.99
☐ FRENCH MANNERS Olivia Christie   ISBN 0 352 33214 X £7.99
☐ LORD WRAXALL'S FANCY Anna Lieff Saxby   ISBN 0 352 33080 5 £7.99
☐ NICOLE'S REVENGE Lisette Allen   ISBN 0 352 32984 X £7.99

BLACK LACE ANTHOLOGIES

☐ WICKED WORDS Various   ISBN 0 352 33363 4
☐ MORE WICKED WORDS Various   ISBN 0 352 33487 8
☐ WICKED WORDS 3 Various   ISBN 0 352 33522 X
☐ WICKED WORDS 4 Various   ISBN 0 352 33603 X
☐ WICKED WORDS 5 Various   ISBN 0 352 33642 0
☐ WICKED WORDS 6 Various   ISBN 0 352 33690 0
☐ WICKED WORDS 7 Various   ISBN 0 352 33743 5
☐ WICKED WORDS 8 Various   ISBN 0 352 33787 7
☐ WICKED WORDS 9 Various   ISBN 0 352 33860 1
☐ WICKED WORDS 10 Various   ISBN 0 352 33893 8
☐ THE BEST OF BLACK LACE 2 Various   ISBN 0 352 33718 4
☐ WICKED WORDS: SEX IN THE OFFICE Various   ISBN 0 352 33944 6 £7.99
☐ WICKED WORDS: SEX ON HOLIDAY Various   ISBN 0 352 33961 6 £7.99

BLACK LACE NON-FICTION

☐ THE BLACK LACE BOOK OF WOMEN'S SEXUAL   ISBN 0 352 33793 1
     FANTASIES Ed. Kerri Sharp
☐ THE BLACK LACE SEXY QUIZ BOOK Maddie Saxon   ISBN 0 352 33884 9

To find out the latest information about Black Lace titles, check out the website: www.blacklace-books.co.uk or send for a booklist with complete synopses by writing to:

Black Lace Booklist, Virgin Books Ltd
Thames Wharf Studios
Rainville Road
London W6 9HA

Please include an SAE of decent size. Please note only British stamps are valid.

Our privacy policy
We will not disclose information you supply us to any other parties. We will not disclose any information which identifies you personally to any person without your express consent.

From time to time we may send out information about Black Lace books and special offers. Please tick here if you do <u>not</u> wish to receive Black Lace information. ❏

Please send me the books I have ticked above.

Name ....

Address ....

....

....

....

Post Code ....

Send to: Virgin Books Cash Sales, Thames Wharf Studios, Rainville Road, London W6 9HA.

US customers: for prices and details of how to order books for delivery by mail, call 1-800-343-4499.

Please enclose a cheque or postal order, made payable to Virgin Books Ltd, to the value of the books you have ordered plus postage and packing costs as follows:

UK and BFPO – £1.00 for the first book, 50p for each subsequent book.

Overseas (including Republic of Ireland) – £2.00 for the first book, £1.00 for each subsequent book.

If you would prefer to pay by VISA, ACCESS/MASTERCARD, DINERS CLUB, AMEX or SWITCH, please write your card number and expiry date here:

....

Signature ....

Please allow up to 28 days for delivery.